Ends and Means

WITHDRAWN FOR SALE

The novels of Stanley Middleton

A Short Answer
Harris's Requiem
A Serious Woman
The Just Exchange
Two's Company
Him They Compelled
Terms of Reference
The Golden Evening
Wages of Virtue
Apple of the Eye
Brazen Prison
Cold Gradations
A Man Made of Smoke
Holiday
Distractions
Still Waters

Ends and Means

STANLEY MIDDLETON

HUTCHINSON OF LONDON

To Philip Davis

Hutchinson & Co (Publishers) Ltd
3 Fitzroy Square, London W1

London Melbourne Sydney Auckland
Wellington Johannesburg and agencies
throughout the world

First published 1977
© Stanley Middleton 1977

Set in Intertype Plantin

Printed in Great Britain by
The Anchor Press Ltd and bound by
Wm Brendon & Son Ltd
both of Tiptree, Essex

ISBN 0 09 131110 1

I

Blue night-sky.

Eric Chamberlain stepped into the grass verge as a car hissed past, and then stood for a moment in the warmth. In an air without breeze, he heard a scuffle at the hedge-bottom, a rasping of grasses. In renewed quiet he pushed on, humming, slightly tipsy.

Reaching the main road through the village he paused again by the lych-gate of the church. St Mary's rose behind, clearly outlined against the sky, but here the lamps in the street, splashing light amongst tree-leaves, darkened the perimeter.

He peered at his watch. Just past eleven. Downstairs-windows were still alight. He sighed, heaved himself onward, silent now. At the top of the lane which branched off past his house he found himself singing again, the last movement of the Beethoven Violin Concerto, a work he did not like. Grinning, he conducted himself, hummed louder.

His house was built some two hundred yards from the main road on a lane that dipped, and then rose again steeply. The brook in the valley made a boundary to his garden and again on the bridge he stopped, touching the coping-stones, still, it seemed, warm from the summer sun. He could not hear the stream. Beethoven too had petered out.

As soon as he turned into his drive, the white gate of which was fastened back allowing half a dozen cars room in front of his garage, he heard the bass-thump of a stereo-player. In the shrubbery by the main door the noise hammered in-sistently but dulled, not unpleasant, as if some workmen set furiously about the day's graft. A small brass plate shone chastely in the porch-light: E. E. Chamberlain.

He swung the front door open, was battered by noise. What had been from outside a repetition of punches screamed indoors, with an electronic harshness, a squeal of metallic pain. There were no lights on, but he could see from the glow outside that the hall was crowded. Figures seemed motionless, leaning on wall or furniture; some waved beer-glasses. One group laughed, heads together, in the distance. The dining-room door was flung back with a burst of light as a young man capered out, whooped Indian-fashion, gibbered, pointing upwards. His face was chalk white, painted, his eyebrows black-arched upwards like a clown's, and in the middle of his forehead a long red cross was bloodily streaked in lipstick. They paid no more attention to him than to Chamberlain, seemingly thrashed into mute petrification by the violence of pulsing music.

'Excuse me.'

Chamberlain, on the stairs, spoke to a couple locked in love. They hutched to one side, all of three inches. On the landing a girl in a long white frock wished him good evening, smiling as she poked among the free flow of her hair. The dining-room door banged shut; darkness completed the hell of noise. Beer-fumes, blackness, racket. He did not switch on the light as he moved along the corridor to his study, but rubbed his fingers on the wall as if to guide himself.

'Hello. Aren't you in bed yet?'

His wife sat by his desk, in his armchair, a closed paperback in her lap. She did not answer. He lowered himself into the rocker opposite, fiddled with trouser creases. Elsa turned her head towards him and her lips trembled, puckered, until he half-expected some cry or whimper of complaint.

'They're enjoying themselves,' she said.

He could not tell whether this was a statement or a question.

The voice, clear as glass, slightly lifted itself at the end of the sentence.

'Let's hope so.'

'Did you see John?' she asked. Their son.

'Not a hope.'

His wife shifted, conveyed a disappointment which, he knew, she would have produced to any answer.

'We'll have a cup of coffee.' She pointed to his electric kettle, and her husband moved obediently.

'I thought you'd be in bed.'

'There'll be a mess to clear up.'

'It'll do in the morning,' he answered.

'And do you think I could sleep when half the house is awash with beer?'

He did not answer the implied criticism, but set out china cups, instant coffee.

'I've no milk up here,' he said.

'We'll do without.'

They sat waiting for the kettle. From here, behind the heavy door, the noise was bearable. Chamberlain, staring at his wife, was startled again by her youthful pallor, and tried to marshal evidence against his impression. Her fair hair was swept upwards to a knot on the top of her skull, but the revealed skin of face and neck was unlined. She paid no attention to him, withdrawn, her eyes half closed, head cocked but not listening. In the light from the one table lamp in this room, she might well have been twenty-five, not forty-one.

He made the coffee, handed over her cup.

'Put it down, thanks,' she ordered. 'It'll be too hot.'

He sipped.

'Nobody interesting down at the pub,' he said.

'There never is.'

He felt at such moments that he owed it to his wife to talk, but she offered no encouragement. Had he come up with an absorbing topic, she'd have ignored it, frozen it off his tongue. At this time of night, Elsa waited for the party to end, determined not to be entertained or instructed or even touched from outside. She would be bored, and bore. Yet, he felt, even in this unco-operative stillness, she was attractive, with a beauty that required neither liveliness nor colour. She sat in a chair, a breathing statue, aesthetically satisfying, a shape to be admired, a touchstone. Puzzled, as always, he wondered how he could have learnt so little in his twenty-odd years of marriage.

'She is not dead, she sleepeth,' he quoted aloud.

Elsa did not reply, in rapt inattention.

Chamberlain finished his scalding coffee, rose, went to the window and looked out over the fields, the dark shapes of trees and hedges, the lights on the road at the top of the rise, the milky arch of the sky. He let the curtain fall.

'I'm having another,' he said.

She moved her fingers dismissively over her untouched cup.

Anger stirred in him. She had no right in his study. Why, if she were here, did she not put herself out to speak to him? He made excuses for her without enthusiasm, not convincing himself, not trying to.

Car doors slammed, an engine revved.

'Somebody's leaving. It's early,' she said.

'Another party to go to.'

She picked up her coffee, and the action livened her into words.

'Did you know anybody here?'

'Couldn't see. They keep the light off.' He up-ended the small kettle for the last drop. 'I thought I recognized Saul Hill's voice. I wouldn't be sure.'

'What makes him so interesting?' she asked.

Again he recognized a rebuke. His wife had suspected, with reason, that he had committed adultery with Saul's mother.

That was four years ago.

'I thought he and Pamela were . . .'

'Were what?'

'Attracted to each other.' He mouthed the phrase, as one writes a slow sentence, unwilling to make progress.

Elsa dismissed the reason with a shrug, a small intake of breath. He poured his second cup, gestured with the empty kettle towards her, without reply. At this moment their daughter Pamela tapped and opened the door, poking round a smile.

'Am I interrupting anything?'

'No, come in,' Chamberlain answered. 'And shut that door. Do you want a cup of coffee?'

'No thanks.' She squatted at Elsa's feet, a tall, well-built girl, but heavier than her mother, good-looking rather than beautiful, placid than withdrawn.

'What can we do for you?' her father asked.

'Nothing. I just looked in.'

'Anywhere near closing-time downstairs?'

'Not too far. We announced twelve for the finish. Some have gone already.'

'Is that good or bad?'

'You always have birds of passage.'

The phrase pleased him; one never quite fathomed Pamela. She lifted words from books.

'Is Peter sober?'

'Oh, yes.' Peter was eighteen, a visiting cousin. 'He's very good really. He won't let 'em do damage. He and Johnny.'

'To the lares and penates?' He repaid her phrase; she grinned acknowledgement.

Elsa stirred, kicking her cup. She swore, ladylike, put it safely inside the hearth.

'Is Saul here?' she asked.

'Yes. And Carrie.'

'Your father thought you might be interested in him.'

'I'm interested in any good-looking young men. Haven't you noticed?'

That put her mother in place, Chamberlain thought, and Elsa returned to her lip-locking, meditation, whatever, unwilling to bandy words.

'I like him. Don't you, Dad?'

'Yes. I do. And his sister.'

Elsa looked up. 'And his mother.' But she said nothing, compressing her lips, uglifying her expression.

'Why don't you go to bed?' Pamela asked.

'Your mother's waiting to clear up.'

'John'll see to that. He'll have his fatigue-party of attendant maidens all ready.'

'When you talk about him,' Chamberlain said, returning his coffee-cup, 'I don't seem to know my son.'

Pamela laughed out loud, but laid a hand on her mother's leg to balance the sympathy she granted her father. Elsa sat still. Chamberlain gathered the crocks, took them outside.

The bathroom was empty, to his surprise, bare of honking revellers. He felt very tired, glumly sober. The noise from below had abated. His forty-eight years weighed on him, reducing him to a weariness that was painful, needling his limbs, and which, he knew, would keep him fidgetingly sleepless. Carefully, meticulously, he washed and dried the pots, determined that if that was all he could do, it would be done well. He received no satisfaction from his efforts, expected none.

When he returned Pamela had gone and his wife had resumed her statuesque cypress. Downstairs sounds of impending departure, door-bell, door-bang, brakes, were heard. While he was still straightening the china there was a tap at his room. Elsa neither moved nor drew his attention, so that he was left to call out the invitation.

Caroline Hill, a white shawl draped over her shoulders, edged in.

'Oh, hello.' She was surprised, but demonstrated affability, when she saw Mrs Chamberlain. 'My father,' she said to Eric, 'asked if you'd call in to see him.'

'Surely. When?'

'Any time. He's not too busy.'

'Tomorrow, then. Morning or evening?'

'Please yourself.' Her bright smile mitigated the brusqueness. Chamberlain asked about health, her visit to Ibiza, her work in the bank. The girl directed her answers towards Elsa, but without result, not even a good-night when she left.

As soon as the door closed the woman wrenched round in her chair.

'Why couldn't he have phoned?'

'I don't suppose it's anything important and he remembered it just as Caroline came out.'

She rose lethargically, examined and combed her hair in the room's one small mirror, slipped on her shoes, went downstairs. He followed.

Certainly the boys had their workers organized, though it was not yet midnight. The vacuum blared, replacing the stereo. Glasses and plates were collected, handed in to the washing-up squad in the kitchen, where party jollity did not impede efficiency. Peter, in charge, stacking and putting away told his aunt that she was not needed. Elsa, leaning on the door-post, asked why he was not using the washing-up machine.

'This prolongs the festivities,' the boy answered, reminding his uncle of Pamela; who handled a tea-towel as she collected glasses.

'Any damage?' Elsa, sourly. The boy reported two breakages of crockery, one major spillage, and a chipped skirting-board. He showed no embarrassment at his aunt's question in front of guests.

'Where's John?' she asked.

'He's taking Lynette back.'

Elsa scowled. John, the elder, paid court to a married woman six years his senior. Peter jauntily passed with plates, winking, whistling.

'Will anyone need a lift?' Chamberlain asked.

'When the chores are over,' said Peter, returning, 'we shall muck up more cups with delicious, instant coffee. And so, until the dawn.' Elsa finger-nailed the wall. 'You take Auntie to bed.'

Pamela, with Saul Hill behind, appeared to describe a pool of beer until then undiscovered under the umbrella stand.

'Are you sure it's beer?' Peter shouted. He led Saul towards mop and bucket. Chamberlain took his wife's arm, and together they walked the premises. Elsa did not remark on the amateurish restoration of the *status quo*, so presumably she was pleased.

'Did you hold beery parties?' he asked.

'Not that I remember.'

'All moderately sober tonight.'

'I wonder Lynette Rockford bothered . . .' Elsa's voice trailed off.

Upstairs Chamberlain stood again by the window, holding the curtain back, enjoying the calm chaos of the night.

'I wouldn't mind squatting there with a glass of ale listening to the record-player,' he said. 'Even now I don't improve. To sit there and be wholly occupied by the present.' He blew breath out, moved, peeled off his jacket.

'What about Lynette Rockford?' Elsa asked, palely naked.

'What about her?'

'John worries me.' She stood luminously beautiful, her body delicious, with not a thought of sexual appeal in her head.

'I know.'

'You never say anything. He's chasing that woman at all hours of the day.'

'Yes.'

'Yes? Is that all?' She turned away from him, peering into the mirror. Light lined the slender back, shoulder bones, buttocks. She was holding her night-dress clenched in her left hand as she touched her face for some blemish with the right.

'You want me to tell him to stop?'

'Do you approve of it? She's nearly thirty. He's not twenty-one yet.'

He did not answer, and she turned. Her nakedness warned him off. If he put a hand on that belly, those globes, the delicate pubic triangle, she'd snarl or snivel. Sex is no cure for sex. She slipped the night-dress over her head, reached for a dressing-gown, went out.

Chamberlain prised an indigestion-tablet from its silver foil, then sat in bed waiting for her return.

'Are we reading?' he asked. He'd no book in front of him.

'At this time? I'm tired.'

'It's no use worrying about John,' he said.

'You're no help.'

'What do you want me to do?'

'I don't know any more than you.' Her voice shook, exasperation uppermost. 'But at least you could try.'

'It wouldn't do any good.'

'You could talk to him, then. You could talk to me. You never say a word.'

'I don't know what word to say.' He pulled the cord for darkness.

'It's always left to me.'

'You mean,' he said, with unctuous emphasis, 'that you interfere.'

'He's our son. Isn't he?'

Troubled, he turned his back on her bed, heaving the duvet to his chin, then kicking out for fresh air. She snapped the light on, shook tablets from her bottle, made for the bathroom again.

2

Lynette Rockford lay uncomfortably across John Chamberlain's chest.

He did not complain, thought himself lucky as he slightly shifted his legs in the front seat of his mother's car.

'Time I went in,' she said, tearing her mouth from his. He murmured disappointment.

'Only twenty past twelve.' She sat up, disregarding him, pulling her frock down. 'Did you enjoy the party?'

'Not much.'

'I told you I'd take you in the house.'

'I've been in before.'

She stroked his face, tenderly, without superiority, held up her palm for him to kiss.

'I like being with you. You know that.'

'I love you.' He nuzzled her, but she, straight now, did up the buttons at the top of her dress.

'You see too much of me,' she said, giggling.

'What's wrong now?' His anger made him seem huge in the confined space, creaking seat springs.

'I'm tired.'

'That's nothing to do with what you've just said.'

'No.' She'd put her handbag on her knee, rummaged in it for keys. 'Unlike some, I've got to go to work tomorrow.'

She leaned over, kissed him, pushed him off.

'Why don't . . . ?' He mumbled disappointment, eschewed words.

'I love you more than you think,' she said, stepping out.

'When shall I . . . ?'

'Has the telephone service broken down? Don't get out. I'm tired.'

She was indoors quick as a cat.

John drove noisily in the deserted streets, hauling at the gear-lever, braking at pointless traffic lights, swearing as a drunk signalled two-fingered disparagement. He was not pleased with himself.

He'd completed three years at a college of education, prepared now for a fourth and a bachelor's degree, but did not looked forward to teaching. His grandfather and father had both been in the profession, the first as headmaster of a village school not twenty miles from this place, the second for a time in public schools in Derbyshire and the home counties. Now, John, without the devotion of the one or the slippery brains of the other, struggled in successful mediocrity, in the top ten of his year at an institution without standards, his father said, or reputation. This spring he had met Mrs Rockford at a theatrical entertainment and this had toppled him into sanity. He'd been occupied then, he remembered, on a close study of two brothers, aged eight and nine, whom he'd taught. This inflated his ego, because the children's parents had shown interest, had invited him down to the house, had rummaged for him, come up with records so that he could exactly date Adrian's first tooth or Julian's earliest word, where holidays were spent, when illnesses or accidents had taken toll.

He had felt, he recalled, proud of this research and though he would argue that it was the merest luck he'd dropped across so literate and articulate a family, he could not help ascribing his success to his own superior insights. At meals he'd bored his mother with conclusions and his father with prognostications; she'd said so, while Eric had chewed his lip, eyed him craftily, looking, his son guessed or hoped, for copy. He felt at such times level with the world, his *métier* discovered. Now he wished he'd pleased his mother and gone to university, followed the academic rut so that, exams safely negotiated, he'd be away to his doctorate, the widening of human knowledge.

Of course, he would not have done better than a third. It was all he deserved. Part-time attention, inability to sit still for long, a dilettante's chasing of Aztec history, women's rights, the art of fugue, the end of the world, God-knows-what, left him ill-prepared for narrow papers whose markers complained of blinkered knowledge, lack of reading, initiative or humanity, but who granted the highest honours only to those who had learnt the notes at the back of the text or the opinions of respected professors and delivered them in a style not too divorced from the original so that they were at least recognizable to examining boards in a hurry. John had often heard his father expatiate on the simple lunacies of academic life.

So the training college was his choice. He'd stumble through that, like everybody else. But that Easter Tuesday he'd done well, even considered spending an hour or so in the afternoon on the project. In the evening he'd driven his mother into Retford, the market town, for a play-reading at the house of Mrs Hughes-Edge, a friend, an enemy.

John had no objection because the trip might well dissipate his mother's overt, continuous disappointment in him. Moreover, there'd be young people there who'd arranged to meet in pubs around the county. Mr Hughes-Edge would creep about in his slippers, purposely stumbling against the girls, steadying himself on their bottoms, at the same time criticizing his wife's pretensions, taste and financial ineptitude. The youngsters pleased themselves talking about 'Hug-us', the girls as openly as the men.

'He gave my rump such a rub,' Meriel Speake said. 'Damn near burned a hole through my frock.'

'And what did you say?' Her husband hawked lasciviously.

' "Oh, Mr Hughes-Edge." '

'Call me Emrys,' they chorused at her.
' "What's the matter, my dear?" '
'And you said?'
'I stared him in the eye, and he looked back as straight as the bloodshot would let him.'

They speculated about his age, sixty-two, his sex-life, his work. Nobody loved him. He ought to be in prison.

That evening they tackled *John Gabriel Borkman*.

A dark girl with a contralto voice had read the ex-manager's wife. She sounded disgruntled, as if she had listened for years to the stomping slippers of her husband above, to the Victorian plink of the visiting pianist. One had not to look at her, for in spite of the dark-ringed eyes, she appeared young, but once turn away one heard the disappointment, one reconstructed heavy furniture, mothballs, the charity-ragged poverty. The girl wore no wedding-ring but had been introduced by the Hughes-Edges as Mrs Rockford. Perhaps, he wondered, this was their pronunciation of Ms.

They read one act, then tea and coffee appeared before Mrs H.-E. came to her majestic own. She allowed them the single act and then pronounced. Others were granted spatters of words; Mrs Chamberlain grew deviously mischievous, but Madame pursued her way undeterred, hearing no evil of her own opinions. The initiatory applause, generous usually, to the chosen actors did not distinguish the superior quality of Mrs Rockford's performance. John, released to dry up with her, said so.

She'd turned; the heart-face, blue eyes, black scooped hair; small breasts under a plain blouse, legs powerfully shapely thrusting from the severity of a navy skirt held him breathless. She was not beautiful; her upper lip was faintly scarred. She was no more alive than he was, or the splashing Edna Eland, or even the futtering Edge with his lecherous mouth open; it was as though, he told himself now, a parcel was delivered with his name on. He'd known this a dozen, a hundred times before. Any nubile female was, for a matter of minutes, in a burst of crude imagination, his, but this time, he did not know why, the mind had beaten some reality from fantasy.

'Have you been on the stage?' he asked. 'Professionally?'

'I suppose I could say "Yes" if I wanted to boast.'

He asked the correct, polite questions, then; he was sufficiently his father's son for that. She murmured; encouraged, he pressed on.

'You were Mrs Borkman,' he announced. 'The others were themselves, no more. They weren't bad. I'm not saying they were.'

'You don't know me,' she said, without heat.

'You're not, to look at you, a frustrated woman, in late middle-age, fixated on your son.'

'You don't know that, either.'

That stopped him, dry, dismissive. Perhaps she had a son, sons. The thought seared him. In two sentences she had disparaged his ignorant assertions, as his mother often dismissed him, the undistinguished son, the callow man.

'Perhaps so.'

'Oh, come on,' she said. 'Defend yourself. I hate politeness.'

He did his best. When Mrs Eland who was washing attempted once to interfere with facetious comment, Lynette blatantly ignored the pleasantry, as if demonstrating her carelessness of convention, pushed him into argument, treating him as adult.

Within five minutes they were at loggerheads about Mrs Borkman's living her life through her son.

'It's not possible,' he said.

'On the contrary, it's common.' The voice schoolma'med it over him. 'How many mothers, with no career possible for them, could live in any other way but through brilliant boys?'

answered, matching her in the

lightly different facet?'

with it so bluntly? My son is
his father's disgrace.'

onvention has to be accepted.
ades' worth of trouble inside an

they put crockery away, arguing
about. As they ended the chore,
she knew a woman exactly like
brilliant, learnt Arabic from a
was still at school, won scholarships
to Ox   Mrs Rockford, excited with each other,
or he   , were content to hear the triteness out.
The pro gy took a brilliant degree, killed himself on a motorcycle, broke his mother's heart.

Afterwards the two sat tidily together to listen to Mrs Hughes-Edge's pronouncements on the younger generation. John, excited by the nearness of Lynette, felt, said diffidently that Ibsen's vision was not so sure, so cut and dried as the hostess imagined. His mother intervened to rout him; nobody proffered a word of defence.

'Ibsen doesn't know,' John said. 'He is.'

'What's that masterpiece of obscurity mean?' Elsa, lighting a long cigarette for herself and Madame.

'He's more like the foolish son, the ruined father, the failed poet, than he is a godlike creator who . . .'

'That's obviously untrue.' Elsa.

'He is a universal genius,' said Mrs Hughes-Edge. 'I think we can say that.'

'Even you must see,' Elsa's cigarette wobbled arrogantly, 'that Ibsen could hardly consider himself as a writer who'd unsuccessfully . . .'

'You see him as . . .'

'Don't interrupt.' His mother, rudely.

'I beg your pardon.' Lynette at his side seemed to encourage overtones of irony.

'Ibsen was a great European figure. Writing in an out of the way language, he had captured the consciousness of a whole continent.' Madame booming.

'A man of his genius knows it,' Elsa said.

'I don't think so,' John argued.

'May we hear why not?' Mr Hughes-Edge raising his leering head.

'The man had enormous talent, but even greater expectations of himself which he couldn't fulfil.'

'How do you know this?' Mrs Hughes-Edge from a great height.

'It's written into every line of the play.'

'The universal mind can comprehend failure as easily as success. He grasps both. His observation of one is as powerful as the other.' Madame.

'Then why does he write only about failures?' John knew pleasure, looked down at the blue skirt next to him.

'Tragedy, our greatest human creation, includes failure, colossal defeat, but moves beyond by the power of wit into triumph, into,' Mrs Hughes-Edge paused to check that the audience listened, 'the great C major of life.'

'Because,' John answered, 'all people of sensibility feel their failures are more frequent than their successes.'

'You think,' said his mother, smiling, 'that John Chamberlain and Henrik Ibsen are the same person.'

'Basically, yes.'

'You deceive yourself.' Cold, curt.

'You disregard his imagination, his art. That transforms.'

'I think,' John said, 'that when he'd written the last word of the play he didn't say to himself, "I'm a marvel." '

'No, I'm sure he didn't.' Elsa. 'Perhaps you'd tell us what he did say.'

'Something like, "I'm a silly, dirty old man." '

They all laughed, some uncomfortably. Mr Hughes-Edge knocked a glass harmlessly from sideboard to pile carpet; his wife, nonsense done, summed up lengthily in her own favour. When the meeting broke up, Elsa Chamberlain walked across to Lynette, offered her a lift home, which meant that John and the girl had to stand together, awkwardly, wanting to talk, washed over by a peroration on art from Madame. Elsa said not a word now, made no pretence of listening. Hug-us hummed tunelessly, pottering, smiling, brushing Mrs Chamberlain's buttocks with a delicate sway.

Elsa commented favourably on her son's performance to her husband.

'He said great art sprang from a sense of failure.'

'About right.'

'He silenced Ernestine. I think she listened as nearly as she could.'

'She'll be giving you the same line herself in a month's time.'

John knew nothing of this, wrote up his chosen pupils' measles and intelligence tests, thinking of Lynette Rockford. He did his mother's errands in town on the off-chance of meeting the girl: two days before his return he was rewarded. She swung out from Boots clutching a paper bag, stopped, smiled magnificently, utterly neat, in human flesh.

'What are you doing here?' Masculine, jocular, conservative, stupid. 'Shopping?'

'About to have my lunch.'

'Oh.'

'You can come to see me eat it. An apple and an orange. Do you like the smell of oranges, John?'

'Not a matter I'd considered carefully.' She'd remembered his name.

They sat on a park bench and he began, for want of better, to describe the life history of Julian and Adrian Pethick. It had never sounded so interesting. Encouraged by her, he sorted out the education of these boys, set them on careers. He talked without hesitancy, full of creative energy, aware of his fiction, unafraid of it, wallowing in technique, spattering textbook jargon.

'They are only nine and eight,' she said.

'Yes.' His deflating mother again. 'Of course, we,' all science behind that, 'can't really tell how they'll turn out. Still, it will be interesting to compare the prognosis with the reality.'

'Won't one affect the other?' Good. Good.

'The parents might not see my work.' He coughed, honesty reasserted. 'I shan't be expected to make all these . . . They're guesses, aren't they?'

At this moment she took his right hand in her ringless left. Hers was warm, clasping, but steady. She leaned closer; shoulders, upper arms touched. His excitement wheeled. whirled into a vortex whose centre stood, froze hotly, revealed visions blindly, statuesque, unmoved, the universe at equilibrium on a slatted bench at one-thirteen, on Thursday.

'I think I love you,' he said. He choked his sentence out so that he jerked, upright, monkey-on-stick, uncertain whether he'd spoken aloud.

'You only think?' Neither looked at the other. The banality was offered to passing schoolgirls in ribboned boaters. He put his left hand lightly in the crook of her left elbow, across himself.

'I only think.'

'That's the best psychology can do for you?'

'Or for anybody.'

She leaned across and kissed him on the mouth. He closed his eyes, but she'd drawn back. The beautiful small breasts had pressed him; lips had silently signed him with a perfection of language. He was lost, or found.

A quarter of an hour later, she kissed him perfunctorily

again and left for the solicitor's office where she worked. They had arranged to meet on his last evening, though he knew his mother would want him at home. He could think of no excuse.

'I met Lynette Rockford today,' he announced at dinner.
'Who's she?' Elsa, socially bright, serving mousse.
'I invited her out for a drink tomorrow.'
Mrs Chamberlain tapped the silver rim of the bowl.
'Why didn't you ask her here?'
'Well, you know how it is. She seemed very pleasant.'
'This is your last evening, John.'
'We hadn't arranged anything. I shall be in tonight.'
'Staring at television.'
The father kept his head to his plate. He lacked convictions.

The first meeting was nearly disappointing. They sat in a chrome-bound pub, excited to be near each other, but too tense to know how to express the joy. Small smiles, little touchings hinted explosive energy that generated there. John looked at her profile, tried to learn it, noticing that she looked almost plain, given a bloom of skin, a wide beauty of eye, a sudden swoop into life as she turned to him. Her fingers were beautiful round a half of lager. Both talked by fits and starts, not knowing each other, needing the wildness of sexual contact to calm them so that everyday sentences about weather or football or fashion-displays would seem sufficient until they had acquired a store of shared interests.

They went out, sat in his car beyond the town, arms locked, mouths wetly receptive. Now she dominated him with a strength he barely believed, opening herself to him, in her time, at her will. His hands learnt the sweetness of her body, but it was he who seemed naked to himself, deflowered, discovered, stripped of modesty and pretension, lifted into abandonment, mauled into atomies while she retained a cool vigour, a unifying power that neither yielded nor cajoled but subjected him to her whim.

He lay, replete or emptied, shirt over trousers, underpants, jacket slung to the floor of the car. She held him, like a mother with a feverish child, with solicitude but on the watch. Her clothes were neat again; passion had flared, was now covered. Any minute he knew she'd rummage in a handbag for her mirror, study in the blue moonlight her composed face. At this moment he recognized fear. He knew her now, sexually, and had learnt that she had huge reserves, beyond that parapet. She had given herself to him and had withdrawn so that he felt he'd lost some battle, some grave part of himself.

'Come on,' she said. 'Get dressed now.' She touched his genitals almost playfully. 'No. No more.' She had felt his new quickening. 'We'll get out and walk for a few minutes.' He struggled into his clothes while she sat tightly looking the other way.

'What's wrong?' he asked, arm round her shoulder, with bravado, guilt.

'Nothing.'

'What is it now? Come on.'

'There's nothing wrong with me. Are you ready?'

The lane where he had parked was muddy, its surface rutted, puddles at the verges bright in the moon, dark under the hawthorn.

'You're going to spoil your shoes,' he said.

'I don't think so.'

She'd been here before. The thought excited him. The body that had received him had slaked the thirst, had generously comforted other loves. He did not put this into words, but fitfully imagined the men, experienced and shadowy, brawny or desperate, who had possessed this girl whose hand he held, who walked so steadily at his side. They passed through a gate, under a tree, an undersized, gnarled oak, skirted a fallow field to mount the crest of a knoll. Here the wind lifted stronger, the lights in distant houses garishly sharp.

'Look out there,' she pointed. 'That's where I was born.'

'Where?' It seemed important to know.

'The tall house. There.' She sounded peeved. 'The one in the middle.' How could one be the middle of four? He questioned no further, kissed her on her cold face. She responded, but was not his, not yet.

He'd returned to the college agonized with pleasure and uncertainty. He'd written and, after a week, had received her replies which plainly said she loved him. She sketched life, in her office, her digs, vividly, but he suspected she put on a show to impress him, that her descriptions covered ephemera, on the margins of a real life she was not prepared to share with him. He had no evidence; the uncertainty was in himself, but it made the lectures he attended, the discos, the casual girls he fondled unreal, unimportant.

Now, this summer, his quandary had not been resolved.

They had revelled in sex, in the bright fields, the shadow of woods, in her room. But she had a fortnight in Spain about which she expressed no regret. Two weeks of sunshine and new faces attracted her more than he did. His company bored her sometimes, and she was not afraid to say so. Sometimes she rejected his sexual advances, or worse, allowed them with a detached interest that once had betrayed him, twisted him into tears so that he lay in her, sobbing. She had not been affected, murmured after a decent interval for composure that he was a funny boy and quickly restored her hair, face and dress to propriety.

He stared at the closed door, her scent still faintly in the car.

3

Eric Chamberlain in dressing-gown, sat in the kitchen sipping tea. Nine o'clock on Thursday. The commuters' cars had hissed past; the vicar, back from the daily solitary eight o'clock communion, would have finished his breakfast and now in his study would be looking over the sermon notes he worked out on Wednesday. In this house there was no sound; summer mist dusted the garden and the fields beyond. Elsa was asleep. John and Pamela had not stirred out of their rooms. In a house on holiday, Eric sipped, displeased.

He plugged in, shaved; washed at the sink, He brewed coffee, poured it into good china cups and delivered to the family. Pamela smiled; John turned and groaned; Elsa called him 'darling'. Downstairs he prepared two thick slices of wholemeal toast which he scoffed. After a second cup of tea, he went upstairs to the bedroom, cleaned his teeth and on tiptoe made for his study, where he walked about for ten minutes before he forced himself to his desk.

Luckily he knew how he'd spend his next two hours. From the buff folder he'd extract his notes, read them and write his review. This might be done before twelve; once or twice recently he'd had it over before eleven and then he'd rapidly type, altering already before squaring the sheets under a paper-weight, stand, remove his glasses and emerge. Lunch would be ready at twelve-forty for him, a silent meal at which he dozed with guilt, while Pamela and her mother chatted, like two sisters, and John sat laconic and glum as his father. At the end, Eric martyred himself helping wife and daughter with the dishes. They dashed, and laughed, splashing, energetic as climbing goats, and, he reflected, as unattractive. Ignoring him, Pamela had now given up her socializing attempts, they talked on with triviality, meaningless as the clatter of plates.

Sometimes his wife would announce her plans. That pleased him, though he did not know why, had no part in them, and he'd kiss her, friendly, while she'd pat his biceps, even press her body on to his. In the lounge, he'd smoke a cigar and wait for the clock to strike two-fifteen when he'd stump upstairs to attack the typescript with a biro.

After Oxford and the army Eric had taught in three public schools. At the second he had written a thriller, *God's Spies*, which had been recognized as outstanding, and was still in print. Two years later he'd published *Another Troy*, which had made his name and managed considerable commercial success. A year later, at his last school, he'd brought out *The Waxwork*, which had, for no reason he could understand, made a small pile and allowed him to retire to his native Nottinghamshire where he worked, half dazed, on his next book. He could grasp the success of his first two novels, felt he deserved it. During his period of army service he'd been lucky enough to work in military intelligence, and he'd used his experience. But these two were works of imagination, with people who lived, who troubled him, who were complex and memorable. The set-pieces, the rapid action, the bloody deaths of hero or innocent bystander daggered the reader into a welter of cowardice and attention, made works of a powerful fiction. The third, bundled into films both in England and in Germany, the basis of a world-wide television series, had nothing of the shattering strength of the first books.

Chamberlain knew this.

He was no fool, and bought good financial advice. With Elsa, his wife, an art student who'd easily given up her career, they'd settled in a house not a mile away from the present home, and he'd struggled for five years with *Swarthy Webs*, producing in the end what seemed to him a patchwork job, its faults hidden by a sharpness of realistic detail, a worthless return to an exhausted vein. The book made money, won critical acclaim. Friends and enemies read into it insights he knew he had not intended. When they lauded the energy of his subconscious, he believed them on one day, lost all hope on the next. His accountant was delighted; he and Elsa with their children moved into this larger house.

At present his main occupation was reviewing in both England and America. He did not altogether despise himself, as he had a sharp pen and was not afraid to praise merit. People feared and respected his critical word; he worked. The whole of Friday, each week, he left to his fiction, though he feared himself finished. Since their move into the present house six years ago he'd written one novel, again successful, and in the last year he'd surprised himself by producing the first draft of another. These, and occasional commissions for film and television, kept him occupied, though uneasily. He drank more than he felt he ought, but was neither alcoholic nor ever drunk. He took exercise; he slaved at his desk some seven or eight hours a day, but felt badly askew with reality. His army experience, his reading or interviewing, had made him superficially expert in espionage and at the same time had pictured the humdrum of the children's education, Elsa's preoccupations, life in the village in such odd colours, such a faded wash, that he walked like a blind man who'd recovered sight miraculously, seeing men as trees walking, unexpected perspectives round every common corner.

He did not understand this.

Inflation bothered him now. He did not earn enough, or properly. One had to report for duty to a classroom or a factory to earn a proper salary. He had done that once, as had his father. The propositions which fell through his letter-box demanded care, research, frustration often, lengthy hours, but seemed unreal. It was as if the headmaster of one of his schools had appeared before he taught the sixth form and had named some vast sum of money, greater than the year's wages, which would be awarded him if he managed one successful period, or one good set of results. Headmasters did not act like that; Chamberlain could not convince himself, in spite of evidence and hard cash, that other authorities did. The harder he laboured, the more misty, insecure, notional his world grew. His savings dwindled; he could not afford a new car.

Elsa, efficient at home, supreme at warding off unprofitable callers while her husband was in his study, believed she knew his trouble. He had lost confidence in his power to write. It was unusual for her to reach such conclusions, but she had heard him say as much once, and had seized on it as the truth. She repeated it to her children, warning them to mention nothing of it to their father, for she knew he was mistaken. His last novel, she was certain, bettered his first. It read more slickly, rang contemporary, dazzled; it made more money. She, therefore, kept Friday a holy day, encouraging him, retyping his typescript herself, talking, making a maker of him. For the rest, he worked himself hard and, in her view, was not overpaid for his effort. Her small private income became a necessity. What he needed was a huge financial success.

Her difficulty, now, lay in expressing her convictions to Eric.

Where his work was involved he was a formidable man. He'd stare through you, cut you glassily down, not speak for days if he thought you had criticized him unjustly. Bruised, he'd maim in return. She, after a bout, would compare this desperate brutal assailant with the vague man in carpet slippers who could not remember where he'd put his glasses or that address. Well intentioned, not unintelligent, she persevered.

Two years ago she had picked up an indiscreet note to him from Madeleine Hill.

It was thrown, carelessly, in an envelope, on his desk, and Elsa had opened it, expecting to find a cheque or chore he'd have to be reminded of.

'God, come again quickly,' she read. 'You made my body into a young girl's. I worship you.' She picked the sentences out from the half-dozen on two small sides of notepaper. 'Darling Ricky.' Elsa knew the huge writing, did not need to turn for the signature 'Your besotted, devoted, mad Maddy'. The language astounded.

Madeleine Hill, the wife of a general practitioner, daughter and grand-daughter of doctors, was a neat, dark, elegantly dressed woman, with hair carefully arranged into primness above her well-cut suits, her smart sweaters and slacks. She spoke precisely, knew what she was about, put up with no nonsense from her children Saul and Caroline, matched her husband's gun-dog image with metropolitan, dull chic, never lost head or temper. She seemed contented with George Hill, a shrewd man under his tweed, compared him favourably with her brother who had recently been appointed to a regius chair of medicine. Her only eccentricity was this sprawling handwriting, in which she delivered instructions to her many subordinates in good works amongst the *haute bourgeoisie* of the county. She attended church, patronized Eric, gave the impression that Elsa was a parasite on society who had even failed with her own children.

Now her body was a young girl's. She worshipped.

The note read so astonishingly that Elsa returned it to its envelope, refolded, before she read it a second time. No change. Neither in content nor in the damning hand. Elsa trembled, felt sick, put her head on her forearms on the desk before she realized what she was about. The day to change character. Integrated, mature Mrs Hill mad in love. Poised Mrs Chamberlain allowing herself to snuffle, not noticing the sob-drags in her breath. She rearranged the note four or five times into carelessness, made for the bathroom, where Eric, unusually, was cleaning his teeth with boyish noise. She apologized, stumbling out, to the second bathroom where she locked the door, sobbed into a thick towel, then made her face up, prudently.

By the time she faced the world again, her husband tapped the typewriter, the sun obliquely roasted the walls of the front rooms, Pamela would be home from school in something over an hour.

She could not believe. Nor could she remember whether or not the letter was dated. It had not come through the post. The envelope was marked: 'E. E. Chamberlain, Esqre', that lengthy, fool's abbreviation. Esbloodyquire. Elsa walked from room to room, touching, shifting familiar bric-à-brac trying to convince herself by the habitual appearance of inanimate objects that the knocking, stumbling, untameable chaos of feeling in every vein of her body did not exist. The power, the colossal weight, of her emotion terrified her; her own powerlessness was new, desperate. In her middle age she had not thought to find such wild-running force inside herself.

Against custom, she walked, without knocking, into her husband's study. Perhaps she hoped for guilty hurry, the scuffling away of some paper. Instead, he turned from his typewriter, pulled his glasses a quarter of an inch down his nose, smiled over them absently, at her. His face was brown, creased somehow; his hair pushed untidily into spikes. She could see his scalp at the crown, sun-reddened.

'I thought perhaps you weren't busy,' she managed.

'I can spare a moment.'

'It doesn't matter.'

He looked surprised, did not press the point. He tapped a line on his typewriter, then without turning his head asked, 'Is it something you're thinking of buying?'

He sounded himself, preoccupied, but kind because he was

doing well. She stumbled from the room, unable to accuse him. For the next two days she could not control herself, cried, muttered, trembled until she expected the family to comment on her eccentric behaviour. On the third day she bought a packet of cheap stationery from Woolworth's and a copy of *The Sun* from which she cut out the letters to make the sentence 'Your husband is carrying on with Mrs Hill'. She was surprised how long the exercise took, but then carefully burnt newspaper and the pathetic lined pad in the incinerator.

It was not until the sixth day that she presented the forgery. They had all been out on Saturday afternoon so that someone could have called unnoticed. The next day Elsa summoned hypocrisy and handed the crumpled sheet over. Eric was enjoying a glass of whisky as he watched football on television. This was out of the way behaviour, for though he never worked on Sunday he often strolled out, or sometimes took a nap. He apologized now, saying that this was the first match of the season. She mumbled something about summer and cricket and then held out the paper, screwed up in her hand.

'This came. Yesterday afternoon.'

He smoothed the paper, read it, nodded, did not speak.

'I didn't know whether to show it to you. I didn't know what to do.' Grey figures flitted about the screen.

'Not by post?'

'No. Yesterday afternoon.'

'In an envelope?'

'Yes.'

'Addressed how?'

'Just "Mrs Chamberlain".' She did not like the dry cross-examination.

'Cut out like this? Or typed? Written? Printed?'

'Printed, I think.'

'Where is it?'

'I don't know. I must have burnt it with the waste paper.'

'I see.' He sounded unsurprised. 'Can you remember anything about it? Did it look like a man's hand? Educated?'

'Not very good printing.'

'Block letters?'

'No.' She hated these lies.

'No initials?'

'I don't think so.'

He cracked on with his questions. She answered with fear that did not show.

'What do you think?' he said in the end. 'Who's likely to be responsible?'

'No idea.'

'You've not upset anybody? I'm trying to think if I have. Somebody who'd like to make trouble between us?'

She denied knowledge and he did not press. From his lackadaisical tone she concluded, and felt relief, that he'd lost interest. For some minutes he watched the football with the sound at low, then roused himself. He scrubbed his chin, bared his teeth fiercely, then asked, in a faintly familiar voice, 'And you're wondering what the truth is?'

Now she sat trembling.

'There's nothing in it,' he continued. 'I know my denial doesn't mean much, that you can't help being suspicious, but that's all I can say. There's nothing to it.'

'There never has been?' she asked, surprised at herself.

He did not look discomposed, but moved forward in his chair, stretching his legs wide and clasping hands on his stomach. He yawned widely, then licked his lips.

'What do you think?'

'Nothing.'

'Nothing?'

'Nothing happened.'

'There you are, then.' He smiled broadly, making his eyes

small and wrinkled, as he held out his hand to her. He had not to lie twice.

Curiously she felt relief. It was nearly a certainty that her husband had committed adultery and had perjured himself, but she was pleased. He was warned and in any case she had learned that he did not want to throw her over. She released his hand, took the paper from the wide arm of his chair, and walked for the door.

'What are you going to do with that?' he asked.

'Destroy it.'

She smiled all the way up the stairs, shoulders back, hips swinging, but when she placed the treacherous paper on her dressing table she dropped to her bed, face white, rigid. She lay down, kicking off her shoes.

Ten minutes later Eric opened the door.

'There you are.' He quietly shut himself in, said 'I know this must have upset you, Elsa.'

'Yes.'

'What puzzles me is who would have gone to all the trouble?'

'I don't . . .' She couldn't be bothered to complete the sentence. What's the sense between liars?

'Do you want to talk about it again?'

'What's the use of that?' she asked, leaning on an elbow.

'I don't want you to feel that the subject's closed. It's all so odd. You and me and Madeleine. I don't even know her very well. Do you think we should mention it to her?'

'Why would anyone bother to send . . . the thing?'

'That's what intrigues me.'

They talked, in circles, two hypocrites, before he knelt at the bedside, stroking, urging his hand under her frock, tenderly touching her sex. She allowed it for a time, passive, taken aback by his brashness, before she sat up, set her legs together, her feet to the floor.

'Not now,' she said.

'You're angry.'

'I don't think so. I don't know where I am. I don't know what's going to happen next. That's all.'

'Nothing will happen.'

She stood up, made her way to the mirror, sat down to tame her already cultivated hair. He watched the comb, the finger-work.

'We'll forget, then,' she said.

'Can you?'

'No idea.' Elsa shrugged. She had made her protest and would not recant. For a moment she wondered how frightened he was or how much Madeleine still demanded of him. The thought of the pair locked nakedly limb with limb seemed outrageous, or laughable. She wished she had seen them at it. Would she, spying, have rushed in or allowed them to continue their ridiculous, middle-aged jigging? She could not say.

'Odd,' he said.

'Never mind.' She rose, patted his arm. 'You get on with your work now.'

'Where are you going?' He was frightened.

'Retford.'

All that had taken place four years before and though three or four times he had tried to raise the matter again she had checked him with the same sentence: 'As far as I'm concerned it's over, forgotten.' When he continued, as she knew he would, she answered, 'You heard what I said. I meant it.'

Now, as he sat comfortably with *The Times* and his morning tea, he knew that soon he'd be at work, notebook to hand, carefully for an hour, then with flagging interest, forced to remind himself that behind the page he found so banal were concealed struggles, some writer's bloody sweat. He doubted that. Most of the books he reviewed were professional enough, competent, even ingenious, but there was no sin, no grief there. Why should there be? He'd joined the entertainment industry. If one poked about in the strip-shows for a Virgin Mary or even a Cyprian Venus one would end disappointed. He turned the page of his newspaper, wrestling. He knew damn well what he'd say in his review before he read this morning's book. All he looked for were the points where he'd push his wounding pins accurately in, and the words which would make his own name memorable for a week. He'd take half an hour off, and see what George Hill wanted. It would do at twelve-fifteen when the doctor came in from his round.

He asked his wife if she wanted to join him. She refused; lunch was in the oven; they'd put the meal back.

Madeleine let him in, informed him that George was not returning before evening surgery. Armchairs and whisky were prescribed for both. An energetic, edgy woman, Madeleine Hill kept the blue-blackness of her hair smoothed over her unlined face, her pale eyes. The small Roman nose stood fierce, and her lip curled back from white teeth immediately she showed animation. Today in a scarlet blouse and an ankle-length skirt she swerved like a gypsy, ready with abuse, wild movement or specious promises of fortune.

'I'm glad to see you,' she said, seated four yards away. 'You've been avoiding me.'

'I've been busy.'

'That's a man's feeblest excuse.'

'It's the truth.' The only way, he'd decided, to handle her was to treat her with a vulgar ordinariness. 'What does George want?'

'Oh?'

'Caroline brought a message last night.'

They sipped the doctor's excellent blend. The sitting room was dark, with windows on one short side only and they overshadowed with a huge rhus, red-dark in the sunlight. Chamberlain could not help recalling that he'd had the woman in this room, on cushions dragged down from chairs and settee. A matter of pride now. Or so it seemed, for she had made the pace, laughing at his timidities. He never understood her. As she sat absolutely still, staring down at her glass, she was handsome but proper, distant, bored by conversation. But her face would break so that she'd squeal, pant, pinch, dash clothes, without modesty, in creases to the floor.

'I've no time for you,' she announced.

'What have I done?'

'You know what you haven't.' Her hard, unmoving face made no sense of the words.

He took refuge in whisky. She did likewise. With nothing to say for himself, he did not enjoy this silence. He could hear her breathe. Madeleine finished her drink, made for the sideboard.

'Another for you?' she asked. He declined. 'You're a rotten sod.'

'So you tell me.'

'Doesn't it mean anything? What's happened to us?' She spoke towards the decanter on its heavy silver tray, without emphasis, grumbling.

'I shan't leave Elsa.'

'I know that. I don't ask you to.'

He finished his whisky, put the glass to the ground, let his arm hang ape-like over that of the chair.

'Put some music on,' he said.

Immediately she obeyed, walking to the record cupboard. The shrillness of a baroque organ rippled round, knuckled the room. Too loud, it distressed him, cut his nerves. He did not complain, but closed his eyes. At the conclusion of the first band, a Bach Pastorale, she snapped the set dead.

'You never talk sense to me,' she began. She held a man-sized drink. 'If I didn't feel about you as I do, I'd despise you.'

'So you've said.'

'It's true. You're not a man at all.'

'No.'

'Why can't you have the courage of your convictions?'

'I've got none,' he answered. 'You've often said so.'

She swigged, inspected the glass, became remote. 'I don't want to quarrel.'

He let it pass, wondering if her outburst was any more than a passing need for excitement, for a factitious quarrel. She certainly did not love him; for some months after their first coitus she had troubled him with letters written and delivered indiscreetly. After that she made a fuss of him in public and contrived to keep out of his way in private. Now and then, as today, she'd lash him with her tongue for no sane reason that he could see. If he made a pass, she'd shriek or run off.

'You're a fool,' she said.

'What's wrong with you?'

She pulled her mouth into a line of prim pleasure.

'Oh, you see there's something wrong, do you?'

'Go on.'

Madeleine drained the glass, turned away.

'When George's not here, you take it out on somebody else?'

'Is that the best you can do?'

He picked his glass from the floor, put it on a table. She allowed him as far as the door.

'I saw that idiot son of yours.'

'Oh, yes.'

'With Lynette Rockford.'

'I expect so.'

'You approve, do you?' She had come up to him.

'What use is my approval?' He suddenly felt sorry. 'He seems very taken with her.'

'It'll come to nothing.'

'Probably not.'

She followed him outside into the porch.

'She spends a lot of time with Boy McKay.' The solicitor son of Lynette's boss.

'So I've heard.'

'Does John not know?'

'He never talks about it. Neither to me nor to Elsa. You know how it is.'

'My children confide in me.'

He kept the smile frozen from his face. If Saul or Caroline heard a civil word from their mother it meant company was present. Madeleine, hand on carved white totem-pole supporting the glass and wood structure, seemed rapt, self-delighted, a loving parent.

'You're lucky,' he said.

At the pretentious gates, out of sight of the house, his daughter Pamela held hands with Saul Hill. Her father stopped.

'Want a lift?'

She kissed Saul, enthusiastically, he thought, to impress, annoy him, climbed in. 'Been there all morning?' he asked.

'On and off.'

'Don't be filthy.' She did not laugh. 'His mother said nothing.'

'She doesn't know.'

'Doesn't she get on with Saul, then?'

His daughter grimaced, attending to her appearance.

4

October sunlight lined the ripples of the sea with uneven gold.

The air, mildly gusty, was not yet chilly as Elsa and Eric Chamberlain walked the promenade at Leaport. They had, this Tuesday morning, come from the hospital where John recovered from an attempt at suicide. On Sunday evening he'd swallowed barbiturates, but a flat-mate, unable to rouse him, had sent for an ambulance. In the hospital they'd pumped him out, called for the college authorities who were represented at this time by their senior tutor, a large-bosomed spinster. She, frightened out of her wits, since the principal was delivering a lecture and the deputy not back from a week-end in Wales, had decided not to inform the parents once she learnt that the young man was out of danger. A fellow pupil had taken it on herself to ring the Chamberlains on Monday, and they had set out at once for the south-coast resort where the college was situated.

The staff-nurse had allowed them to see their son shortly that evening. He sat, abashed perhaps, sulky, but perfectly well, if unwilling to talk. Elsa had pressed him without qualm, and he stonily refused to answer. They left for their uncomfortable hotel, where Eric drank in a bar underneath the room in which his wife tried to sleep. When next day, at eleven according to instruction, they reported at Drake Ward, they found John up and about in pyjamas and dressing-gown. He was more communicative, admitted he'd been a fool, blamed Lynette Rockford and informed them that he'd been back to Nottinghamshire the week-end before without calling in at home.

'But why?'

'She wrote and told me it was finished. Between us. I had to see her.' He mumbled, ashamed of himself, but staring them out, flesh puffy under his eyes.

'Where did you sleep?'

'With Tom Angelo in Retford. On the floor.'

They scowled about the room.

'What's happened between you and Lynette?' Elsa asked.

'She says she's going to marry Robin McKay.'

'He's married.'

'He'll get a divorce.'

John shrugged, shuffled, searched the pockets of the gown, peeled chewing-gum, settled to jaw-work.

'What was between you?' No answer. A slap of hands on thigh. 'Were you expecting her to marry you?' 'Is she divorced?' 'What made you try to kill yourself?' They sprinkled angry, mystifying questions, rephrased them, re-emphasized, wasted their breath as he chewed or grumbled non-committal, sullen jerks of words.

'What are you going to do now?' his father demanded in the end.

'Don't know.'

'You'll start back at Lord Dacre?'

'Suppose so.'

He was like a five-year-old. Any minute now he'd suck his thumb.

'Do you want to come home with us?' Elsa.

'No.'

'You'll be all right?'

He did not bother with that.

'Your mother means you won't try suicide again?'

'No.' Shoulders lifted.

Elsa took the boy's hand as it lay on his lap. She seemed calm, young, delicate, while John hunched, his jaws ugly in heavy mastication.

Chamberlain saw the moment as ludicrous, because he could not believe that Elsa did more than go through an expected act, which she'd rehearsed on the way here, and was allowed only because she was more beautiful than most. The wet sound of moving gums, teeth, tongue, lips answered her but she did not release the hand. Then he recalled photographs of John in pram, bath and high-chair watched over by his mother; the woman herself, blonde-bright, in love with her child. She did not look much older now, held herself as handsomely, seemed slimmer.

The memories, against his will, roused no emotion in him; because the chewing lout loomed too ungainly. Elsa perhaps was made differently, felt through the flesh of her hand the helplessness of the son she'd reared. Her face showed a quizzical calm, as if she assessed him, herself, the boy. She repeated her question and the voice had nothing spurious about it, spoke breathily, breaking the rhythm. Elsa could at this minute be in crisis while her husband, two yards away, fumbled for cynicism.

'We're going to the college, then home if you think you don't need us.'

John looked at her.

'Would you like us to come back after lunch?'

He nodded, chewing still, as her eyes shone suddenly wet.

'We'll come then. Won't we, Daddy?' God.

'Is there anything you want?' Shaken head. 'Anything we can do? Arrange, you know?' Nothing. 'While we're at the college?'

'I sent Lynette a letter.' The words sounded crumpled near incoherence. His father was through the door.

'Telling her what you ...'

'Yes.' He'd said the word, surprisingly. With a bitter vigour.

'And you want us to let her know how . . . Go to see her?'

John blew breath out, rudely, not recognizing what he did, unhearing.

'And you will be all right, won't you?'

'I think so.' Sane, in haven. Eric looked in.

'Smile, then.' She used to say that years before after a bloody knee, a tantrum. John complied, his face a full moon lined and thatched.

'We'll be back at two-fifteen.'

Chamberlain admired his wife, knowing she'd won a battle, but as he walked two steps behind her down disinfected stairs and corridors into sunshine he did not speak, had nothing to ask.

On the sea front they headed into the wind, Elsa's coat-tails wildly alive. Chamberlain asked about lunch, but his words were blown off. He admired his wife's bearing; her ruffled hair showed fetching imperfection. He did not love her at this moment, he was too scarred, but he knew he had chosen the right wife. She had conveyed their love to the boy, their love, not merely her own and had maintained her poise. He had shuffled, scruffily ineffective. Outside a steel-framed menu she stopped, rapped the glass, indicated they'd eat here. He followed her into a dining room with heavy starched tablecloths and serviettes, massive cutlery, waitresses with lace caps.

Though the service was slow, the meal was substantial and they could sit in the sunshine by the first-floor bay window and look out at the diminished breakers in the distance and the lashing twigs in the street.

'What did you think of him?' she asked, with the soup.

'He seemed normal.'

'That's what I thought.'

They did not speak for a while, though both were uncomfortably aware of the other's presence.

'I wonder if he'll try again?' Chamberlain asked, fork blooming with cauliflower.

'Why do you say that?' They ate again.

'To tell you the truth, I didn't think he felt anything as, as strongly as . . .'

'We don't know our own son.'

'I don't, certainly.'

That about summed it up. They spoke between mouthfuls or courses, then with coffee, about Lynette Rockford, John's revolt at school over cross-country, their own ignorance. The conversation disturbed them so that he felt guilty that he could eat heartily; she left half-helpings on the side of the plate.

The Lord Dacre College of Education was close, three Victorian villas with some nondescript concrete blocks packed into the garden of a demolished mansion. Students in denim drifted about notice-boards or walked smartly away from the foyer, in the new building, a place of orange and green arm-chairs and revolving glass-doors. The Chamberlains discovered the discomfort of black chairs while a girl in the office, packing away her sandwiches, went off in search of the vice-principal.

Mr Denton, discovered, proved to be a tall young man, hair grey already, his throat alive with adam's apple. He apologized for the delay, and expressed sympathy. The parents understood, of course, that John would be welcomed back, to finish his course. The man consulted his brief; a good student, shaped well on practice, an excellent study of two brothers had gained a mark of distinction. This, this aberration had caught them all napping. His voice, with its slight Welsh lilt, comforted them, forced them back from reality.

'Do you have many suicide attempts?' Elsa asked, bright as water.

'Not many, no. Not many. But . . .' He was away again until she cut him short.

'Do they usually come back.'

'That varies. By and large, I'd say they do.' Mr Denton

embarked on a story of delayed success, throwing in questions for good measure. 'And do you know where that young man is now?' They shrank, hearing the glad tidings. Doctor of Philosophy. Principal Lecturer at a polytechnic. He gabbled on, remembered to ask how they had found their son, confessed he did not know him personally, but, finger-nails a-flick on the paper, here was evidence of quality.

'You didn't let us know,' Chamberlain said heavily.

'I beg your pardon.'

'The college authorities did not get in touch with us.'

'It was a friend of John's,' Elsa said.

Denton became quieter. His colleague, the senior tutor, an excellent lady in her way, had not much experience of these matters. Hostility unnerved him. She knew all about, rabbit-toothed giggle, pre-menstrual tension, but. Had he been on the spot, now. Of course, in her defence, John was an adult, and once it had been established that he was in no danger, then perhaps he should have been consulted about his parents. Yes, yes. Had he been on the premises there would have been a phone call. It was not his place, however, to malign his colleague who had done what she thought best. His adam's apple bobbed like a float. Elsa despised him.

'We'd be grateful,' said Chamberlain, 'in any repetition . . .'

'Certainly, certainly. The principal and I unfortunately on this occasion were . . .'

They escaped under the great horse-chestnuts and limes round the building, made again for the hospital. John now seemed more sullen, or less talkative, showing no pleasure when told he could return to Lord Dacre. He muttered, pulled his mouth elastically about, walked away from them towards a window. His mother followed him.

'Is it what you want to do?' Elsa asked. He shrugged.

'What else is there?'

'You could come home with us, and look round when you felt better.'

'What would my dad think of that?'

'You can come home if you want to.'

'No.' He'd go to Lord Dacre; there was nothing else for it. Chamberlain closed the gap between them, asked John if he was all right for money. He had no sooner spoken than he felt degraded by his question. The other two stood apart, morally, superior.

They left, driving the Rover hard for home.

Though they hardly spoke in the first hour after a preliminary inquest for five minutes in the car park, Chamberlain knew he must praise his wife.

'You did well with the boy.' The roads flew past deserted; the country green still undulated charm as on a calendar. She looked up.

'You got across to him. I couldn't.'

'Were you angry?' Elsa asked.

'No. I don't know what to say.'

'Neither do I.'

'No. You were very good. I think you, you helped him. He wanted to please you.'

She did not even look at him.

'Thank you,' he said.

'He doesn't seem like our boy,' she argued. 'He's coarser.'

'He must be frightened, if nothing else. I mean, will the college recommend him for a job?'

'I can't think,' Elsa began again, 'what sort of state he'd be in to do such a thing.'

'Desperate.'

'Can you see yourself in such a, such . . . ?'

'No. At one time, perhaps.'

This conversation was repeated, in bursts, throughout the journey. Each time Chamberlain complimented his wife, who shook the praise off, tried to make him talk about John's distress. Each time the conversation faltered.

When they arrived home, dog-tired, they sat together over

a sandwich and a drink. Elsa fidgeted, crossing and recrossing her legs, frowning.

'We should get in touch with Lynette Rockford.' There burnt her anxiety.

'Yes. I suppose she knows. He sent her the letter.'

John had confided that to his mother, who had passed it on to her husband as they waited on the black chairs of the college.

'Will you go to see her?'

'Oh, well.' He'd taken it for granted Elsa would. 'I don't know her. I've never met her.'

'It would be better coming from you. I don't take her seriously. She's nothing. But you're a man. And you'll perhaps see what it was that drove your son to such a thing.' She spoke with loathing, as if she hated suicide, as smirching, fouling her.

'What am I to tell her?'

'What's happened. So she knows what she's done.'

'It may not be her fault.'

'No it may not.' Elsa jerked her crossed right leg up and down, violently from the knee, kicking out. 'But she should learn. She's older than he is.'

'But she might have acted very sensibly. John could be the one who . . .'

'John could. That's for you to find out.' Elsa's lips were thin. 'You don't want to do this, Eric. I see that. But it's a man's job to make her see, understand what's happened. She'll think I exaggerate. She'll listen to you.'

'I doubt that.'

'Women like her listen to men.'

She had decided. Next morning, grudgingly, he rang the office of McKay, Son and Roberts to ask for Mrs Rockford, who answered demurely, as if she'd been expecting the call. She agreed to see him that day, in the park if it were fine.

He drove to Retford without lunch, sat in his described

car where she joined him. Her legs flashed beautifully, but she wore too strong a perfume. He introduced himself; she expressed sorrow about John.

'I, my wife and myself, thought someone should come to see you.

She hummed soothing noises.

'He seemed,' Chamberlain said, 'to be over it physically, but we don't know how he'll shape otherwise.'

Now she inquired about the attitude of the college, John's prospects, the possibility of continuation of his training. Her voice was high, sharp, like that of a social worker ticking rapidly through the standard questions on a form. He did not like it, but he answered civilly.

'He wrote to you on the evening he . . . ?'

'Yes. I was away. I got it on Monday when I came home from work and rang your house. You'd gone. There was nobody in.'

'He has written from the hospital?'

'No. Still, it's only Tuesday.'

'You expect to hear, then?' he asked.

'How do I know?' She appeared flustered for the first time. He waited; for nothing.

'You had told him you had finished with him?'

'Yes.'

'And he came over last week-end?' Like blood from a stone.

'Yes.'

'What happened?'

'Mr Chamberlain, is this doing any good?'

'I've no right to expect answers.' He spoke pacifically. 'You have been kind enough to meet me. We're trying to help the boy.'

'Didn't you question him?'

'To some extent. We didn't press too far. He looked fragile.'

'But you don't mind interrogating me?'

'We can hardly call it that, can we?' He thought he knew how to deal with her. 'We aren't in any way blaming you for what's happened. I'm sure you realize that.'

She turned full face, smiling with her teeth white as an advertisement. He looked, unimpressed. She seemed soiled, second-hand, and momentarily he was sorry for her.

'Go on,' she said.

'Was there anything between you?'

'We were fond of each other. We used to meet.'

'You were lovers?'

'We had sex, sometimes. That's not what you mean, though. There was no permanent commitment between us.' The formality seemed natural.

'No mention of marriage?'

'No. I'm older than he is. I've been divorced.'

'Not even on his part?'

'Not really. I wouldn't allow it. He seemed dependent on me. In a way.'

'He read into the relationship more than you would have thought sensible?'

She sat quite still, staring at the windscreen. A gust of rain rattled it with thick drops.

'It would be silly to say that. He thought he loved me. I was fond of him.'

'He did speak of marriage, then?'

'Yes. He said that as soon as he'd finished and found a job . . . I wouldn't hear of it.'

'When you told him you'd done with him, did you expect anything of, of the kind . . . ?'

'No. I expected letters. Him bursting up to see me. We have to take it, put up with it, don't we? My husband told me once to my face that he was going off with another woman. Mind you, I wasn't surprised.'

'But John was?'

'He's young for his years. Don't you think so?'

Lynette did not appear ill-at-ease, nor notice her contradictions. It was, now, as if she enjoyed the company of this distinguished man for a short while.

'In some ways, yes. Was there any particular reason why you wanted to break off the relationship?'

'I'm going to marry Robin McKay.'

'I didn't know. I hadn't seen any announcement.'

She stared, put out. The pose did not suit her, with eyes protuberant, too large for the face.

'When he's got a divorce.'

'Does he know about John?'

'Not about what happened. Why should he?'

'About the affair, then?'

'Mr Chamberlain, I don't use such words. Sex is easier. Even in your day it didn't mean if you slept with someone you had to marry her. Did it now?'

'Easier or not, John tried to kill himself.'

She hadn't thought of that. She clasped her hands between her knees and huddled herself round them.

'It's sad,' she said after silence. He could hardly believe his ears. 'He's such a nice boy.'

'You told him about Mr McKay?'

'Yes. We'd made this agreement. As soon as his divorce comes through, then . . . You know. I couldn't carry on with John, really, could I? It wouldn't have been fair to him or to . . .'

'If you thought anything of him . . .' he said.

She flushed, frowned, jerked so violently he thought she'd fling the door open, fly out.

'I don't have to answer your questions.'

He apologized, explained that he wrote books of investigation, spent some part of his time listening to cross-examinations in the Assize Court. She seemed satisfied with this foolery, relaxed into her seat, head back, thighs bared bright.

'Perhaps it was my fault.' She improvised incompetently on the theme, attracted compliments from Chamberlain, lit a cigarette, saying she must be off.

'Is there anything I can do for you?' he asked.

'No. Not really. I'd be grateful if you'd not talk about it.'

'I see.'

'It's no use my writing to John. It wouldn't do any good. He's got to accept that it's all over. You see that don't you.' Choking smoke clouded, knifing.

'It's finished?'

'Yes. I'm sorry. I liked him. We had some good times.'

She held the door open, bent on the pavement, white breast-tops to brown throat, to hear his speech of thanks. He watched her go, buttocks shifting, head in air and thought for some seconds like his son. Recovering untidily from the age of twenty-one, he made for the nearest pub.

The lounge where he sat with beer and beef sandwiches stretched large and empty. The landlord, a taciturn man, offered pickled onions or sauce, moved into his other bar. Chamberlain recognizing he had wasted his time, that his account would not satisfy his wife, decided to hurry home, get unpleasantness over. By the time he brushed the last crumbs off it was raining hard though the western sky was widely patched with blue.

'What did you have to eat?' Elsa's first question.

'A sandwich, in "the Star".'

'With Lynette?'

'No. She'd gone back to work. We sat in the car to talk.'

'I thought you'd be back for lunch.' He'd gone wrong again.

'I didn't say so.'

He was displeased with himself, determined not to let her harry him. She led him to an armchair, provided whisky which he tried to wave away.

'How did you find her then?'

'Co-operative in so far that she'd say something. She's going to marry Boy McKay.'

'He's married already.'

'He's divorcing his wife.'

'They still live together.'

'That's what she said.' He paused. 'She and John had been sleeping together.'

'Didn't you expect that?' Elsa asked, face smooth as ivory.

'I suppose so.' He would not be outdone. 'She made it clear to John that it was all over between them.'

'When he came up?'

'Yes. She told him about McKay.'

'I can't understand John coming back all this way,' Elsa said, 'and not calling to see us. You wouldn't have been pleased, though, would you? If he had?'

'No.'

'He must have been desperate. And we're no help.'

'I should think that's not unusual.'

'He needed us.'

'He wouldn't think so.'

He picked up his whisky in displeasure. It would have been better if he could have left it untasted. For two or three minutes he reconstructed the interview and she sat unkindly silent. He toyed then with his glass, waiting for her to question him.

'What did you make of her?'

'She's quite attractive.' Lips thinned. Now he would please her, because she'd deserved his consideration. 'There was something about her I didn't like. She was shabby.'

'Her clothes, do you mean?'

'No. They were nothing to write home . . . No. Perhaps that's the wrong word. Tatty.'

'What's that?'

'She didn't seem straightforward with me. Wanted to ingratiate herself, if she could. It was, I don't know, not right.'

'You didn't expect to like her?' Elsa asked. 'She was the cause of John's...'

'I didn't connect her with that. Not in any emotional way. It was her manner. It's wrong to say such things, because I might just be picturing my own misgivings, unloading them on to her, but she wanted me to like her. Not just me. Any man. And that was more important than John's suicide.' He finished his drink. 'Now I've said it I don't know whether it's right. I didn't like her.'

'She makes out she's been on the stage.'

'Is that wrong?'

'I don't know.' Elsa gave up there. Her husband had been pushed by her into action and his results bored her. There should be action rewarding or retributive, not dull recitals of the already known.

'She won't get much out of Boy McKay,' he said, aiming to please.

'Why not?'

'He's a sod. Clever and idle. Drinks, I'm told.'

'His wife... I feel sorry for her. She's for trouble.'

'Where's this Lynette girl from?'

'She's local. Her father had a farm. Or an uncle.'

'And where's Rockford, the husband?' he asked.

'Away, somewhere. She married away.' Elsa seemed at ease now, on some pleasurable tack. 'She's not been here long.'

'Are the parents still about?'

'She doesn't live with them.'

They sat, the two, unobserved of each other. Chamberlain made his gesture of goodwill.

'I'm sorry,' he said. 'I didn't get much out of her.'

Elsa considered that, disregarded it, nodding to herself before she walked out of the room.

5

Eric Chamberlain swayed over his beer in the Royal Oak.

He had done little work, which annoyed him, left him guilty. In the hour or two before dinner, after the interview with his wife, he had tried to read, but found that though he jerked his eyes over the same page, he learnt nothing, could not even blot out the incoherent tumbling of his thoughts. Uncomfortably he'd summed Lynette Rockford up but found words worthless. This afternoon's performance with those two women had been, God, his best; nothing short of the miraculous would have altered the outcome and yet he sat in discomfort, his head waspish with self-criticism.

When he, against judgement, had invited Elsa to join him on his trip to the pub, she had not put her refusal into words. Pamela, his daughter, back from work to read a magazine in front of a television set had jerked straight with surprise.

'You go, Mummy. It won't be too crowded.'

Elsa removed herself from the room, diminishing father and daughter.

A shadow darkened Chamberlain's table so that he, immersed still, dragged himself back to the world and Robin McKay.

'May I join you?' McKay, carrying a large whisky, waved with his left hand towards Chamberlain's tankard, offering dumbly. At a headshake he pulled a chair about, chose a position, sat down.

'I came on the off-chance of seeing you,' he said. 'I heard you, er, patronized the place.'

Chamberlain made no answer, not sorry to be disturbed.

McKay sat very upright on his chair, very still. He was tall, with hair that covered his ears, slightly greasy, beginning to grey, but his face caught the attention, thin, lined near the nostrils, with cleft chin, dark round small, blue, lively eyes, an untidy nose, his forehead and cheeks slightly pitted. He did not smile; his features might have been set in concrete, so that one had no idea of his mood, searched for expression in vain.

'Lynne Rockford said she saw you this afternoon.'

Chamberlain nodded; McKay sipped. They did not hurry each other.

'Is your boy all right?' Glass replaced. 'She told me about him.'

'As far as we know.'

McKay put together some phrases of regret. Both picked up drinks. Chamberlain, by now both interested and at ease, examined the speaker's face. The nose was lumpy and large, but smooth, waxier than the darker cheeks.

'Was it unexpected?'

'Yes. We were caught out.'

'Had you any idea he was . . . going around with Lynette?'

'We knew. Yes. That he saw her.'

'But not that it was so serious?'

'Does one know that sort of thing?'

Silence again, while Chamberlain wondered what the man wanted, sitting there, straight as a dog up for a bone.

'He wrote to Lynne. To say he was about to . . .' There was a courteous, old-fashioned air about the way he allowed the phrase to tail away. He spoke with a bass voice, rather quietly. English public-school. 'She didn't get it until, well, late.'

'So I understand.'

'She was upset. She hadn't expected anything like this.'

'No. I'm not surprised.'

'He seemed a well-balanced boy, she said.'

They sat. Chamberlain finished his beer, rose, asked what the other drank. McKay drained his glass. Whisky and water.

After a wait at the bar, conventional brief toasts, Chamberlain did not find conversation easy. McKay stared at the table, not in gloom, but noncommittally. He squinted at, lined up, read a beer-mat as if it were important. Both drank, like paupers, wetting their lips.

'I understand you and Mrs Rockford are getting married.'

'She told you that?'

'Yes. Isn't it so, then?'

McKay suddenly relaxed, like a deflating balloon. Stiffness deserted him; he stuck his legs out; arms dangled ape-like alongside his chair. He tried to smile, not with any success, as he lolled.

'It's not so easy.'

'You mean you're married already?'

McKay rubbed his hand through his hair, disturbing disturbance. He stared his disbelief.

'No. It's not that. Not my wife. She's well out of the way. I live with somebody else.'

'Does Lynette know?'

'Yes.' He came back to ramrod. 'Oh, I see. She told you. Some story. Some ... Lynne's a good girl, but she romances.'

'Tells lies, you mean?'

'Yes. Put like that.' McKay took no offence. 'She believes her own account. At the time.'

'So there's no knowing what she told John?'

'Hard to say. There's a kind of coherence about her.' The word had gravitas, the solicitor's cachet. 'She's sensible within limits, our Lynette.'

Again the pause while Chamberlain shuffled his ideas.

'But you won't marry her?'

'I don't suppose so.'

They gloomed into their glasses, comically.

'She's a local girl,' McKay said, voice deep and slow.

'From Leenside Farm. Lynette Smith. The parents have retired now to a housing estate. She went to work in London, office, married a research student there, then to America with him for a year, but they didn't hit it off. She came back, did a bit of acting, I believe, so she says. Then she joined up again with her husband. In London, at first, then in Wales where he had some sort of job. But she left him, came home, was recommended to us.'

'And Mr Rockford?'

'Divorced. By consent. He'd found somebody else.' Sipping. 'There's something sad about it. She's very lively, I think. Attractive. And without trying to be. You met her.'

'Not my type.'

'No. She wouldn't put a show on.' Chamberlain raised his eyebrows, reached swimmingly for his tankard, plopped with his lips like a pipe-smoker.

'But not the sort of wife you want?'

'I don't want any sort. I've one too many now. And another bloody woman round my neck.' He laughed, awkwardly. 'I'm a prize . . . No. I get out of life what I put in, and a bit more. I'm a woman-chaser, in a small way. And when an attractive crumpet turns up in the office, ready and waiting, I'm first in.'

'But you've problems?'

'I'll say.' McKay yawned, widely, rudely, not covering his mouth. 'They're not insoluble. There's nothing tragic about me. Or mine.' Now he looked handsome, and intelligent, a cut above the average. 'I've deserved what I've got.'

'What'll happen when it becomes clear to Mrs Rockford that there's nothing doing?'

'I don't know whether she'll believe it, for a start. But she's lively. She won't . . . At least, I think not.'

'It's a risk. I wouldn't have said that John . . .'

They lifted glasses; each man locked from the other.

'Why did you want to see me?' Chamberlain began in no hurry.

'See you? That's just the word. See. I know your wife slightly. We've met. She knows my wife. But not you. You're one of the famous. I'm curious. Lynette praised you; you were polite and calm. Perhaps she fancied you.' That seemed gratuitous. 'I thought, "Here's the opportunity to say hello. Perhaps I'll hear something." Don't want her hurt.'

'Is she upset about John?'

'Seems so.'

'She feels responsible?'

'I wouldn't say that. I don't know. It's an odd thing for a young man to do.' McKay stroked his dark chin. 'All right for poetry. Plays. That sort of thing. It doesn't happen much. I shouldn't have thought so.'

They exchanged sentences about the two young people, interesting trivia, offered as if to keep themselves amused, or up to scratch. John's motor-bike. Lynne's Viola with the Grafton Shakespeare Players. His football. Her clothes. His quietness. Her loquacity. They justified their existence, the next drinks, with these confidences. Neither man knew if he liked the other. In the end both fell silent and Chamberlain, earning a glance from the landlord, left for home three-quarters of an hour before closing-time.

Elsa sat, a large gin at her elbow. She looked at her watch, but made no remark. He opened a can of beer in the kitchen, brought it in.

'I wanted to talk with you.'

Twice in one day. He dipped his lips in the froth.

'John rang while you were out.'

'How is he?'

'Back in college. He's going to see some psychiatrist. They want him to.'

'And in himself?'

'He said he was well. I didn't press him. He sounded absolutely normal. Cheerful.'

'Did he mention Mrs Rockford?'

'No. Nor I.' She snapped at that, voice crackling.

Slowly, picking his words, he described his conversation with Robin McKay. She listened, but interrupted neither with comment nor question. When he'd finished she waited, proffering further scope, but at his silence she swigged her gin, poking the slice of lemon about the wet curve.

'Can I get you another?' he asked, relieved.

She handed the glass over, holding it with a straight arm.

'Never mind about lemon,' she said, as he moved doorwards. 'Sit down.'

'But, ice.'

She waved him to attention.

'No sooner had you gone off,' she began unpleasantly, 'than Pamela announced that she was going to marry Saul Hill.'

'Oh.'

'Is that all you've got to say?'

'Listen.' He spoke angrily, low, temper banging his pulses. 'I've heard just about all I can . . . Either get on with it, or leave it to Pam to tell me.'

'She won't.'

'I'll do without then.' He glared; she sat unmoved in stalemate. Elsa lifted the glass to her lips.

'They're going to get engaged.' Now she spoke coldly, smooth as cream.

'But they want our permission?'

'No. Information only. I think they'd like our approval. But she won't ask you. "Daddy'll fly off the handle." I have to break the news.'

'What do you think?'

'She's nineteen. At work. People get married at that age.'

'He isn't. He's still at university. Then he'll have to get his professional qualifications.'

'You don't approve?' she asked.

He did not reply, fearing the consequences of the alternatives. Elsa was out to rile him, because they were tired of each other, had no means of reconciliation. He puffed his lips forward, slipped lower into his chair, pushing his belly upwards to appear as uncouthly froglike as he could.

'They sleep with each other,' she said.

'They've told you so?' He would not be provoked.

'Yes. She admits it. And what are you going to do about it?'

'Nothing. That's obvious.'

'You won't say anything to her?' Elsa asked.

'No. I don't need confirmation.'

'You don't mind?'

'Yes.' He dawdled on his answer. 'Yes, I do.' He shoved himself upright. 'One's daughter is unique. She's a child to me.'

'You're wrong, then?'

'Yes. Yes. I am. The world doesn't work as I want it to. You don't need to rub that in. One plans, has plans.' He stood up, marched to the far side of the room, where he stood stupidly in a corner, aghast at the strength of his feeling. He put a hand flat on the wall-paper which felt cool or damp. After a moment's not-thought, but release from jarring, he knew he'd like to comfort Elsa with a word or two. He turned, still in his dunce's niche.

'This must have been a shock to you,' he said, mumbling.

'No. Not at all. It's what one expects.'

'But Pam's such a nice child, so, so . . .'

'I don't deny it. That has nothing to do with it. Young people think differently. You ought to know. Your books are full of adultery.'

'You blame me?'

'Not for that. I'd be surprised if she's read anything you've written. No. For your attitude. You say nothing; you keep out. And when you are involved you lose your temper, and go red in the face and shout.'

'If,' he said, advancing one yard, 'I'd have acted differently, would Pam?'

Elsa shrugged as if at stupidity.

'I don't mind,' he said, 'your taking it out of me. It's all to the good if it makes you feel better. But you might tell me what you want?'

She considered, playing with her glass.

'A little consideration, sometimes.'

'Here we go.' He slithered back to his chair, stood by it. Not loudly, not displeased, he hummed the tune of 'Tell me the old, old story'. She did not appear to listen, having no notion of its significance.

'I know it means nothing to you because you're so utterly selfish. You lock yourself away with your books and writing, and when you've finished with that you sit in the pub. It's not as if you go down for social reasons.'

He made humming noises, expressing, he hoped, sympathy.

'You've no idea, have you, what I have to contend with?'

He did not answer.

'You don't seem to care that John nearly killed himself. I have to do everything. Make the arrangements. Talk to him when we get there.'

'I drove you down.'

'Why do you say that?' she asked.

'I didn't just do nothing.'

'You'd drive twice that distance to lunch with your publishers or have a fishing holiday.'

'I see I shan't get any sense out of you.'

'No, you will not. I take the brunt of it all, and you, as long as you put money in the kitty, think that's all there is to be done.' She waited, an expression of distaste twisting her mouth, until she turned more sour when she saw he wasn't going to speak. 'What about Pamela, then?'

'I'll speak to her.'

'But what do you think?'

'I'll wait till I hear what she's got to say for herself.'

Elsa did not spit in his face. 'She's in now,' she said, 'if you're sober enough.'

Chamberlain bowed ironically, went upstairs to his daughter's room, where he found her in front of a mirror, doing nothing. It was obvious that she had been crying. He bent and kissed her, his arm round her shoulder. Physically she made no response, neither flinching nor in warmth.

'Well, young woman,' he asked, 'what's all this your mother's been telling me?'

Pamela studied her lap.

'You and Saul, isn't it?'

Still nothing. She looked like a sullen ten-year-old. He tried again. He loved this child.

'You didn't think I'd be angry, did you?'

'You usually are. Either you or Mummy.'

'I see.'

He pulled a chair up, said he liked Saul, thought they might make a go of it, though it was for them to judge that. The sentences flowed plausibly, comforting, so that he found himself lulled in benevolence, pleased with his performance.

'Mummy's angry.'

'Do you know why?'

'She just doesn't like Saul. He tells her what he thinks.'

'And that's bad?'

'She's not very happy, anyway, is she?'

Pamela began some cosmetic campaign, opening jars, lining up implements.

'Is there anything I can do?' he asked.

'Shouldn't think so.'

'Shall I see Saul? Ask him what his intentions are?' His injected joviality pancaked flat. 'I can't see much against it to tell you the truth.' He rubbed his hands. She'd finished her preparations, but started nothing. 'What do his parents think?'

'He's not told them.'

'Is he afraid?'

'He just says, sensibly, that's it's no use looking for trouble. You know what Dr Hill's like . . . And Saul's mother. Well.'

'They're worse than us, you think?' He tried to lighten her load.

'In a way. I didn't think you'd mind I, us, being lovers.'

'What made you say that?' His anger flustered him. Pamela, hearing the change of voice, looked up from her task.

'There's plenty about it in your books,' she answered, without emphasis.

'You mentioned that to your mother?'

That caused embarrassment so that she dropped a file, clattered a small bottle away.

'I think I did.' Defiant.

'It's not very sensible, is it?'

'How do I know?' She burst into tears, tolerably at first, then putting her face on her arms to sob. Another vial tippled before blind fingers.

Chamberlain, belly laden, lungs taut, was afraid. His skin prickled, shuddered while his eyes were wide with tears. He forced himself, against mild nausea, to speak.

'I don't like it. I love you.'

She sobbed, not looking up.

'You're my daughter.' It took him all his time to get that out. The last word, old-fashioned and desperate, choked him, and he coughed, lying. 'Whatever you do.' Crying. 'It hardly seems any time since I was giving you baths or donkey rides. I thought you liked me.'

'You shout at me.' She half-lifted her face.

'I'm sorry. I didn't know I did.' He sighed, regaining control. 'Your mother always complains that I never intervene; you say I bully you.'

'You're always pressing me.'

'No. That's not true.'

'You want me to be what you want.'

He pulled himself together, half scared at the discoloured blubber of her face, and said quietly,

'I don't think I've been a harsh father, have I?'

'You're always on at me. Telling what I ought to think.'

'It's not so, Pam.'

'What about that painting course? What about a bank account? What about driving lessons?'

'But I hardly . . .'

'You think you didn't. You don't know what you're saying. You don't care how much you show me up in front of other people. You bawled at me in the street.'

'I had explicitly told you which forms to bring.'

'I thought . . . You'd no right to rave like that. Saul doesn't. I made a mistake.'

'I was a bit sharp.' Nothing. 'But I'd given absolutely clear instructions.'

She'd stopped crying now, looked almost interested.

'I don't approve of indiscriminate sex,' he said. 'I will say that. But when I have said it, it's not the end of the world. You and Saul want to get married?'

'Mummy doesn't like him.'

'So you've said.'

'You know it's true.'

'I don't really.' He coughed, pacifically. 'No man's good enough for our daughter. We both think that. But I expect we're willing to learn.'

'I think you're selfish,' she said, quite quietly, unemphasized.

'Oh?' No answer. Anger bit, but he kept his face down. 'Go on. Explain yourself.' She did not. 'Why do you say that?'

She smiled, almost comically, reflecting, elf-sharp.

Attracted by that grin, he felt amiable, charitable.

'You don't mind about Saul and me because it doesn't

affect you. You'll go on tomorrow as you did today. If Dr Hill comes round, raising hell, you'll be pleased, won't you? But if I failed to bring down some forms you ought to have remembered to hand in to your accountant the day before, you'd blow your top in public.'

'I seem to have made an impression there.'

The door opened. Elsa came steadily forward as Chamberlain rose to his feet.

'Have you spoken to her?' the mother asked, before she had come to a halt.

'We're talking.'

'Have you reached any conclusion?' Elsa looked about for a chair, found none, moved a pile of ironed underclothes to sit on the bed.

'Not really.'

'No. I didn't suppose you had. Is she to marry Saul?'

They sat; Pam, elbows on dressing table, supported her face to peer into the glass.

'That's not really for me to say.'

'Do you take responsibility for anything?' Elsa snapped.

'Yes. I do. Financial matters. I keep the house paid for and warmed. I buy the food.'

'You provide money for it.' That seemed a small enough score. 'You know I'm not carping about that. I do everything else. Who do the children run to if there's any snag?'

'I agree. But isn't it wise? You understand them as I don't seem to.'

His wife crossed her legs, folding her hands into her lap, in a modest, middle-aged gesture of acquiescence so out of keeping with her bright slimness, her beauty, that its irony was lost.

'But do you understand what I feel about it?'

'Yes. I do now.'

'Go on.' She twisted her wedding-ring. Small movements writhed.

'You think I leave all the responsibility to you. And it seems unfair.'

'Don't you?'

'No. I don't ask you to do my work.' His promptness of response, its firmness startled her.

'Who says it's my work?' she asked.

'I do. You took it over, presumably because you wanted to, or saw it as your duty, or thought you were good at it. I was content, I'll admit. But you did. And you didn's complain.'

'And now I've had enough.'

The three were silent, immobile, pricklingly conscious of the others outside their own carapaces of discomfort. Finally, rather slowly, Elsa rose, walked towards the fireplace over which hung a reproduction of Paul Klee's 'Fishes', at which she peered, moving her head from side to side, following the dim reflection of herself before making for the window. There she stood, back to them, but not ignoring them, thrusting her personality through the well-cared-for suit, tights, polished shoes, shining hair-do, so that father and daughter waited, chidden for her next word. Elsa thrust up a hand, cuffed the curtain six inches apart, edged to the gap. The two waited, an audience, for the performance to conclude, to flower; to climax.

Elsa turned.

'In this case,' she said to Chamberlain, 'you'll decide.'

'There's no need for you to feel guilty about John,' he said. At the name Pamela caught her breath in a croup of pain. 'There was nothing either you or I could have done about that.'

'We could have known.'

'We did know. We talked about it. We even, if I remember, invited him to bring her to the house if he wanted to.'

'But . . .' At that she stopped bitterly, unedifying. She braced herself. 'We might have known how he felt.'

'That's not likely,' he said.

'You're supposed to be a person,' the definition unrolled like a bad examination answer, 'who uses his imagination.'

He ignored her, standing there in appeal, elegantly beautiful, begging for what she feared did not exist.

'Did you know, Pam, how bad John felt?' he asked.

'Leave her alone,' Elsa said. 'Don't try to push it off on to her.' She had turned, leaving the curtains apart. 'Whether she knew or not is not your concern. We should have noticed.'

'I didn't know,' Pamela answered.

'I see.' Chamberlain.

'He doesn't talk much to anybody. Well, not anybody here. I'd seen them out together. They bought us a drink in the Swan one night.'

'Did they seem happy?'

'That night? I don't . . . All right as far as I could tell. She seemed a bit restless.'

'Thank you,' he said. 'I'll have a word with Saul if you don't mind.'

'I can't stop you.'

'What will you tell him?' Elsa asked, very cold.

'I shall ask him what he thinks. Do you want to be there?'

'It's your responsibility.'

Elsa left the room, without a further word, while Pamela fiddled, began further cosmetic ceremonies, wishing her father out of the way.

'Good night, then.'

'Good night.' Not a smile; rattling of lids.

'When I come back from London, I'll see him. If that's . . . When he's over.'

He stood outside on the landing, in bright warmth, his face in a paroxysm of grief. No tears flowed; he cried in hurt dryness until he composed his face to appear downstairs at the whisky decanter.

6

Chamberlain's first call in London was to his publisher where he reported on the progress of his novel. Over an excellent lunch Charles Martin hummed the advantages of completing it by the end of the year, but Chamberlain promised nothing. Hope cut no hawsers; he feared the book, lacked confidence, felt his skill diminish as he worked. Here in a clash of cutlery, the savour of hock, the pleasure of choice, he knew strength, a factitious optimism, that would warp as he lifted the cover from his typewriter.

Elated, for Martin knew how to praise, he left the office at about four to visit Eli Dunne, one man he admired. Every time he came to town he dropped a line to Dunne, asked permission to call, received by return a list of trains from London Bridge, the latest fare-increases and an apology for this solicitude. 'You are capable, I know, of finding all this out, but it gives me pleasure to save you a few minutes.' Eli used the same phraseology and, Chamberlain guessed, in about three letters' time would begin to apologize for that. A hugely bearded man, Dunne, in his Victorian villa on the Woolwich Road, had the look of some Herbert Spencer or Carlyle, though easier, unforceful, edging his way past, laying neither curse nor blessing on you, but whispering the time of the next bus or the nutritional value of milk and raw cabbage. A former orchestral violinist, he now taught in schools, hutched out on winter's nights to lead or conduct amateur orchestras. He was not content; he could grumble with extraordinary speed in his breathless sputter of voice, but he moved on in life, went from place to place, encouraged this talent or that lack of it, putting his boots to the floor as if God had ordered it.

Chamberlain's case was extremely heavy, not with his laundry or washing-gear but with reveiw copies for Mrs Dunne. She loved books, piled them from floor to ceiling on white shelves so that, according to her husband, there'd shortly be nowhere to live. She did not mind his complaint, touched his arm smiling so that he reduced the volume of his grousing and, as he stumped away, seemed to congratulate himself on his extraordinary wife.

The garden in sunshine lay unkempt but beautiful, its grass littered yellow with the spent leaves of silver birches, horse-chestnut, lime trees. The bushes were stripped to wands or glowed red still; michaelmas daisies, yellow chrysanthemums stood bright with antirrhinums, roses, nicotiana spared from summer. Chamberlain kicked leaves, noticed the latch on the drive gate was still unmended, as he made for the hideous panels of stained glass in the pagoda-roofed porch. He rang the bell which no one answered.

Not without effort, he pushed the porch door inwards, scattering flakes of rust from the inefficient hinges, and hammered on the lion's-head knocker of the house door. A female voice, loud but preoccupied, invited him in. As he humped his case over the threshold, the same shout instructed him, 'In the kitchen.'

He could smell baking, but in no rush he examined the reddened palm of his carrying hand, rubbed it bloodless, stretched it nearer comfort before he moved on. In a sweetness of warmth, Mrs Dunne bent by the stove lifting a tray of congress tarts, her hands cased in a white oven-cloth, her hair untidy over the flushed face. She looked at Chamberlain, blue eyes wide, asking:

'What time is it?'

'Getting on for half five.' He did not consult his watch.

'I didn't think you'd be here yet. El's not back. From work.'

She carefully placed the tarts on the table, examined the next tray, shut the door before hanging her cloth and throwing her arms about Chamberlain. Her mouth fastened wetly on his, with such weight that he edged a foot or two backwards to regain his balance. Now he was into the sweetness of her body, held and locked, as they kissed deeply one into the other, loving and upright, yielding or erect, man and woman in a practised spasm, a drilled prelude of lust. He pulled her buttocks in to him and she snatched breath wildly, like squealing, into her lungs, fastening on his mouth in ecstatic liquidity. He straightened, moved her shoulders back, patting; she reached up with a hand, without much purpose, touching a wisp of her hair back across her forehead.

He held her at arm's length.

Blue eyes in a slightly stupid face, roundly pretty, stared not so much at him across the room, dazed, wild perhaps, as if she had been clobbered or delighted beyond measure.

'I've come.'

'So I've noticed.' The voice belied the vagueness of face, robbed her features of prose. He pulled her in and as they nuzzled he stroked her back, her body, breasts and belly through her dress, with skill, with tenderness, but all too neat, a prefabrication of caresses. It was she who shrugged away.

'Eli won't be long.'

She moved round the kitchen, filled the kettle, clattered out cups and plates from cupboards, knives, spoons on a tray, moving with speed, gracefully, like a dancer. She was plump, but delicately so, with unstockinged legs perfectly calved, swelling in perfection.

'Try that last lot from the oven,' she said. He reached for the cloth.

They were lovers, had been so from their first meeting. Nearly ten years ago Eli Dunne had written Chamberlain a fan-letter of four sides, minuscule script in black ink, praising *Another Troy*, but suggesting an alternative ending, ingenious enough, but aready considered and rejected by the author. Chamberlain replied explaining why he had done so, and by return more clerkly pages apologized, offered two more endings, both good, but both finally condemned by Dunne intelligently and in six lines. It was as if in minutes he could create plots, see their flaws, correct them, polish and wreck the new versions. Chamberlain, who struggled from one fullstop to the next with bloodied front, was impressed, suggested they should meet.

There followed the first of the timetables, and an invitation to stay the night. Chamberlain agreed not willingly, as he enjoyed the impersonal comfort and large whiskies of good hotels, feared damp sheets in cold bedrooms, a breakfast of watery eggs in bacon grease. Eli Dunne compelled attention. His praise was directed at real strength; he saw the bone and muscle of a book. His criticisms were exactly made, almost wittily, in brevity, depending on a recognition of the power of the novel. It was as though he were the master, Chamberlain the tiro, and yet his praise was so grave and lucid that there was no sense of condescension, rather one expert's view of another. Eli had wasted no time, had discussed the novel at an excellent tea, had continued jovially but sharply over the washing up before announcing that he had to go out for an orchestral rehearsal.

Chamberlain, shaken by the forthright line of Dunne's criticism, was now abashed that he had been abandoned like this, and, uncertain, mumbled as much.

'No,' Mrs Dunne was embroidering a cushion-cover with huge spiky flowers, 'he knew he'd got to go out. But he said he'd manage to fit in what he'd got to say. And if you're a late bird, so's he. And, anyway, there's breakfast time.' She smiled so complacently, this shapely woman, poured him so large a tumbler of whisky that he relaxed by the stove, in the kitchen. When she rose to mend this, she'd not spoken again, she poked, rattled and at the end of the commotion had nodded at his glass, muttered, 'Give us a sip,' so indistinctly that he'd begged her pardon. Without shame, she'd repeated her request and he held up his drink, towards which she bent. When she had wetted her lips, she said, 'I don't like it much. Do you?'

'Well, yes, I do.'

He stood, as she stood above, in front of him, shadowing him from the light, and settled his glass on the shelf to take her in his arms. They had gone up almost immediately to the bedroom which damped their nakedness with chill; they had lain shuddering, then afire, then goose-pimpled, he in her. They had dressed in an embarrassed silence, or fussily ignoring the partner, but once downstairs she'd slopped more whisky into his glass, laughing, saying, 'You see where it gets you.'

'Good luck, then.'

He did not even know her Christian name.

Each time they had met since then they'd made love, until he suspected that she and not her husband worked out those timetables that stranded them together. In between they did not correspond much, and their conversation was minimal. Once he had brought her a present, a cut-glass bowl, which she had refused, saying, 'There's only one thing I want. Books.' And that time she led him upstairs in the draughts to see the white-painted shelves she had built herself. 'I'm not good, so I asked El. He's a craftsman, but he hasn't got the time.'

Chamberlain had inquired from Dunne about this penchant of his wife. 'D'you get review copies you don't want?'

'Yes.'

'Send them to her, then.'

'They're mostly criminal affairs, thrillers, that sort of thing.'

'That doesn't matter. She'll have 'em.'

'Is she a great reader?'

'Yes.' Doubtfully. 'She does read.'

Chamberlain could not help wondering if Dunne knew what was going on, and staked this innocent claim for recompense. He could imagine Beth, that was her name, confessing that she and Mr Chamberlain, she called him that for long enough, had rolled on the bed, making it sound innocuous, as if she had given him a cup of coffee. So every few months he'd pack a box of books and send it on, and each time he visited The Limes damage his soft hands lugging a heavy portmanteau to fill up expanding shelves. Beth never wrote in thanks, angering Elsa.

'You'd think she'd say they'd arrived after you've taken so much trouble.'

'I don't know. It's the only way I can pay Eli back for the help he gives me.' This wasn't true, as well he realized. Dunne three or four times a year made, as a result of prolonged thought or off the cuff, some suggestions in a downright manner that livened the listener. But the ideas, Chamberlain knew now, were those he would have come upon on his own in the end, more slowly, more painfully perhaps, but they would have been reached without doubt, and rejected or developed. During his evening in Kent, Chamberlain rested, kept himself alert, used a notebook and made love, not furtively, not impersonally, but in a muted splendour of technique with this delicious, compliant, silent woman.

'What sort of person is she?' Elsa demanded.

'Early thirties. Blonde. Round-faced. A bit fat.'

'Attractive?'

'Yes. Yes, she is.'

'But not to you?'

'I'm not there long enough, am I? She makes me comfortable, I'll say that for her.'

Elsa had seemed content, but once asked for a photograph, which Eli provided. It showed the pair of them, hand in hand, in the glittering shallows of the sea at Swanage.

'She's not fat,' Elsa said, handing it back.
'No, perhaps not.'
Thus adultery was condoned, or missed, he did not know. Now drinking tea, eating a warm scone, waiting for Eli's return, he sat on a stool in the kitchen eyeing her energetic laying of the table.

'His favourite tea,' she said. 'Hot-pot. Fancy it?'

Her conversation never varied from this banal norm; creature comforts, snippets of randomly chosen information, small in-sucks of delighted breath and girlish thanks when he opened his box of books.

Eli burst in, laying a battered fiddle-case on the sink, to shake hands with the visitor, and was off immediately as he stripped overcoat and packet, deposited the violin elsewhere, munched a congress tart; on an account of the strengths of Chamberlain's typescript which had been posted a fortnight before in anticipation.

'It will sell,' he said. 'That death at the winter-sports in Grenoble was as good as anything you've done. The whole thing is publishable now.' Dunne liked such pseudo-professional lexis. 'My objection would be this, and I don't know how you'd surmount it.'

Off he swung, returning to drag his tie loose from his collar, drape it over a chairback, bang down hard on the seat and heave away at his shoes, leaping upwards to cant the huge brogues off, reappear slippered.

'You haven't,' he said, 'frightened yourself enough.'

'What's that mean?'

'You haven't considered what you'd feel like if you were convinced Elsa was trying to murder you, was in fact an enemy.'

'It's unlikely.'

'It's happened here, in this book. Edward Winstanley knows, and he's used to such bizarrerie, that Gisela will shortly try to murder him.'

'She never does,' Chamberlain said, 'because she has no such intention.'

'He convinces himself, because he's beginning to break. It's the conviction that's important. Here's a man under such stress that he thinks his wife will kill him. It sounds and exciting idea. It is good. But you don't believe in it; not enough.'

'What must I do?'

'First you frighten yourself to death, then you'll frighten me.'

Beth put down a Lancashire hot-pot which she served into deep soup plates.

'Don't burn yourself,' she warned. They laughed, remembering from his first visit a scalded tongue.

'You've got to consider Elsa,' Eli Dunne said, shovelling into his beard. Sitting he appeared enormous, broad as a house, short legs hidden, and his arms seemed in perpetual motion, cutting or forking, reaching for salt or bread, knocking back his glass of beer, wiping froth away with one great back-hand motion. 'In her everyday, humdrum passages.' Dunne had never met Elsa, knew next to nothing about her, but used her as his thick left-hand fingers broke up a slice of bread, rushed it to his mouth. 'How would you know?'

'Only when I felt ill from the poison. Or she went after me with a knife.'

'Wouldn't there be signs?'

'I don't . . . Yes, if it were a planned thing. But the point about this is that she's no intention of . . .'

'What would be the signs?' Dunne pressed, scratching the hairy barrel of his chest.

'Unaccustomed nervousness. Or questions about comings or goings, so she could choose an opportunity. It would depend on her. Her temperament. Wouldn't it?'

'Suppose it was Elsa and not Gisela Winstanley.'

'I've told you. I can't imagine that.'

'You'll have to. Or it'll be a fault in the book.'

They chewed over it, Dunne filling in pauses as he scratched amongst his hair and beard, finger-nails like tortoises.

'I could murder you sometimes,' Beth said.

'How would you do it?' Her husband.

'I don't know. I'd go for you from behind with a knife.'

'Would you know where to put it in?'

'The heart, or somewhere.' Now she faltered.

'Would you have the nerve to shove it through my clothes and flesh?'

'I never . . . I only meant I felt angry.'

They laughed, she like a forward child, together and settled to eating. Chamberlain, interested, would not let the matter rest. 'It's the motive, isn't it? Why would a wife want to get rid of a husband?'

'Very common,' Dunne said. 'Divorce laws not withstanding.'

'Besides, she'd be caught,' Beth said. 'She'd go to prison.'

'This woman, Gisela, doesn't want to murder anybody. She's an ordinary housewife, whose husband has this job that's unnerved him. That's all.'

'She's got a German name,' Dunne said.

'She's as English as we are.'

'Her grandfather was a Dutchman.' Eli poked a hair-blackened finger at his wife. That he could play a violin with such sausages seemed impossible. Conversation rambled, but all were satisfied. Chamberlain knew he must rewrite the book, beginning with Gisela, shivering through her. He felt the stirrings of fear, looked round to anchor them. Dunne had cut a hunk of bread, was wiping his plate clean. Beth, dainty-handed, half-moons clear on each finger, speared a slice of potato, added a circle of carrot, bottomed them with meat and lifted the fork, chewed with her mouth prettily closed.

'Fetch yourself some more,' she said. 'I put the pot back in the oven.'

'Thanks.' Eli wiped his face with a silk handkerchief. 'This book'll be superb, once you've . . .' He belched, politely. 'But you see what I mean.'

Chamberlain did, knew the excitement of creation, was already at work on the revision. Pleased that he had an occupation for the next few months, a justification over and above the journalism, he did not consider failure, recognized his imagination as capable of scrambling over the newly erected obstacles.

'You're right,' he said.

Dunne, returning with a second plateful, began to demur; the book was excellent as it stood, technically very adroit, advanced, and quite possibly if Chamberlain pushed it further, frightened himself with the readers, he'd lose ground with reviewers and public. 'They don't,' Dunne worked a huge spoonful towards his mouth, 'like to get too far from the convention they understand. If you write a masterpiece, they'll condemn it.' The food disappeared as the mouth took on a meditative smile. Both men, warm, fed, delighted with each other, discussed scenes. Chamberlain admitted where he'd plagiarized other works, but claimed he improved as he stole. Dunne confessed that he rarely read a word of fiction outside his friend's typescripts.

'Don't believe him,' Beth said. 'I see him at my shelves.'

'The motive.' Her husband's beard shook like a leaping fire.

The men washed the dishes before settling to more talk, while Beth kept out of their way. Disappointed, Chamberlain saw no inclination on Eli's part to go out, but at seven-thirty Mrs Dunne came downstairs, in a dove-grey dress, very sedate, perfumed and powdered.

'Are you not going to change?' she asked her husband.

'No. Should I?'

'Please yourself.' She explained to the guest that Eli, for once, had neither orchestra nor pupils to oversee, and she had therefore insisted that the three of them visited the Bells. Dunne described the place as Edwardian rubbish converted into Elizabethan sewage, but seemed pleased enough with the project. It was, however, well past eight when they set out; and Dunne wore a suit, shiny navy constricting his great shoulders, as if at any moment the cloth would split from the muscles into tatters.

They drank until ten in a noise from dart-board, one-armed bandits and domino-table that made lengthy speech almost impossible. Chamberlain, slightly tipsy, dozed in the warmth, leaning on Beth, exchanging no confidences with her, even when her husband made his long-drawn-out sallies to bar or lavatory. Once when the visitor handled her thigh she smiled.

As they came out into the street at ten-thirty, Eli Dunne staggered, though recovering quickly. He led the way along the back-streets, his peaky cap awry, singing 'Blessing and honour, glory and power be unto Him, be unto Him, that sitteth upon the throne', in a beautifully pitched undertone to which he conducted wildly. The effect was incongruous, as if a windmill in full gale directed a solo recorder. Beth, who had made three glasses of lager last the evening, walked as soberly as she had sat in the pub, where she had shown a detachment that seemed almost critical. Now and then Eli lurched across the pavement, unfastened duffle-coat out like huge archangel's wings, but always regaining the point of departure to resume course and another burst of triumphant *Messiah*. At the door, he had difficulty finding and then using his keys; his wife neither helped nor complained, stood there amiably, ready when he was. 'That sitteth upon the thro-one', Dunne delivered as he burst through into the kitchen, slapped bar-lights blindingly on. He sang with utter sobriety, each note exact, each word enunciated. 'And unto the Lamb.'

They sat to coffee by the stove while Eli explained that

this time he had been determined not to desert his friend. Mrs Dunne sounded laughingly cheerful at his protestations so that Chamberlain began to lose his composure, to decide that she had arranged to drop him. Husband and wife spoke with a joviality that left the other man uneasy, uncertain whether he was victimized by conspiracy or by a chance that pleased the woman.

He slept badly, but was woken at seven by Dunne, carrying tea. Eli apologized for the early hour, but said he had a start to make on the other side of London at eight-thirty. He'd already breakfasted. Ten minutes after the door had banged Beth appeared, tousle-headed, climbed into his bed and sitting there had removed her discoloured dressing-gown. They made love, shedding, shattering Chamberlain's reluctance, before she offered her apologies. Well, no, she couldn't say, could she, that she knew El was leaving at the crack of dawn? She mothered him, holding his head warmly between the huge breasts, certain that he'd be comforted in the end, quiet as a baby with a dummy-teat.

'Does he know?' he asked, out of pique.

'No idea. I shouldn't think so.'

'Would he mind?'

The soft nakedness at his side moved, more for her own relief than his, though her arms dominated him.

'Why bother yourself?' she yawned. 'That pyjama button's sticking into me.'

'He's a decent man.'

'So are you.' She laughed. 'You're very nice.' She gently slapped his bare rump as if she reminded herself of some tune.

'How many men have you got?' he asked.

'That's rude,' she announced.

'I want to know.'

'Well, find out, then.'

He sulked, but she did not mind, wrapping him in her ease, kissing him as if he were a sugar-mouse, smiling all the time, obtuse and secret. Uncomfortable in the plenitude of her comfort, he touched her but without delicacy, thinking that this is how Winstanley would stroke his wife who planned his death. When she jumped groaning and jovial from the bed, leaned Rubens-naked over him to rescue her night-dress and tuck him up, he eyed her with suspicion, knowing that the relationship was marred for him.

'You're to stop there until I bring your breakfast up. Go to sleep again. Is that clear?' He heard her splashing in the bathroom and wished as he dozed away that she'd come in to dress in front of him. Poached eggs and coffee were presented this time. She sat on the bed, said she took no breakfast these days, invited him to stay the day because Eli would not be back before five and would be off again an hour or so later. 'But he'll be chuffed if you're still here. He talks about you all the time. When you're going to come, you know.'

She sounded naïve, child in schoolyard.

'He'll suspect . . .' Chamberlain's answer grudged.

'He won't do anything of the kind.'

'Then he ought to.'

She frowned, hardly managing to wrinkle the smooth skin between her eyebrows, eyes blue and wary.

'That's not nice,' she said.

'Is what we do nice?'

'That's up to you, isn't it?'

She pulled the cord of his pyjama trousers, poked his belly, left him munching, but he was persuaded. Beth warned that he must ring his wife, then pleaded that she be allowed to overhear the call.

'Why?' he snapped.

'I'd like to listen to what you tell her.'

Elsa showed no interest in his delayed return, said nothing had happened, mentioned, on instruction opened, two letters, both of which contained dull cheques not glowing promises.

She made no inquiry about how her husband spent his time, though she remembered at the last minute that Dr Hill threatened to storm over.

'I see. Tell him to save it.'

Beth listened to this hands clasped, with a facetious concentration. As he talked to Elsa, Chamberlain realized that Beth had had her hair permed into a rough semblance of curls, which he'd noticed without verbally describing to himself. She'd wasted her money.

Coffee appeared. This house provided an endless miscellany of hot drinks served in mugs. He tinkled with his spoon as she told him that Eli and she often discussed Elsa, whom they had never met. They had seen two photographs, one in a magazine, one Chamberlain had pulled from his wallet, and had decided that she was exceptionally beautiful. They had tried to discover whether she was intelligent, or literary, played golf or followed country pursuits, had any part in her husband's books either by typing or licking stamps or picking at the sore-spots which pained him into composition. She was, Mrs Dunne claimed, their favourite character and they had a fantasy about her in which Beth made her eat new-baked date buns while Eli played the D minor Chaconne. 'I hate those things, and she'd know they were fattening and wouldn't look at them in any case, and Eli can't play the Bach now, if ever he could.' Chamberlain had never heard her so loquacious, thought it worth his time to have stayed to have heard this rigmarole, which was not well delivered, but gained from its shy spate.

'Now I've actually heard her voice,' she said. 'Only over the phone. And I couldn't make out what she was saying.' She burst into embarrassed then subdued laughter as he now clasped his arms about her to put her at her ease. Cooking and making love apart, he decided, she was a big schoolgirl. The phone rang; she answered, exactly detailing Eli's movements for the day, issuing finally an explicit instruction about the collection of instruments and stands for this evening's rehearsal. He did not know her, he realized, except as a provider. Of flesh. Cooked or naked. Enjoying the conceit he rubbed his hand along the white casing of the boiler, a comfortable man, satisfied with himself for once. The pair ran upstairs again before lunch, but after her soup, salad and cold meats, home-made bread, he'd fallen asleep, failing even to help with the washing-up.

At tea Eli savagely outlined Winstanley's fear of his wife. She needed to change habits, personal and domestic, to choose a new brand of soap or detergent, to shop at different times, to alter the positions of pictures on the wall, to take up correspondence, especially with men, that had been allowed to lapse. This, he claimed, forcibly, laying the law down, would sufficiently rip her husband's shattered nerves. Move the television set to another room; shift the armchairs, especially his, round, and the secure world of a help-mate, a supporting partner, was splintered into smithereens.

'Why would she do it?' Chamberlain asked.

'Boredom. That's likely.'

'Why not before?'

'He's the dominant partner, you said. She's not been allowed.'

Beth sliced the cobs, ladled and cut food, adding not a word to her husband's exposition, allowing him to clear his system. Chamberlain wondered again, with a frisson of guilt, if Eli guessed their adultery. A man who was so inventive with fictions must surely allow the idea to cross his mind. No sign. A ravel of words; a fountain of suggestion as his smiling, seduced wife saw to his creature comforts.

After the meal, Eli lit a cigar, hitched his trouser legs and stroked his ample belly in front of the BBC newsreader.

'I heard Elsa,' Beth called, clearing away. Chamberlain already stood at the washing-up sink.

'Who?' Blue smoke expanded, expended. 'Heard who?'

'Elsa. Mrs Chamberlain.'
'What did she say, then?'
'I couldn't make out a word.'
'Well, bloody hell.'

Eli filled the room with the richness of his cigar, pressing his wife for details of the conversation. In the end, satisfied, he grunted, fell asleep, chin into chest, ash over his pullover, the stub burning between his fingers until she prised it out, hurled it firewards, gently swearing at him once she was in the scullery, teatowel flying.

'Are we going with him,' she asked.
'Where is it?'
'The Morrison Hall. It'll be worth it.'
'We'll go, then.'

He snatched a kiss, and she blushed down to neck and bosom. He fondled her crotch to see the blush deepen. In time Eli woke, searched for his cigar and swearing went away to wash. On his return, beard and hair damp still, he asked for music which Beth immediately produced, naming the works, and once explaining why there was only one cello copy. She must have prepared and looked through the papers during the day, packed them into cases ready for transport, though he had noticed nothing.

'We're coming with you,' she announced.

'You're not?' He beamed, made it clear once Beth had gone from the room how much he depended on her. 'She's a memory like an elephant. It's a good job she has, because I'm bloody hopeless and there's so much last-minute chopping and changing at this job.' When she came down, she wore a plain blue coat with white buttons, and smart shoes; Chamberlain did not like the effect. Only a fool paints grass.

'Ummh,' Eli mocked. 'Honouring the guest.'

She picked up a shiny plastic handbag, snapped its clasp close.

The Morrison Hall, brick-built in the early fifties, smelt

of stale polish and dust, but was warm. Already two schoolboys were manhandling trestle tables out of the way, and setting up stands. A young woman played to herself *molto allegro* on a viola, her face surprised at the agility of her fingers, or the sounds as they emerged. She sat on the end of a double-row of chairs and wore a wide black skirt which swept the floor. Five minutes after the announced time of rehearsal, the room seemed crowded, but no one moved towards the arc of stands and seats. Dunne emerged from behind the stage carting a rostrum in one hand as easily as if it had been a brief-case or a loaf of bread. He set it down, adjusted his own, superior, wooden-topped music-stand, called for a start. People edged towards their chairs only when they'd satisfactorily completed their conversations.

'Tune,' Eli said. The oboe brayed; leader bowed A; the rest dashed to approach it, or dumped instruments to rosin bows.

'I don't know how he's got the patience,' Beth whispered to Chamberlain.

'Handel, Passacaglia,' Eli called. The noise did not noticeably diminish. 'Come on, ladies and gentlemen. There's a lot to get through.'

'What are we doing?' A cello.

'Handel's Passacaglia.'

'You said last week you'd start on the Mozart.'

'Handel.' This time he tapped the stand, raised his arms, bent the first chord in. It staggered, a boneless grotesque. 'Bloody hell.' They stopped, abashed. Now there was some scurrying to open music, to raise instruments. The second attempt sounded strong, sinewy, broad, all there. Eli allowed them a line or two, then called for another start. 'Sloppy still. Come on.' This time bow-arms swept and pushed together, so that Handel spoke. Now and then the conductor shouted an instruction, tautened the rhythm, once encouraged. At the end of the piece he muttered a few words of lukewarm praise, then loosened them on the Purcell Chaconne in G Minor. This they repeated, with no noticeable improvement to Chamberlain's ears, then tackled the Mozart *Eine kleine Nachtmusik* in which Eli took more care, stopping the players, demanding, insisting on perfecting what seemed to the two listeners unimportant passages, starting the last movement five times to establish the tempo. There followed a slapdash skate through the Elgar Serenade, and during this two women appeared with trays full of mugs of tea. As sluggishly as they had congregated, the members rose for refreshment.

Eli consulted with the leader, directed tea towards his guests, borrowed a violin to bow some disputed bars, altered his copy, then sauntered across.

'A good turn-out,' Beth said.

'Not bad. We're getting near performance.'

'Are you pleased?' Chamberlain asked.

The conductor grinned, sucking his drop-laden whiskers, not answering. Immediately the secretary brought a register for scrutiny, and a three-way argument began about the printing and distribution of tickets. After a time, Beth intervened, outlined a plan, disposed of an objection, and straightening the matter, sent the officials away smiling.

'They listen to her,' Eli said.

'You don't need a musician for these,' Beth answered unemphatically.

'A wet-nurse.' The secretary turning round.

'And straitjackets.' Eli.

When the rehearsal resumed, Dunne worked carefully over the Tchaikovsky Serenade for Strings, and once marvellously demonstrated how to play a run of harmonics. The orchestra's ghostly squeal of imitation did not flatter. Without heat, he muttered a sentence or two on the value of practice at home. He did not stress the point, made them repeat, begging a fiddle to show again, and violin in hand played with them. He could be heard, bell-clear, sharp-jewelled above the rest. 'It's the beard,' he apologized. 'It vibrates in sympathy.' They laughed, some of them, exchanged sentences.

At almost ten o'clock he dropped baton to stand, dismissed the players, though there followed a quarter of an hour of administration or socializing. On the way home they stopped once so that Eli could fetch a packet of chips.

'That's his biggest treat,' Beth said, only when he returned. 'He does it on the nights I go with him.'

'Isn't that often?'

'Only when she thinks I'll get it round my neck.'

They sat up until the early hours, not drinking much, but happy in a bemused fug, discussing Tchaikovsky or Winstanley's murderous wife or what Chamberlain was really about in his novels. This was a long, slow, broken monologue by Dunne, cropped as it were from a ouija board so painfully did it emerge, explaining that the world was mapped in these thrillers, that conscience and morality played a part as powerfully as in Spenser or *Paradise Lost*. Chamberlain, who'd heard this thesis before and countered it usually by dismissively saying that even if it were exactly true it did not make his work equal in quality with that of those masters of epic, enjoyed it this evening, humming and haing, eyeing Beth who, up and down, ministered, that archaic word suited, to them. She was large and beautiful, had left a button of her dress sluttishly undone but still wore the high-heeled shoes. She aped an expression of interest, which wrote stupidity across her face, but the visitor, having glimpsed for the first time her efficiency, was unable to make up his mind. He threw her a question.

'I haven't read *The Faerie Queene* or Milton,' she replied.

'Are my books morally based, then?'

'That's not how I read them.'

He was dashed at that, wanted them to be so, at least in her mouth. But she'd outed her bit of truth, not considering its effect, or perhaps judging it would have none, and he would have to put up with it. She should lie naked in his arms, not forced into nude opinion.

Next morning Eli drove Chamberlain to the station, pleased with visitor and visit. Beth appeared distant, concerned with the evening meal, or the larder she was going to clear and paint, smiling, but her own woman. Chamberlain felt wretched to be wrenched away from this place, pitched back into work's uncertainty, at Elsa's iceberg, the clatter of demand, the children, the onset of winter and depression.

Elsa did not meet him at the station so that he had to wait more than an hour for the local train, and then walk a mile and a half on muddy roads. He had not, deliberately, bothered to phone, while she would not take the car out on an off chance, as he knew well. Pamela poked her head through the kitchen door, made a bright inquiry whether he'd enjoyed himself, but did not offer even to fill the kettle. Her mother was upstairs somewhere.

He found his carpet slippers, sought out his wife who chided him for not ringing. Uncomfortably he asked for news; mentioned Dr Hill's projected visit.

'John's in hospital again,' she said, not looking round. He wondered what it was she fiddled with at the dressing table, some notebook, elaborate list of telephone numbers which she made to hiss as she thumbed over papers.

'Has he . . . ? Has . . . ?' He could not spit it out.

'Acute depression. They're treating him, but they want us to fetch him home at the week-end.'

'Isn't he better off in hospital?'

She sneered, as if the question damned him.

'Apparently not.'

John had consulted his own doctor, who in view of his history had referred him to a psychiatrist; after a week or so, they admitted him to a mental institution. Again there had been some delay in informing the parents because the hospital authorities were certain the patient himself had written home. Now drugs were improving his condition, but all considered he'd be better off in Nottinghamshire until Christmas. If he were well enough, he could continue with his thesis; if not the change would be beneficial and his case would be attended to by a local consultant.

Elsa delivered this rather slowly as though the paper in her hand had more interest, or even outlined the facts she offered, but in abstruse language which she could not construe fluently. She did not elaborate, showed no sympathy, retailed the affair as if she were calling out boring details from a newspaper account. In a huff, he walked across, took her by the shoulders, not roughly.

'How bad is he?'

She tried to shrug his hand loose, saying, 'Don't be silly. He won't die.'

At the end of the second sentence, muttered after a long pause during which he had not budged, not shifted his hands, the kettle downstairs whistled. She struggled up.

'See to it,' she ordered, promised.

He did not understand the grammar of this, only her rejection of him, or her self-sheltering from trouble. Stumbling down the stairs, he noticed that she did not follow and that someone, Pamela, had turned off the kettle. His daughter stood by the stove, making herself coffee. Did he want one? Or tea?

'Yes, that's what I put it on for.'

'Oh, like that, is it?' She reached for, unscrewed the jar.

'What's wrong with John?' he asked.

'He's depressed,' she said, stirring. 'As if we all weren't.'

'What's up with you, then?'

'Oh, everything. Nothing.' She passed the drink across.

'You and Saul?'

'And everything else.'

He waited. For nothing.

'Come on, then. Let's hear.' He took a stool, so that he

could look at her, but from the distance of a protective yard or so. 'Father Hill?'

'Mother Chamberlain, sod her.'

'That sounds bad. What's happened?'

'Nothing.'

'Come on. Either say something or shut up.' He grinned companionably; she disregarded him.

'She sides with the Hills. We're silly. We're too young to know our minds.'

'I see.'

'That's what you think, is it?' she asked this, coffee masking her mouth. 'Except you don't like Dr Hill.'

'I can see some force in the argument; yes.'

They sat in awkward silence, Pamela quite beautiful, with a high colour, dark hair curly. She was dissatisfied, but saw no sense in continuing the discussion.

'What's wrong with John?' she asked. She blurted this out, his own question, so that he recognized it as a small triumph on his part and a powerful social effort on hers. 'Really?'

'Badly depressed.'

'Has he tried to kill himself again?'

'Not so far as I know. Depression's not just feeling down in the mouth. It's long-term. In the system. Needs digging out. Not just miserable for a good reason. Like you and me.' She at least raised her eyes at this, then lifted the covering mug. 'That's why your mother's so, so sharp. She's worried about John.'

'She thinks more of him than of me, and you.'

'I don't know.'

'He was the first.' Once this girl learnt to compromise, to care less, she'd be magnificent socially. 'It makes a difference.'

They had exchanged a few more non-committal sentences when she skipped away, leaving him to wash out the mugs.

7

Chamberlain drove down to collect John on Sunday.

The boy looked pale, but not ill, was up and dressed at the college, not in the hospital. He had packed his bags, and insisted that he should hump the heaviest out to the car. After the first, almost effusive, replies to questions about his health, he became so quiet that the rest of the journey was uncomfortable. The break for lunch brought no relief. On his arrival, he greeted his mother with exactly the phrases he had used to his father, delivered with a spurious energy. Elsa was pleased, made an effort with the sherry decanter, and when John declined to drink, blaming his drugs, they laughed together, screechily, about the devious routes to sobriety. Thereafter silence settled and the son opted for early bed.

Elsa went up to see him, took a careful note of his medicaments, made herself responsible, removed all the bottles. When she returned she showed a new cheerfulness towards her husband, insisted on his taking sherry, which he disliked, and on giving a full account of the journey. This frosted the atmosphere, because he had so little to report, had already done his best, knew his taciturnity would be held against him. She stood up, after an interval, helped herself unusually to a third glass and leaned against the mantelpiece, superb, a marvel of smooth fairness, her old silk dress clinging, head proud, blonde, raised, disdaining, despising his grudging utterance.

'What do we do about Lynette Rockford?' she demanded in the end.

'Do?'

She walked, swept a step or two to express her scorn, posed herself statuesque again.

'Will she be round here when she knows John is back?'

'I doubt it.' Her question seemed naïve, rough, wasteful. 'She's still in Boy's pocket, isn't she?'

'Will John want to see her?'

He had not the faintest inkling of John's wishes. He had on his hands a pale, laconic figure, who before had been flatly unremarkable, one of life's shufflers. Very carefully Chamberlain explained this to his wife, stressing the ordinariness of the son, a father's crumbling ambition for the boy, the final sense that there was a run-of-the-mill schoolteacher who'd end typically in his neat detached house with carpet-slippers, two children and a street-fouling terrier. Elsa watched, began to probe, demanding why she'd heard none of this before.

'It wasn't until he tried suicide that I realized that he wasn't like that, and bothered to look round for a description.'

'What are you going to do? Now you know?'

'I shall get on with my work, if I can.' He wanted to impress her. 'That keeps us solvent. We let the doctors do their best for him, and we rest him and feed him. Talk to him. Make a fuss.'

'I do all that,' she said. 'Not you.'

'Right. You do my reviews, get this bloody novel written for me, and I'll put him rice-puddings on trays.'

'Why are you angry?' she asked.

Chamberlain did not answer immediately, acted out the thinker, tapping the chair-arm, crossing his legs.

'I may be wrong.' Her face assumed an expression of long-suffering matching his words. 'I get the impression. You seem to blame me for what's happened to John. As if my omissions, or commissions for that matter, are responsible for his ... unbalance.'

'Aren't they?'

'No, they are not. However you've convinced yourself.'

'You've never shown any interest in what he's doing. To you he's a nonentity. You say so. You can ignore him. Or offer him a drink, give him a present at Christmas.'

'That's what he's like,' Chamberlain said.

'Nobody's like that.'

'If we worked,' he began, 'on the assumption that everybody is unique, needing special examination, care, treatment, the world'd stop in no time.'

'I didn't ask it for everyone. Only for your son.'

He sat back; she'd made a point.

'Good for you,' he said. 'Good for you.' She did not acknowledge his acceptance of her touch. 'But that's where . . . I was wrong. I'll admit it. He was humdrum, mediocre; I'd no more idea than fly-in-the-air,' his mother's expression, 'that he'd try to kill himself. For love.' The stops spelt out his embarrassment. 'It's incredible. I can't believe it, even now. I would have said that every person has in his, her, life two or three, perhaps more, happenings, crises of this kind. When they are rebuffed by somebody they love. I don't deny the importance, or try to minimize the pain. I'd say, if I were pressed, that one perhaps never quite gets over these traumas. The scars smart. One wants to get one's own back. I know all that. It's happened to me. But most people come to some kind of compromise, go on living, marry somebody better for them. Most people don't rush off to cut their throats.'

'John . . .'

'I know. He was the last I'd have expected. I was wrong. I expect suicides to be highly strung, unusually sensitive, not middle-of-the-roaders like John.'

'And so?' Was she friendly?

'He's got a bad defect. Amongst all the rest of his middling bits and pieces. I don't know whether I'm to blame. Genetically, perhaps we are. I don't understand it. It isn't what I expected, I'll tell you.'

'It's done you good to visit those people.'

'What people?'

'The Dunnes. Is that their name? In Woolwich.' She enlarged on her topic. While he worked he cooped himself up, lived inside his own head, only emerged to sit in a pub with people with whom he'd nothing in common. Now he'd stayed with this interesting pair, it had livened him, to his own wife, his children. He'd not spoken to her in this frank, searching way for years; he appeared to be exploring, seriously, rarely not backing away behind a polite expression of interest.

At first Chamberlain felt a stab of delight.

He and his wife were getting on, for once; the relationship kicked, was alive. Though Elsa retained her distant beauty, her poise, sat inviolate, she spoke warmly. The delivery did not heal, only the content, but she sought him out, met him, unusually, praised him in her lukewarm style. Nodding, he could only be pleased. But. He grinned to himself, sour, chin-scratching. The whole foundation of the argument was cracked with his hypocrisy. In the new honesty, or involvement, she claimed to see in him, he should out with the fact that he'd seven times committed adultery with his host's wife. That would demote her from 'interesting'. And what he'd said this evening had no connection that he could see with those naked bodies belly to belly, mouth glued to thirsty mouth in south-east London. A spurt of anger had fetched the words up from his spleen. The same small outburst may have scared her, he did not know, cowed her into congratulation or compliance.

Such things did not bear saying. He admitted again to her he'd been wrong about John, said it had unsettled him, left him uncertain what to do. Again, he confessed, smugly, that she'd have to bear the brunt, and though he saw the unfairness of this, she was better able to cope. As he talked like this, ambivalence flickered, was extinguished as he began to believe his own argument. He rose, topped up her glass, poured himself a large whisky, walked about, a man justified, hypocrisy buried.

As he moved around the room, he touched furniture as he stopped, gripping a chair back, bending a forefinger to a right triangle on the surface of a desk, realigning a table leg with a slight movement of a shoe. Elsa watched him, smiling, apparently wary, and he realized that she was drunk. He moved behind the chair, knuckles white on the corners when she put her head back to look up at, to him. He reached down, fondled her cheek, and immediately she snatched at his hand, conveyed it to her mouth, covered the palm with light kisses.

He bent to touch the top of her head with his lips, realizing that she did not mind his mussing her hair. Uncertain, he eased his fingers down the front of her dress to the delicious, small breasts. She rolled in cat-like pleasure, smothering a wrist with kisses, groaning, beautiful and intact from him. When they moved to the bedroom, where she stripped with neat speed, she seemed two persons even in nakedness, an object, *objet d'art*, inside which a living woman squealed, half-mute from habit.

'I love you,' she told her seated husband.

'It's strong drink.'

'It's truth.'

Comparing her with Beth, even as he lay in her, he believed he could believe it, trusted some lucky star to slit his darkness. Chamberlain dressed, went downstairs, brought coffee, sat on the bed to talk again, not so easily now, not perhaps sensibly, but as mates. The word crossed his mind, with pictures of bricklayers' hods, scarfed football scruffs, a lorry driver, milkmen. This entirely tidy, golden woman sipping from china ought not to be so designated, but that's what she was, his help-mate, with the roughness of relationship there, the swearing and the sweat and spit. He lolled against her quilted legs, pleased.

Next day, on which they kept John in bed, they exchanged

cheerful sentences as if to acknowledge a new relationship. Elsa came to the study, interrupting him, to ask if it were convenient for Dr Hill to call round this evening. In the ordinary way a pencilled note, small enough to be overlooked, would have been left on the pad, but this signalled the new earth if not the new heaven. Hill was left waiting at his phone, while she stopped her husband's imagination, and as this happened she showed her pleasure, laughed, mocked men.

Hill, accompanied by his wife, arrived at seven, since with no surgery they had eaten their evening meal early. Elsa guided them into the drawing room, poured drinks, asked them to wait for her husband who was struggling upstairs into a clean shirt. On Chamberlain's arrival, Madeleine Hill made suitable inquiries after John while her husband, who was not the family's physician, gruffly outlined the increasing success rate in such cases. Neither visitor looked uncomfortable, nor seemed to mention John to discompose his parents. A discussion about re-siting a hedge at the village bowling-club, in fact, became so animated that Hill had accepted a second whisky before he reached unpleasantness. He squirted soda with neat-fingered skill, so that one could almost see the swabs, smell the disinfectant.

'You know what we're here for, eh? Elsa?' Afterthought and awkward. 'Saul and young Pamela.' That sounded straight from the twenties, stiff upper lip and m'horsewhip's outside. 'They're talking about engagements.' He waited pulling at his tweed jacket, pouting, but finding no encouragement continued. 'Now, I'll tell you frankly, I see no sense in it. I've talked to Madeleine and she agrees.' He turned towards her; she did no more than blink rapidly at her gin.

Chamberlain did nothing to help out.

'Pamela's just left school. Saul's got his degree then articles to clear before he decides where he's going to settle. It's premature to talk of marriage.'

'You've nothing against Pamela?' Chamberlain.

'Not at all. Nothing. Why should I? Very nice girl. It's just their age. As I see it, it's like this: while I'm supporting Saul, he's no right taking responsibilities of this sort on.' Bluster.

'And they're not capable of understanding this? I take it you've put it as plainly to Saul as you have to me?'

'You can take it.' Hill guffawed, rolled in his chair.

'Madeleine? What do you say?'

She smiled as if she'd been concerned elsewhere, put down her drink and stared. This from the woman who could not leave him alone.

'I tend to agree. It'll do them no harm to wait. Children have it too easy these days.'

'But if they did marry?'

'How could they?' Hill bristled, upright. 'I wouldn't support them.'

'They'd support themselves. Pam works now. They could live somewhere, find a room.'

'You mean,' Madeleine asked, 'you'd let them lodge ... ?'

'But suppose she became pregnant?' Hill again. 'They're unthinking enough.'

'The relationship's sexual already.'

'How do you know that? Has she? Have they told you?'

'Pamela's on the pill.' Elsa's first intervention.

'She let you know? Just like that?'

'I found out. I guessed. I looked. Then I faced her with it. She's been on the pill for a year now.'

'And you approve?' Hill.

'I had no chance.' Elsa.

'One of your know-all colleagues provided the prescription,' Chamberlain said. 'As I expect you would. Nor did he inform us. Again, like you.'

'I tell you this,' Hill said. 'There'd have been some straight talking between me and the girl. She'd have known exactly what she was embarking on.'

'Are you suggested that Gilman neglected his duty? When you'd finished your fatherly advice, what then? If she'd insisted, you'd have issued the prescription. And said nothing to the parents.'

'There's no alternative.'

'But there is. If you felt as strongly as you apparently do now in this case, you'd have refused.'

'She'd go elsewhere.'

'Yes, but you'd have made your gesture. Pam's a decent child. She wouldn't find it easy to go down to Gilman's surgery and tell him what she wanted. And if he put one more obstacle in the way that might have deterred her. He, if it was Gilman, didn't try very hard, any more than you would. If it's somebody else's daughter, it doesn't matter so much.'

'This is all very old-fashioned, Eric,' Madeleine said. She was one of the very few who called Chamberlain by his first name.

'You can say so. I'm pointing out the inconsistency in your husband's behaviour. He'll huff and puff this evening because he's personally involved. Elsewhere he'll slide into line with Dr Gilman and the rest.'

'And that's wrong?' Madeleine waved her husband down.

'Inconsistent. Right or wrong, I don't know. I don't know whether I approve of what they're up to. I rather think I don't. But I'm not sure. It may be prejudice. Or envy. Or jealousy. I don't know.'

'Now, listen,' Hill leaned forward, leering in an attempt at rationality. 'It's all very well your absconding from responsibilities with your don't-know and your don't-care. I know what I think, and I'll say it.'

'Habit.'

'I beg your pardon.'

'I don't want to be rude. But it's a professional hazard. You doctors spend so much of your time laying the law down that it's damn near second-nature.'

'Come, Eric, that's stupid.' Madeleine. 'And we might as well face it, that you and George don't get on, and that you're only too willing to goad him into saying something more than he meant to.' She moved a hand policing him to silence. 'But that's not why we came. George's here to be helpful.'

'But if I open my mouth I'm hindering.'

'Roughly.' She laughed, black-haired, sallow-skinned and handsome.

'You're not in agreement with us?' Hill asked, surprisingly pacific.

'I'd say we are.' Elsa. 'But we aren't going to threaten.'

'Presumably because you think Saul is a good catch for Pamela?' Madeleine.

Elsa grimaced over that one, not answering.

'Are you going to do anything or not?' Hill asked.

'I'm going to fill your glass, George,' Chamberlain said, 'and talk to you.'

'Well, none of your bloody foolery.'

They laughed aloud, suddenly at ease. Chamberlain talked across to Madeleine. 'In fact, I'll go round with the hat myself. And none of that will stop them breaking off the engagement, if and when they feel like it, any more than it'll stop them belting for the divorce court when they get bored with the marriage. We may not like it. But I guess we just make them more obstinate if we get in the way or threaten sanctions. Keep our mouths shut. That's us. Say nothing about this little meeting...'

'Do you think they don't know?' Elsa.

'I'm sure they do.' Madeleine.

'We tell them to do as they like?' Hill sounded doubtful, his chin, grossly double, pressed into his collar. 'Is that it?'

They tentatively agreed with each other, swigged spirits, swayed jovially, decided on cheese and biscuits. Noisily Dr Hill proposed he should accompany Elsa to the kitchen. As soon as they had closed the door, Madeleine snapped, 'One of these days George will hit you.'

'He will?'

'He thinks something of his son.'

'That he's too good for my daughter?'

'I don't mean that, and you know I don't mean it. He's prepared to tell Saul, or you, or me, or anybody else what he thinks should be done. I know you don't consider it very intelligent, or sensible, but at least he makes an effort, comes across here, nags me.'

'And I don't? Won't?'

'Because fundamentally you're selfish. You are interested in yourself. Now, isn't that true? Your son tries to kill himself. What do you do? What have you done? Nothing. You drive down and make soothing noises. Pamela wonders about Saul? The thought of them never crosses your mind from one day to the next. You're so preoccupied with your own devices or depressions or schemes...'

'That?' he mocked. She did not answer. He waited, taken aback. 'You sound off, Madeleine. Unpleasant. Nasty. Put out.'

'My husband is a decent man.'

'Agreed.'

'There you go. Sneer again. You wouldn't basically give a damn if our children went round preaching cannibalism.'

'Basically?'

'You can score, with words. George has done well tonight. You haven't.'

'Yes. Perhaps so.' He stood, straightening his jacket. 'What's wrong, Madeleine?' He'd no idea why she'd spoken so. She frowned; red spots inflamed her cheekbones. 'Come on. Spit it out.' He sipped his whisky, which soothed him, closed his eyes so that he wanted to take her in his arms.

'Nothing you can help with.'

'You shouldn't say that. I know I'm a bastard sometimes. But I don't want you doing your nut. Not on my behalf, anyhow.'

'It's not for you.' Her eyes stretched large.

'Look, Madeleine, for God's sake. Be a good girl. I owe you something, and if I can make it up to you, I will.'

'Why?'

'You bloody well know why.' He crossed, took her hand.

'Give me some more gin,' she said, perhaps to rid herself of him. Dr Hill, the tray held in front dwarfed by his bulk, burst in, laid it on a table, sea-dogged it out for the kitchen. 'It's all bloody,' she said. 'Bloody.'

'You know what to do.'

'Know? What in hell are you . . . ?'

'You know what you think about Saul. Or Pam. Or me, for that matter.'

'You're wrong. Sometimes I'd like to talk to you, but it's no good.'

'Ummh?'

'We shouldn't talk for long enough. You know that. We'd be on the floor with our clothes off like a couple of adolescent screwdrivers.'

'I recommend it. Does good.'

She smiled, as if she'd gained complete control over herself, held her glass cupped like an acolyte with a chalice.

'Talk,' she said. 'Exchanging words, and ideas. Thinking. You're intelligent, aren't you? You don't know what to do because you see the obstacles. It'd be marvellous if I could just sit opposite you and know you were concentrating on Pamela and Saul and me as a distressed area and not mentally shoving your hand up my skirt.'

'I don't think I could.'

'That's not a compliment. I want somebody to sort me out.

Some Jesus.'

'Shove your hand on the hem of his garment, eh?'

Hill and Elsa, beaming, brought in the coffee-pot, the china, a great cheese dish.

'A picnic,' Hill said. 'I think my greatest pleasure in life is a cup of coffee, with a slice of brown bread with blue Stilton cheese.'

'And they are all there,' Elsa said. 'Every ingredient. And what's your pleasure, Madeleine?'

She did not answer.

'A sober conversation,' Chamberlain said.

'You drink too much whisky.' Elsa glanced, puckish, at home as she began to sort out cups and saucers. 'Now, how do we like it?'

They did not speak much for the next quarter of an hour, but Hill's enjoyment was great enough to influence the others. He buttered his bread prettily, carved it into squares on which he meticulously knifed cubes of cheese, a seventh-day God with his handiwork, a belly like Buddha's, the contentment of a Ganesh.

Chamberlain, slightly tipsy, looked him over, not displeased.

'I tell you what,' he said. 'If you haven't brought your car, we'll walk back with you. Or part way. How's that, Elsa?'

'Why?'

'Exercise and the pleasure of our neighbours' company.'

They decided on the outing, fortifying themselves with more spirits, so that when Elsa and Hill washed up, they laughed excitedly in the kitchen. Chamberlain and Madeleine sat apart, unspeaking, staring at the electric fire as it twisted boring smoke behind red glass. Once he looked up, but she shook her head.

Outside under a blue night-sky the wind swooped warm as Elsa and the escorting Hill made great pace, clacking away on the asphalt, arm in arm. They took the short-cut through Hemmingham's Wood, shouting and signalling back, but the other two kept to the road, apart, silent if not unhappy. Chamberlain would have taken her hand, but she seemed like a runner determined on her pace, concentrated on her steps, apart from him, trained to move alone, to notice only his rivalry. The walk lasted an uncomfortable quarter of an hour; the others waited under blazing lights, unstoppering decanters.

'You will talk to me, won't you?' Madeleine said. 'Just talk.'

He shook his head, unsure of himself. Hill crashed in genially, rebuked their long faces while Elsa watched in detachment from the door. When they made their way back home, she questioned him about the other woman's conversation, chaffed his glumness, blamed him as she hung on his arm. When they entered the wood she made him stop and kiss, said they were lovers in the sheltered darkness where she could not make out the blankness of his face.

8

Five days later Lynette Rockford turned up at the house.

She faced Mrs Chamberlain, brazenly. 'Could I see John, please?' and was shown in. Elsa ran upstairs to where her son lounged in front of his portable television set, announced his visitor, asked angrily if he'd invited her. He crossed immediately to the mirror, worked with a comb at his hair, changed his jacket and only then replied as he switched the set off. 'Yes, you could say that.' He left his mother standing.

She stamped to the landing, rapped her husband's door.

'Now what do you think?' she said, flinging the girl's name at him. He looked mildly up from his book, eyebrows high at the sharpness. No fishwives here. 'He asked her.'

'Yes, I suppose he did.'

'Did you know, then?'

'No. Sit down, Elsa.' He removed his reading-glasses, marked and closed his book. 'It's what you expected now, isn't it?'

'I did, I . . . It crossed . . .' she said.

They talked for half an hour, during which Elsa's anger stirred again as she blamed Lynette for the attempted suicide. Chamberlain spoke gently, argued that the Rockford did not know what she was about, nor could have any idea of John's condition when she ditched him. Elsa, certain that the boy would be bruised again, here, tonight, fluttered about the room, determined on intervention. He, cheered by his wife's disquiet, and, oddly, by Lynette's appearance, said dully that they could not keep their son in cotton wool. They argued, volubly, then fell to silences which nagged both, in that there they realized the other's fears and resumed talking out of pity. At the end of thirty-five minutes they had repeated it all three times and were as uncertain as at the beginning.

'Tell you what,' Chamberlain said. 'We'll go downstairs and put the kettle on, and I'll barge in to propose coffee. How's that?'

In the sitting room John, presumably, had reduced the lights to the small wall-lamps over the mantelpiece and the standard behind Lynette's chair. As she sat, her face, her front were almost totally in shadow, though her hands, not prettily, caught the light. Chamberlain had listened at the door before knocking, had heard no sound. Nobody answered his signal, and as he entered, John on the chesterfield did not turn.

'Your mother and I are having coffee. Can we get you some?'

After the moment of quiet, Lynette heard, so that her face emerged into light, and he saw that she was smiling. The effect charmed, warmed the room.

'Yes, please,' she said. John stumbled to his feet. Dazed, he dashed the hair back from his forehead.

'I'll give you a hand,' he said.

'No need. You stay and talk to Mrs Rockford. Biscuits and cheese?'

Lynette was up, now, handling her skirt straighter. The room lacked mirrors, but she knew her beauty without reminders. Chamberlain ordered them to sit down, proffered a remark or two.

'They were just sitting there,' he informed Elsa, 'dumb as pigs. Put 'em plenty of knives and plates out, so they've got something to play with.'

'Is John all right?'

'As far as I know. But it'll take the pair of us to carry this lot in. You can see for yourself.'

'You're pleased she's here, aren't you?' Elsa said. She made an effort with the cheese tray.

'Yes. Not displeased. It had to come. I'd sooner it happened here.'

'If she said . . .' Elsa's smile crooked, 'that she'd have him, would you object?'

'I don't dislike her.'

'You wouldn't, then?'

They discussed her divorce about which they knew nothing because it kept them clear of argument. The cheeses, the biscuits, brown bread and butter on flowered china on lace were beautiful, amongst the silver of knives. On the second tray, coffee-pot, cream-jug, two cups, saucers matching the plates, spoons, seemed sober in comparison, sparse, spartan.

'Are you ready?' he asked his wife.

'Yes.' She took the smaller.

'They're waiting for us to come in. That may encourage them to talk. I don't want them there stiff as dummies, Elsa.'

She shook her head, puzzled, but she led the way, tapped the door, stood straight for the invitation. The young people rose so that for a minute the room seemed full, before John and his father moved a table, switched on lights. Elsa, by Lynette, directed subordinates without a movement, a general.

'That's it then,' she announced. 'We can leave it to you.' She turned to the visitor, asked if she were warm enough. On the gush of the reply, she ordered John to let her know if they were short of anything. 'Look after Mrs Rockford now she's here,' she warned, swept from the room. Chamberlain, grinning, winked at Lynette and stumbled after his wife.

'Well, then?' he asked.

'I don't know what he sees in her.'

'A sex object. A mystery. Another young mother.' She bridled, happily enough. 'What one person sees in a second rather than a third constantly flummoxes me.'

They sat to their coffee, not in mugs, but in flowered china like that in the sitting room.

'I wonder what they're saying.' Elsa. He shrugged, drank. 'Come on. You're a purveyor of fiction.'

' "Where does your mother buy her clothes, John?" '

'You're a fool.'

But she was not displeased, though nobody appeared, even to return the dishes. At ten, an hour later, they sat in the kitchen, alert to the doors, eyes lethargically on the old monochrome screen.

'Time the meeting broke up,' he said.

'Give them five more minutes.'

He went in, collected the crockery, suggested the invalid should retire. Lynette fiddled with her watch, miming concern, but within ten minutes had left the house. John did not look in on his parents; they left him alone. When Elsa asked in the morning if Mrs Rockford would be coming again, the son answered that he didn't know, cheerful and composed.

On the next day but one Chamberlain, to his surprise, received a call from Lynette; she must see him. Outside the Crown at eight-thirty. Yes, outside.

As soon as he stepped into the car park she emerged from the shadows, said she did not want a drink, urged him into her car, reversed, dashed beyond the lights of the pub, out towards the main road. She drove badly, clashing gears, swearing at error, and when asked where they were going answered, 'Where nobody knows us.'

He sat intrigued in her battered car, in a draught. She turned off the main road some four miles this side of Retford, drove more steadily, then parked by a farm-gate.

'If we'd have gone in the Crown, the first person to have come barging in could have been Robin McKay.' He was pleased she'd settled that one for him. 'I want you to talk to me about John. Then I'll tell you why I asked.'

He described the latest bout of depression, the treatment, its effect on his career, how the boy seemed. She did not interrupt, but tapped quietly if impatiently on the rim of the steering wheel.

'Will he get better?'

'We hope so.'

'This wasn't another suicide-attempt, was it?' She did not turn.

On his denial, she slumped, hands clenched in her lap, chin to chest.

'Will he ever be any good?' she muttered. Lips stiff.

'What do you mean by that?'

'Will he be able to hold a job down, live a normal life?'

Chamberlain now told her how well John had done on his teaching-practices, how highly his tutors praised him. 'Last year,' she interrupted. He acknowledged her point, expressed optimism. Angrily, now, she demanded how he could be certain.

'I can't. I can only hope.'

'Is that any use?'

The two sat in silence, under a blue-black night-sky swept by the rapid shift of clouds, with hedges alive, the grassy summit of the hillock to their left combed with a wind that rattled the car, blurred puddles.

'How did you find him?' he asked, in the end. He did not want the answer, wished to cower, in a fantasy of idleness, half uncomfortable.

'That's what I want to talk to you about. The other night, up at your house, he asked me to marry him. I don't suppose he told you. Did he? Well.' She allowed speed to ooze away.

'What did you say?' He could wait no longer.

'That's it, isn't it?' The fill-in question jarred. 'I said I'd think about it.' Then hitting the steering wheel, grasping it. 'That's all I could. He said if I refused, he'd kill himself. I needed to think. He told me I was free. He seemed very quiet. We sat there for long enough not saying a word. It frightened me. He tried before because I told him about Robin. You knew that, didn't you? I said I needed to think, that I'd been so desperate in my marriage to Joel that I wasn't sure I was suited to anybody. Silly things like that. It didn't seem right. He didn't.'

'Would you marry him? Or consider it?'

'What the hell . . .' The words screamed, squealed into tears, which were dashed dry in seconds.

'What about you and Boy McKay?'

'He won't marry me.'

'So you're ready to break with him?' he asked.

'I love him. I know that.'

'Doesn't that cut marriage with John right out of the picture?'

He waited for her, feeling an importance in this. She must talk herself into sense. They sat, unbudging, staring at, through the windscreen. Lynette shifted uneasily before she began.

'I think he might do it. John,' she said. 'He means what he says.'

'I see.'

'He's tried before. He's really set; his face showed it. It scared me. He looked weird.'

'Is that a good reason for marrying him?'

'I'd be to blame if anything happened. You'd blame me.'

'Now, let's be sensible.' Chamberlain tried to sound so. 'Marriage is an agreement to live together because both parties think it would be to their advantage. Threats don't come into that category. No, don't interrupt for a second.' He flapped her down. 'Are you attracted to him in any way? Sexually? As a companion. As a nurse, even?'

'I might look after him.' She sat straight. 'I could.'

'I'm pleased you've talked to me. We can be on the lookout. I honestly don't know what to say to you. But don't marry him because you think you're saving him. That's wrong.'

'He's . . .'

'Never mind what he is or what he isn't. If you can make a home with him, and you want to, that's different. His prospects aren't marvellous, but . . .' Chamberlain noisily scratched his neck. 'I'll talk to his mother about this.'

'Do you have to?'

'Why do you say that?'

'She doesn't like me.' She stopped his explanations. 'No, she doesn't hate me. I'm not worth considering.'

'I sometimes feel like that,' he said, 'with Elsa. It's nothing but surface mannerism.'

They went through the motions of argument, as he explained how his wife felt abandoned, unloved. She'd hedged herself with independences so that weakness within showed the blank reverse side of defence. He confessed that he could barely, sometimes, answer her politely, stay in the same room. 'This,' he maintained smiling, 'started as a love match.'

'She's beautiful.'

'She is. But she does not think so.'

Again he tried, his own confession done, to explore whether she'd any affection for John, and when he'd failed to make head or tail of her evasive answers, he puzzled himself why she'd fetched him out. He pressed, angry in catechism, but he met vagueness. 'I'm frightened. He's capable of it.' In the end he suspected she wanted him to take a hard line. 'Marry him.' 'Drop him.' Chamberlain persisted as he enjoyed bullying the girl, though soon he lost the savour of this as she answered dully shrill. In the end he demanded what steps she was taking to get Boy McKay to the altar.

'That's not on,' she said. 'He won't marry me.'

She was an attractive girl, hair curling under a felt hat, with a tip-tilted nose, a slightly open mouth, an illustration from a ladies' magazine. He offered to buy her a drink at any pub of her choice.

'We haven't settled anything,' she said.

'We are not likely to. You decide for yourself.'

'You wouldn't want me as a daughter-in-law.'

'It's what you want. You and John.'

'But you and Elsa . . .'

'We've no real chance of stopping you.' He almost believed that, after he'd repeated it several times in face of her dissenting sentences. 'You decide. Be selfish. That's that.' He put a hand on her thigh, but she did not flinch.

'I don't want a drink,' she said. 'Let's just have a little walk. You won't get your shoes muddy.'

They got out into the wind, which cut icily from the east.

'By God,' he said, 'winter's early this year.' The ground was iron-hard. As they walked, not quickly, between hawthorn hedges, they did not speak and Chamberlain, regretting the venture, dug his chin down to a scarfless chest. Suddenly his eye was caught, in the level roar of the gale, by a leaping shape, blackly square, above a gap under a tree. He moved towards the thing, glad of an objective, found it was a piece of plastic bag, caught, fixed, at the top of the hedge on a spur of barbed wire, wound high round a post. Its movement was violent, wild, a demented bat, an agony. His breath stopped, so that he stood, stiff, mouth gaping, unable to breathe.

The temporary paralysis lasted for so little time that Lynette did not notice; in the wind she pressed her hat to her head with one hand, and wrestled her coat down to her legs with the other. Chamberlain knew immediately what had stopped him. Under control, now, he watched the material flick and drive against the blue-dark sky, corner-pinned. She had turned bending, shouted for information. He bawled that it was a piece of one of last year's fertilizer bags. She demanded what was so interesting about that. He stretched his arms, shrugging.

He knew.

First he replied to her with some generalization about aesthetics, shape, chiaroscuro, variable geometry. She showed no interest, perhaps was unable to hear, but stood holding down her flapping clothes.

As a schoolboy he had sometimes walked out at night, when house and family had riled or bored him past bearing, and he had no work to dull his smarts. Then he watched the moon race through clouds, stood with the wind tearing at his hair, a monarch of thought, a king of love. Back home he'd dash down a banal line or two of free verse on the back of a French translation or a Latin prose, and sometimes he'd produce the finished article to one of his friends. He'd prided himself on the silver polish of his snatches, but had expected little praise from elsewhere, so that when the captain of rugby had, in ginger manliness, said a gruff word of admiration, he'd been taken aback. His first literary success, tainted, doubtless, explicable somewhere in the schoolboy welter of sex.

One such night he'd stood perched above a railway cutting, its banks striated with shadow, the straight length of track soft-steel blue and the signal lights blinking in the uneasy shift of wind. Beyond in the valley street lamps, renewed after the war, shone, but uneasily, expecting catastrophe. The new electric lights on the main road swung on their transverse wires. Soon he'd leave school, join the army, see the world; here, alone, breeze-battered he created it.

Turning his back to the pole-star, he looked along the rails where a dark bridge, black-blue even in daylight, showed clearly against the milky sky. He had decided to walk that way because it took him past the house of one of the three girls he loved. It meant an extra couple of miles, and her garden gate would be shut, no light glowing in the front windows. But he would see the front door with its porch supported by totem poles and read, if he were lucky, 'Alma Villa' cut into the lintel. Anti-climax roused poetic art. 'These ghosts of cloud haunt moon and heart,' he'd mutter. 'She does not see. It cannot hear.'

He stared again towards the bridge.

Signal-lights changed. Distant and home on green. The Manchester express would be along shortly, running downhill, regulator cut off until they were right through the station when the driver would open up again with a plume of steam. Eric delighted in his vigil, knowing the shriek of the whistle, the different hammer of wheels as the train left a viaduct for the solider earth of an embankment. As the carriages scuttled past, lighted now, rattling, he saw a movement on the bridge, a black moving shape, bat-ugly, up on the parapet right over the lines. The figure writhed, half-lost in darkness until it stood, a quarter of a mile away, more perhaps, upright, a man in a top coat, still waiting the approaching train. At the whistle the figure toppled forward, down, headlong, he did not know. Perhaps the youth, now Eric imagined him as one of a gang, in bravado had jumped backwards, one could not see which way he faced, not forwards, to safety, on to the pavement of the road across the bridge. The train surged through, tail lights disappearing, clacking away into the tunnels and the city station. As Eric Chamberlain stood, trembling, he conjured up the black shape, like a ruined kite, or a scarecrow, a paper bag on the bridge, scrambling up, balancing, unbalancing, outrageously clear, not to be thought.

He did not go that way home. The wrought-iron gate of Alma Villa kept its latch untouched that night by this passing lover. He ran home, panting to expel fear, sat so dumb by the radio that both father and mother asked him what was wrong. Next day the local paper ran a small column: Man found dead on railway line. Rumours bloodied school conversation. The body was decapitated, legless, cut in two. A small boy whose father swept the station platform passed solemn information to a circle of admiring, wiseacre seniors. Later still, an account of the inquest named the dead man as

Ernest John Naylor (52), factory hand, married without children, of Newark. Evidence of depression, unemployment. Balance of mind disturbed. A leaping kite of black on the parapet of a black bridge against a sky and above the darkness round stars. Within a week he'd begun to dismiss the image, but he had not spoken of it since, huddling in cowardice.

At Oxford three years later a man on his staircase had committed suicide.

They were not friends, but knew names, spoke them, once or twice had sat together in hall. One evening Francis Bulleid had invited Chamberlain in, for no reason, had made coffee, produced a huge tin of arrowroot biscuits, talked about his camera, fetched out an album of photographs. Eric, watching the movement of white, bony hands, the flapping forelock, half-envious of the public-school whine, had expected some homosexual overture, and had, rather bored, speculated about its form. He was in no way frightened, could have toppled Bulleid, shoved his way out of the place, but there had been no need. The photographs were beautifully mounted, and all large, one to a page. Francis developed and printed himself and now explained about optimum size, horizon lines, the purpose of shadow. What impressed the visitor most were the silver corner-mounts, standing up from the pages, embossed, rich; the photographs, to his philistine eye, were interesting enough, but their setting in the padded, pre-war album compelled, attracted. Even at that time he had sense enough not to say this, kept questions fluent. Francis talked about skiing, the French Alps, flipped back to *Geographical Magazine* mountains, boasted and confessed, but at the end of half an hour the pair were dumb, had nothing left to say, staring uneasily. When Eric finally forced himself to his feet, the other man did not detain him. Outside on the staircase Chamberlain danced light, let out of prison.

He heard later that Bulleid had been homesick, but noticed

nothing untoward when they acknowledged each other occasionally. One morning he was preparing his washing-kit, for he had to cross the corner of a quadrangle to enjoy hot water from a tap, when his door was thumped, flung open. Peter Leitch, a small, auburn-haired Scot, with glasses, gaped in at him without apology.

'I can't wake Bulleid.'

They stood locked in silence, before Chamberlain put his towelled bag on to a chair, moved out.

'He's breathing. He won't wake.'

Bulleid's room seemed exceptionally untidy compared with his own. A portmanteau reared like a hurdle in mid-floor. Books, shoes, a coat-hanger were haphazardly scattered. Bulleid had thrown his clothes across a chair as he'd undressed. The room was stale with cigarette smoke, cold-damp. Hastily drawn curtains let in a thin, zigzag pillar of light; the electric bulb shone dirtily.

Bulleid lay, pale, cheek on pillow, his overcoat thrown blanketwise on top of the bed. A smear of vomit down the side of his mouth, on the sheet had dried, thinly. A brown bottle, empty, had overturned, lay on the table with a glass jug, a cup, an ash-tray, empty, a box of Swan Vestas, a packet of Players.

'Wake up.' Leitch pushed at Bulleid's shoulder, shifting the head.

'Is he breathing?' Chamberlain asked.

'Yes. Not deeply.' Leitch pulled the figure upright. 'Wake up, Bulleid. Wake up, you silly bastard.' Still holding the torso, he looked over his shoulder at his companion.

'Put him down.' Chamberlain knew a cold excitement. 'Get over to the phone and ring emergency. No, I'll go. Keep him warm.'

He dashed out, shouldering a dressing-gowned figure in the corridor who swore sluggishly. Down in the porter's office he was surprised at the ease with which he summoned the emergency service. Militarily he informed the porter what was happening, ordered him to watch out for the ambulance, numbered the room and corridor, asked who he should speak to now.

The porter scratched his white head, unhelpful. 'Well, what's wrong with him, then? Appendix, is it?'

'Can't wake him.'

He ran back, found Leitch at the window. Somehow he'd expected a crowd. Leitch said he'd taken a cup of tea in; he had a gas-ring and liked to work early. Since Bulleid had returned from home, he called in every morning at seven-thirty. 'He's not been well. It's damned cold here. Give him time to wake up slowly.'

'Did you see him last night?'

'No. Was he in hall?'

They shrugged. Chamberlain went back to his room, dressed at speed, slouched back to the lodge, where the porter announced he couldn't raise Dr Markham, Mr Bulleid's tutor. The ambulance arrived; Chamberlain reported; the two attendants, noses red with cold, pulled out a blanket-covered stretcher. Within five minutes it was over. Now there were people about asking questions, faces wise and white. Sick to his boots, Eric, after shivering in the queue for a sink, shaved, shuffled back to his room. He went down to Leitch's; nobody. Across at breakfast people glanced inquiringly, but no more.

Bulleid died that day.

Markham, dark-jowled and judicial, allowed them to learn that the dose was massive, as he grappled for reasons. No one knew anything. It could not have been work, or Oxford. Love? No word emerged. The college was represented at the funeral. One or two, not Chamberlain, wrote to Bulleid's parents, received unilluminating politeness in return. Eric recovered, made his way in the world; the authorities saw him as responsible, told him so, granted him small privileges.

Lynette Rockford and he passed the flapping square, walked in gusty noise along the lane.

'Where are we off to, then?'

'Nowhere.' She stopped. 'You're not going to answer me, are you?'

'You want to marry him, don't you?' He wasn't involved.

'I don't know what I want. Somebody to bother about me.' She pressed up against him, mouth on his. He understood this, pulled her in, but made no attempt to hold her against her will as she heaved away. 'You, you,' she said. It barely sounded angry. He thrust his hands deep in his pockets, turning his back on her. Over the fields under a stunted branch of an oak tree, he could make out a road, a house or two. She joined him.

'I'm sorry,' she said.

'I feel like that often enough.' He took her in his arms. A squall of raindrops whacked them, dispersed itself as quickly. 'Let's get out of the wet.'

They hurried back to the car, hand in hand.

9

Every day up to Christmas Elsa found jobs to keep her husband busy.

She'd allow him to occupy himself in the study until lunch time, but then he was ordered out on errands, set to decorating, minor repairs, once or twice dispatched in the car with presents to her friends. He did not mind this, did his reading over whisky in the evenings instead of walking to the pub, and salvaged pride when he claimed the whole of Friday for the rewriting of his novel. Why Elsa had begun domineering he did not know, and though he tried to feel aggrieved realized that he had often spread his work into the afternoon for lack of occupation.

'You're bossy,' he said, half joking, 'these days.'

'You're idle.'

'I don't think so.' She did not relish seriousness from him. 'I need to...'

'Mull.' She mocked, then outlined his afternoon programme.

Five days before Christmas she sent him to the coast with a present for an old harridan they both detested whom he was to invite back if he judged it unavoidable. He spent an hour or two there listening in relief to a diatribe against Lady Hargreaves's nephew who was coming on Christmas Eve to fetch her for the holiday. The old woman crackled with malice, seemingly well, fed Chamberlain with a thick boiling of chicken soup which scalded his tongue, criticized the embroidered cloth Elsa had sent, saying it was bought from some charitable organization who were the biggest commercial cheats in existence, and thoroughly enjoyed herself making her guest uncomfortable. Her present to them, a bottle of grocer's port, fetched up from the larder, she wrapped in newspaper.

'How would you know,' he asked her, 'that somebody wanted to murder you?'

'How would I know?'

He explained his dilemma, but she had no interest. One wouldn't know until the first attempt; one never knew what other people were about. There followed an anecdote or two, malicious and irrelevant, about a former colleague of her husband, like him a knighted local politician and former Lord Mayor, who for years suffered from the delusion that his wife, impeccable, an Anglican, was putting arsenic into his food. He was sick after meals at home, took to eating out, and locked away his supplies of tea and coffee, his own pots, kettle even, in a specially installed safe.

'What did she do?'

'What could she? In the end, because that's what he wanted, she neglected him.'

'I thought you were going to say, "murdered him".'

They laughed, though her cackling was maniacal, unconnected with his sentence, he thought.

'It was quite a scandal at the time. My husband was approached to bring him to his senses. Arthur and a doctor, another Conservative councillor. They asked him how he knew his wife was poisoning him. He said he did know now that she wasn't, because she didn't have the chance. He could laugh about it. Arthur was taken aback.'

Lady Hargreaves sparked on, voice like radio interference. The man grew seriously ill, and that stopped the silliness. He had to depend on her. Chamberlain quizzed about evidence, but the old dear seemed convinced that human behaviour was so eccentric one did not need anything so banal as supporting circumstance. She moved to the nephew whose hospitality she was about to receive; he had loved a married woman to distraction, had twice deserted his bride during the first year of their marriage, on his honeymoon even. Now he was a dry stick in his fifties with too much money and too many fears he'd lose it.

'Has his wife forgiven him?'

'As far as I know. Why shouldn't she?'

'She never tried to get her own back?'

Lady Hargreaves's mind had flitted elsewhere. She had not allowed herself to conceive of the distress, shame, anger of the deserted woman. Stanley had been wild, yes, madder than most, she admitted, but over thirty years ago. She had no idea what had happened to the other woman, either, except that she went in duty and submission with her husband to Brazil, or the Argentine. 'They'll be back now, if they're alive still. I've heard nothing of them.' No, Stanley never said a word these days. The thin face smiled round the aristocratic nose, she was an ironmonger's daughter, the false teeth. She seemed never to have considered the right questions. In her stories people acted with high eccentricity which made them memorable; she never mentioned, let alone ferreted out, their motives. She must, Chamberlain concluded, have interested herself in such matters at the time, but now only the mummified corpse of the action remained, hard as locust root, degutted, heartless.

He left her house later than he intended, at seven o'clock, for the two-hour drive home. His mind was alert, resurrecting these stories, preaching to himself, putting himself as he raced along dark lanes into the highly polished shoes of Lady Hargreaves's protagonists. A year ago, he'd met Stanley Watson, a bald, pig-faced, squinting man, six feet three and broad; they'd talked about conservation and the public school Stanley had attended, where Chamberlain had taught. The voice had been cultured, admirably modulating.

As he drove he concocted metaphors for the old woman's

talk. One picked up a scrap of newspaper in a foreign language which one understood except for two or three key phrases. Lady Hargreaves fluttered, a butterfly in an expected gust, forced into wild flurries of action, all wasted.

He arrived home in the drizzle without much enthusiasm. There would be food available, provided he foraged; a pound to a penny Elsa would not even leave off whatever idleness she was about to ask how he'd fared. Wrong again. Pamela opened the front door before he'd wiped his feet; John appeared from the drawing room; Elsa, hand to banister, descended the stairs.

'Reception committee,' he said.

They all smiled. Pam and his wife led him into the kitchen, explaining that a friend of his had called. Eli Dunne. They seemed excited, competing to tell the tale as they prepared his supper. He caught their enthusiasm, began to question. Miles Teeman, the conductor, had been unable to direct the County Youth Orchestra's course and had recommended Dunne; he'd come up overnight, had a two-hour interview with education officials, ten minutes of handshaking and coffee with the director and his deputy, on appointment, and had then tried to contact Chamberlain by phone and failing, typically, had driven over, arriving not a quarter of an hour after Eric had left for the seaside. Elsa, out of character, had invited Dunne to lunch, and the meal had lasted an hour and a half, while the four had sat round the table in conversation. Pamela had already arranged that John would go with her and Saul Hill into town for last-minute shopping, but they came back early. Elsa had spent the afternoon in Eli's company, had enjoyed herself. He'd now gone off to meet heads of sections, but would be returning to stay overnight, they'd no idea when. Elsa was unusually animated.

Intrigued, Chamberlain pressed. They answered, cheerfully willing.

Lunch had been very attractive in that they had all talked

to each other, a family. John had really spouted, Pam said, about a performance of *Macbeth* at his college, and about an orchestra at the junior school where he'd done his last practice. He'd been really interesting, lively. 'He seemed different altogether.' What had Eli told them? Both women spluttered, bursting to inform him that Dunne had produced nothing out of the ordinary, and then to laugh at each other, surprised that they had appeared mad keen to say so little. In the end, Pam went off to phone Saul, to invite him over in case the visitor arrived back in time for more unmemorable uplift.

'You liked him, then?' Chamberlain to Elsa.

'Yes. I did. I don't know why, now I come to think of it.'

They'd spent an hour together in the afternoon, over one gin, while he'd explained what the course entailed and she'd described a day's work in her husband's life. Each had been more interested, she claimed, in the other's topic. Chamberlain said that he'd have guessed that anyone got up as casually as Dunne wouldn't have had her favour. She seemed pleased with his bluntness, did not take it amiss, let out in the end that though Eli had worn a workman's donkey-jacket for driving he'd worn a very respectable grey suit. As they laughed trying to argue whom this sartorial sobriety would impress, both began to be circumspect, sure now that the visitor had made an impact, that Santa Claus had turned up.

'He really was delighted he'd got the job. Miles Teeman had to go into hospital, without much warning, and had put his name forward. But he said the interview was very sticky because he thought the music adviser wanted to take over himself.'

One of the afternoon's topics had been Chamberlain's novels. Elsa, hearing for the first time that her husband discussed his books with Dunne, began to ask if Eli was helpful, clever, a good listener. She seemed so unlike herself that he was tempted to rib her on this conversion, but did his best for her. That afternoon she'd learnt something.

Dunne arrived soon after eleven, rather tired, not altogether cheerful. He'd met the people he'd work with, found them unforthcoming, and in one case obstructionist, because he was not Miles Teeman. There had been little to discuss, as the programme had been chosen and the music ordered, but he'd done his utmost to placate, without, he thought, much success. 'I shall have to go my own way,' he said, 'whether or not they like it.' After the meeting he'd gone with three of them into a miserable pub with yellow walls. 'Like heaven,' Chamberlain said. Eli swore comically. That, too, had been an error, because the poor beer had loosened tongues and he realized that his companions were a minority group of neither influence nor power. The old brigade would already be condemning him as a drunkard lacking judgement.

'What'll happen then? On the course?' Elsa, enthusiastic.

'I shall please myself. If it means getting across them, I shall be bloody rude. I shan't see the job again. They'll want Miles if he'll come. I only got it this year because the notice was so short they couldn't find anybody better known.'

'There'll be trouble?'

'There'll be sixty-eight kids who want to work and learn something. They're my concern.'

'You'll do well with them?'

'God knows. It depends. I'm not promising.'

The family supplied him with coffee, whisky and pork pie. He ate and drank heartily, beaming, soon wooed from his dumps. Before long he, John and Saul Hill shot headlong into a discussion on fame, pseudo-notoriety, the television, films. For the first time Chamberlain realized why tutors had praised his son for his ability in the classroom; he was quick on the uptake, but angelic of temper, ready with a question to keep argument moving, not short of sense. Dunne sat benign now, glass in hand, a provider of anecdotes, delivered without malice, of nepotism, sharp practice, marvellous luck or patronage. Pushing circular spectacles up to his eyebrows, beard skipper-sized, broad as a house, he held his trunk upright, a Buddha, but neither godlike nor inscrutable. Saul Hill, on the other side, was soon furious, hoarse, leaning on injustice; in twenty years' time he'd be like his father, a bad-tempered conservative, Chamberlain thought. Pam did not seem to mind, or notice, but supported him with emphatic nods, glances to indicate her understanding, short sentences of approval.

This was family life, was great, warmed.

They staggered to bed at ten minutes to one, John and his father pushing upstairs together.

'You're late, young man.' No criticism. 'I've enjoyed that.' They could hear Elsa explaining to Eli about towels, morning routines. 'And your mother.' He congratulated his son on his performance, said he'd like to ask about films.

'You know more about it than I do.' That meant he'd written scripts, helped massacre his books.

'No. The pictures to me, that's the place where the brainless go to pass time. Like the billiard-hall.'

'The clever people at college are more interested in films than books.'

'Typical, now all the cinemas are bingo-palaces.' They laughed, in brotherhood, whisky, amity. 'It's a pity Lynette wasn't here.'

'Yes. Her mother's ill. She's down there every night.'

'Serious?'

'Think so. Bad bronchitis. The father's useless.'

'Will she be able to come up for Christmas?'

John shook his head, suddenly tired, a pale scarecrow again.

Elsa bustled into the bedroom, the hostess still, dusting her hands like the manageress of a hotel.

'Eli's going to ring his wife tomorrow to see if they can come up over Christmas.'

'Doesn't he know?'

'Seems not. It's such short notice. She's probably filled the house with turkeys.'

'They've a deep-freeze. I know that.'

She took him in her arms. He smelt the gin on her breath, but she stood energetically beautiful, dominating him, confident. Happy enough, he kissed her mouth, himself her sexual object, objective, created by Dunne and the spirit bottle. They fell, raged into sexuality, love, sleep.

Beth Dunne made no demur, pleased that she and her husband would arrive on Christmas Eve. The idea seemed flat now, organized in drink, not regretted, best neglected. Lynette Rockford's mother was taken into hospital. Hearing this, Elsa barked inquiries, said that Lynne and her father must come on Christmas Day, that Eric could fetch them, that John was to check details.

'She must be pretty ill if they have her in now. They're trying to clear the wards for the holiday. And if you say her sister's out, then get them here. Phone her. Go on down to see her at lunch time.'

'You're not taking too much on, now?' Chamberlain worried his wife.

'Four more. What's that, once? Besides I've got Elsie in eight hours today and tomorrow morning. And Pam. And you and John to run errands.'

'Good-bye, work.'

'Christmas comes but once a year.'

She was magnificent, like a campaigning general, with her lists, her curt efficiency. She ordered her husband upstairs to his desk, and when he complained, reminded him his big moment would arrive with the bills she ran up. 'You earn some money.'

He wondered how long the mania, the radiance, would last. Lunch was, certainly, no more than soup and cheese sandwiches, but eaten like a picnic, with a bottle of champagne. He was dispatched to collect the Christmas tree from the forester at Welbeck Lodge, and then commanded to get it erected. 'And no midnight crashes this time.' Last year it had collapsed, noisily, so that he'd armed himself, fearing a clumsy burglar.

The hall sparkled when the Dunnes arrived, with polish, with fairy lights, massed greenery, bunches of dried silver honesty, Cape-gooseberries and garlic-head golliwogs. The kitchen was a place of talk which did nothing to impede the bustle; glasses clinked all over the house so that when Saul ushered his parents in it seemed an event, worth lining up for. John, who had accompanied Lynette and her father to the hospital, returned before nine, and by half past eleven Elsa was filling a pair of Pam's football-type sockings, yellow and black, with the traditional childish gifts for her son and daughter.

'Not next year. This is the last time.'

'Pity.'

'These things are so expensive.' She handled a bar of soap, bundled it down to join the chocolates, the orange, the tights, the talcum-powder.

'They like it. Don't they now?'

She'd go out in a few minutes, lay the bulging sausage across the foot of each bed, order, 'No touching, now, till morning,' and be obeyed.

Christmas Day began slowly, suiting the mild cloudiness outside. Presents crowded the base of the tree, but there'd be little ceremony, a mere five minutes for handing out when everybody could be collected, after which Father Chamberlain would pick up, fold and burn the torn wrapping paper, the string, the sellotape. Smoke would rise foggily, sadly for him in his anorak away from the house.

Mrs Dunne assigned herself to the kitchen, where, as an underling, she slaved cheerfully. At half-twelve Lynette arrived with her father, who was taken to the drawing room for fuss and a glass of beer. Ernest Smith was a tall man, thin, with rough grey hair cut short, and a walrus moustache, who, as he sat, squinted his suspicion at the people round him. He'd not expected this: the large house, the young people, their affable elders, glasses in hand. One saw his like, cloth-capped, tight-lipped, silent, in the corner of any pub, in, not of, the crowd. Like some old dog, incapable beyond a snarl or yelp, he eyed them inhospitably, if not with hostility. Lynette, whisked away to the purdah of the kitchen, proved useful, singing 'My lovely Celia' to herself, until encouraged by Pam, then Elsa, she full-throated 'Oh, let me gaze/On your bright eyes' so that the hot room rang with her clarity, and Dunne looked in.

The meal, early and short, so that Lynette and her father could visit the hospital, was noisily successful. Elsa, congratulated, praised her aides, ventured on port. Her fairness, her beauty, seemed to her husband becomingly matronly; she had filled the hungry with good things and knew it. That she looked no older than Lynette lacked importance; that she could coax answers out of the silently chewing Smith, the imperturbable Beth, the ever-ready Eli, gave her status, position, the lady of the house. Chamberlain, eating meagrely and taking pleasure in his abstinence, founder of the feast, smiled round his table. He sat next to Beth Dunne, within touching distance, but they kept apart, in a seasonal propriety. When John went off to the hospital with Lynette and her father, the two remaining men set about the dishes with a will, chaffed by the women, who squared up, found them work, plagued from the periphery.

The afternoon was spent glazing on the television screen, munching.

At six, now that Lynette and party were back, they took high tea, sandwiches and wedges of iced Christmas cake. Leaving Smith in front of the fire with a glass and decanter of port, the rest trooped out for a walk, along the lane, through the village, then for a short time into the plantations where they decorously kept to the grass paths and sang carols.

Back home, with drink and crackers, they found Ernest Smith almost talkative. He described his life as a farmer, with a kind of grim energy, like a machine shaving metal. It had been damned hard work, the lovely Midland vowel screeched, werk, no other word for it. He missed it, but it wasn't bad to retire, to keep to bed in the dark mornings, to have your milk delivered in a bottle. The man seemed delighted that they listened, and yet spoke as if they'd no chance of understanding; he sneered their approval away into further craggy sentences about mud and cold and bruises. Just before ten, when the cheese and mince-pies were fetched out, he fell naturally to sleep, slumped there ugly as a sod of clay. He'd not spoken then for above an hour; he'd said his piece, earned his welcome and had sat aside, apart from the repartee, the Jumbo crossword, the *Statesman* quiz, the blank telly, a man in the past so that his sleep developed easily from his silence, his distance.

After they'd eaten again Elsa asked Eli Dunne to play his violin. He shrugged, politely, but his wife said unemphatically, 'He'll play us the Preludio from the E major Partita.'

'I wish I knew enough to say things like that,' Pam blurted out.

Dunne did as he was told, tuning carefully, lacing his bow with rosin.

'What is it?' Elsa asked.

'Bach,' he answered, cocking the fiddle. 'Unaccompanied Bach.'

The tumbling, flying notes scythed the air, bounced big from the walls, as Dunne's fingers danced the strings. The speed was steely, underpinned in the whirling to a foundation of power so that it seemed in no way wild or demented, but quick and brilliant in a great sanity of movement, that dipped and curled in velocity like light, like a dazzle of reflection, heavenly nimble, in frolic, different, removed from the player with his handkerchief under his bearded chin, his bulging pockets, his planted shoes, the heaviness of his bearing.

He lowered the violin, as they applauded.

'The Loure,' Beth ordered.

Dunne played with extraordinary strength, the double-stopping clear and strong, the rhythm steadily beating. Now he seemed concentrated round his instrument, a part of it, a moving sea round a wooden island of sound; he pushed his tone, thrusting it at them, in six, not hurrying nor dallying, forward to complete Bach's work, to re-create it. As he swayed he no longer stood the smiling, quiet man commanded by his wife to performance; he seemed vast, a maker of giant's song, a mountain of music. He finished, held his violin under his chin still as he said, diffidently, himself again, 'Loure's a word for bagpipe.' They applauded. 'The Gavotte en Rondeau and then I'm done.'

The bow bounced, dancing their faces into smiles now as if marvellously glad to be caught up in the formal, masculine beauty of line, the taut accent of the chords, the orchestral breadth of one instrument strong as a dozen. Their heads jerked with him, shoulders squared, backs like ramrods. He ended, flourishing his bow, had the fiddle into its case and wrapped away in no time. The listeners clapped, shouted, taken out of themselves, excited beyond measure.

'I don't practise enough,' Dunne said, unscrewing his bow.

They congratulated him; Beth blushed with her pleasure. Eli, broad as a house, stroked his beard.

'I heard that Gavotte on an old seventy-eight we had at home,' Chamberlain told them. 'An arrangement by Henry Wood and the Queen's Hall Orchestra.'

'Segovia played it.' said Pam.

'None as well as Mr Dunne.' Elsa exactly right. They filled glasses, drank to him. Smith, wakened by the violin, sat in a daze, peering at them, scattering icing sugar and pastry from the mince-pie they shoved into his hand. His face was puckered as if he'd begin to cry, but he smiled, thanked them gruffly, demonstrated awkward politeness, especially towards Elsa. Dunne's performance had warmed them to this stone of a man. Without condescension, he'd be no mascot, they looked after him, pleased to be of service. When Smith went off with Lynette, the rest accompanied him to the door, and chilled outside they bawled 'O Come, All Ye Faithful'.

Next morning all rose late, set out for the Hills' at midday, returning singing at three-thirty for turkey sandwiches and and Christmas pudding. The young people disappeared to a party, Eli ventured on a walk in the dark, while the three roasted themselves in front of a coal fire. Not much was said; they hadn't the heart even to drink deeply. Eli returned, full of the frosty night, with the story of a couple he'd met who'd begged two pounds from him.

'On Boxing Day?' Elsa asked.

'Were they down-and-outs?' Chamberlain.

'No, they were, as far as I could see, respectably dressed. A young couple, in their early thirties. Quite well spoken. The woman wore a wedding ring.'

'What did they say to you?' Elsa again.

'Something like "Could you give us money for a drink?"'

'Perhaps,' Chamberlain conjectured, 'they'd set out for the pub and found they'd not brought any money out.'

'Would you have begged?' Eli crossly, it seemed.

'I shouldn't. I'd have gone back home.' Elsa.

'Muttering, muttering all the way.'

Elsa and Chamberlain surprised themselves with a dramatic vignette of a quarrelling couple. They had never done any such before. Beth laughed, joined in once, but Eli would not sit down, mooched about the room.

'It's wrong,' he said. 'Bloody and wrong.'

'What is?' Chamberlain still elated from his histrionics.

'Young people. Middle class, I guess. Begging on a country road.'

'Perhaps it was for a bet. Or they were having a competition with another couple on another road to see who could collect most.'

'No. It didn't seem like that.'

'Tell us again.' Elsa.

'I saw this pair coming along. Together. Not arm in arm. When they were nearly up to me, they stopped. I thought they were going to ask me the time or the way or something. Then the man said, "Could, would you give us money for a drink?" I was a bit taken aback. It wasn't what I expected. Then the woman said, "Something for a drink." She put her hand up to her face. I could see her clearly. She wore a hat, an old-fashioned felt affair. I had two pounds in the top pocket of my jacket. I pulled the money out, gave it to them.'

'What did they say?' Elsa.

'Just "Thank you".'

'Nothing else?'

'No. "Thank you." Not "very much" even. Took both notes. Then they went on. I heard them clumping off, down this way, past the house.'

'There's no pub here, on this road, for ten miles.'

'It was rotten.' Eli shook his head. 'I hate it.'

'You're being superstitious,' Beth Dunne said.

'I'm being some bloody thing.'

'It's silly,' Beth said. 'The gypsy's warning. He thinks now there'll be some sort of catastrophe on his course.'

'I don't know what I think.'

Eli was shaken out of his equanimity, that was clear, but they stood drinks up for him, cheered him. The four remained in for the rest of the evening, listening to the *Christmas Oratorio*, hardly speaking, in bed by ten-thirty.

Next morning Elsa tried to persuade Beth to stay with them while her husband directed his orchestra, but she was adamant, pleased to be away.

Weather cold, sleeting outside; the festivity withered.

10

Mrs Smith, Lynette's mother, died on New Year's Day.

John made up his mind that he would return to college in the second week in January. His doctors did not oppose the decision. The boy himself spoke calmly, planned his future and courted Lynette most evenings; he had helped with arrangements for the cremation, packed Father Smith off to a sister in Mablethorpe. Elsa did not like this, niggled her husband.

'He doesn't seem fit,' she said, bursting into the study. 'He's never as quiet as this.'

'I rang Carfax.' The consultant psychiatrist had been unenthusiastically in favour of the return. 'I can't do any more.'

'Talk to him.'

'I've done so. I'll do so again. But what can I say? "Are you sure you're well enough to go back?" "Yes, Dad." "Put it off a bit. There's no hurry." "I shall be all right." '

He knew he'd be driven to this exchange of uncertainties and convictions, but now, snuffling with a cold, worried about his work after a lay-off, he miserably eyed his wife, wishing he could reassure her.

Chamberlain rang Lynette, who calling back by arrangement from a public booth in her lunch hour expressed satisfaction at John's recovery. Without much fervour she said they'd agreed, her word, to get married as soon as he'd found a job. In her view, John had recovered, seemed normal.

Closeted with his son, Chamberlain managed nothing.

John said not a word about the agreement with Lynette,

but cheerfully claimed the break had righted him. Chamberlain, short-tempered from the clichés, pointed out that not many months before the young man had nearly killed himself. John said circumstances had changed. He'd be, father snarled, in the same place, away from Lynette. John knew that. Things were different.

'In what way?'
'I'm steadier.'
'You'll marry Lynette?'
'I expect so.'

Nothing more concrete. John, hands in pockets, was rounder in the face, had grown a moustache, which did not hide the fatuity of his smile. His mother tried and failed with him, but insisted that the parents should drive him down. Lynette accompanied them, the whole journey spoilt by an early start, a disappointing lunch in a starred restaurant, some January fog. By the sea the air struck milder, but his room, different from last term's, was mean, dampish and white, with an awkwardly, steeply sloping ceiling in one corner. John seemed satisfied, not needing them, not Lynette even, shuffling about, hanging jackets, lining up books. His gas fire popped. Elsa made a miserable cup of tea. The Chamberlains called on his tutor, giving their son a last half-hour with his fiancée, but when they returned, the two had brewed coffee, slurped it down at either end of the lumpy bed.

They drove back in the dark.

Lynette refused to stay, dashed off into Retford in her own car.

Elsa walked helplessly about, for the first time in her husband's eyes a middle-aged woman. Pamela had waited up with a meal.

'That room was dreadful,' Elsa said. 'Poky and damp.'
'He seemed satisfied. He knows where he is going.'
'The paint. It was leprous. And cold. He'll be ill.'

'He'll survive.' He had no idea.

His preoccupation these last few days had been with people in extreme situations. The pub explosion, the gunmen at the door, the murderous knife in the common street, on the football terrace.

'What would you do if someone walked in here now and killed me?'

'Who?'

'Somebody you didn't know.'

Elsa's face twisted stricken, into a scream of flesh.

'Why are you asking me that?'

'It's happening tonight. All over the world. Not far from here. When you see those farmhouses where men have been killed, the Irish lanes our troops have been ambushed on, what are they like? They're comfortable, and cosy. Picturesque. Nice. Good places for a holiday.'

'You must be mad.'

'We're worried about John. But tragedy's flung into the faces of people no more or less ordinary than we are. They've got death, bloody death, there on the hearthrug.'

'You fool about with your books until . . .' She stopped.

'What?'

'Nothing.'

'No. Something. Ordinary people cut and shattered bloodier than cannibals. And you and I stutter about. Suppose somebody smashed their way in here, used us as hostages.'

'I can't think what that's like.' Elsa, quite cool now, ready it appeared to take him on. 'I don't know how I should behave. It doesn't mean we should forget about John, does it?' She paused. 'Sometimes you act and talk without sense. I'd sooner you sat there dumb. What is all this?'

'It's what I think about when I wonder about John.'

She snorted scorn, flounced about.

'You're a funny devil, Eric. Sometimes.'

'I expect so.' He pondered, gave it a fling. 'Do you know what I'm considering now? How you'd act if you were going to kill me.'

'I see.' She sat down.

'The book I'm writing.'

'I know that.'

'How come?' He must master the situation with small idiocies of words.

'Eli spoke to me about it, told me that's what you were worrying about. I was furious. Blew up at him, because he knew and I didn't. He said an odd thing.' She laughed. 'When I asked him why you showed your work to him and not to me, he said it was that you wanted me to see the finished piece, as near perfection as you could get it. Is that right?'

He massaged his forehead.

'It's good,' he answered. 'Very good.'

'You spoil every bloody thing, don't you?' She didn't sound too displeased.

'It may even be true. We can't always know our motives.'

'Do you ever consider me when you're up here?'

'Of course.'

'Of course.' Elsa laughed now, but bleakly, like a pianist whose fingers ran through a work learnt years before. 'Eli said that in the middle of a rehearsal he'd remember his wife. It refreshed him.'

'Were you surprised?'

'That he told me? That it was so? Yes, I was. In a way. He was worth twenty of her.'

'But he didn't think so?' Chamberlain asked.

'Who's to say? I thought she was dull. Didn't you? *Gemütlich?* He'd been unfaithful to her.'

'Oh?'

'He told me openly.'

'Not ashamed?' He mocked her with tenderness.

'He said he was. And that was curious.'

'Wasn't he afraid you'd run off and tell his wife? Or did she know?'

'It wasn't mentioned.' Elsa, legs together, neatly beautiful, in the trim.

'Was he sober?' She nodded, smiling as if he'd complimented her. 'What about Beth? Did she reciprocate?'

Elsa giggled, almost childishly but without losing poise.

'He thought she fancied you but hadn't the courage to do anything about it.'

'I see.'

They laughed uncomfortably as Chamberlain blushed. Elsa did not press her advantage. He wondered if Eli had had made a pass at Elsa, tempted her with his infidelities. Perhaps the man had discovered Beth's adultery and handed on his knowledge in this roundabout way. He did not know, scowled there, not troubled.

'How did you like Eli?' he asked.

'Very much. Really interesting.'

'Is he attractive sexually?'

'Yes. In a way. Why do you ask?' Elsa straightened her back, pert, bright.

'I wondered. With all that beard. Can you tell what sort of face there is underneath?'

'Enough.'

'Curious.' He pushed it no further.

'I shouldn't think,' she began, 'that he's as interesting as you are. But he put himself out to talk, to make a fuss of me.'

'You're attractive.'

'You don't say so very often. Do you think . . . ?' She waited.

'What's that?' He looked up, apprehensive.

'Nothing. I just wondered if the Dunnes were happy. Have they got money?'

'Not a great deal. And he's out a fair time in the evening.'

'How does she occupy herself?'

'Second-hand books. She collects, and reads. I send her review copies.'

'That's right. I'd forgotten. She'd her head in a book, given half a chance, here.'

Conversation meandered, returned to the subject of wives planning to murder their husbands, petered out. He felt that the exchange was unsatisfactory in that she had wanted to talk to him about John, or about his work, or her own preoccupations, had nearly managed it. They never made contact. He did not know how.

Next day, cold with sunshine, he invited her out for a walk. He'd done a day's graft before lunch, put in a powerful hour afterwards, and, elated, sought her out. She appeared to be dusting, squaring up in Pamela's bedroom, round her daughter.

'I ought to make a cake.'

Pamela, leaping up, volunteered for the stove.

'Go on out with him,' she ordered.

'If Saul comes, we'll have nothing for tea.'

Chamberlain, surprised at the rapport between the two women, their joviality, kicked heels while his wife took to warm clothes. They turned off the road, out into the fields, and sheltered, faces burning for January winds, in Cresswell's Wood.

'It's cold,' he said. 'Too windy.'

The path through the wood shone faintly wet, and here and there amongst the wintry shrubs a jagged tear of newspaper, a sodden bag, a packet of Silk Cut were bundled. Bracken, frail and rust-coloured, thrust statuesque amongst the trees, but high up twigs knotted, wrestled, whipped.

'I've never been in here before,' Elsa said.

'You're going to get your shoes muddy.'

Elsa walked ahead, pleased with herself, while he stumbled, catching his coat once on a bramble, tripping again on a root across the grey green slime of the path. His wife turned, elegant in trousers, raised her eyebrows, saying nothing.

At the edge of the wood they could see, at the bottom of the slope, the A-road to the north. Cars crawled silently on the dual carriageway, for on the margin of the wood here the wind whooped and blustered.

'How far's that?' she asked.

'Mile. Mile and a quarter, as the crow flies.'

'We must have seen this place as we drove up to Scotland, then.'

She was searching for something to say. Without show, he placed his arm deeply into the crook of hers, waited for answering pressure, found none. He was awkwardly entangled now, forced to bend his knees to maintain the pose. In his adolescence he'd trailed his girls into places such as this, snatched kisses or fondled their breasts. Then, enjoying one minute, he'd anticipate the next, dread the rebuff. Now with arm linked into his wife's he had no idea what to expect of himself. He kissed her cheek, and again, but she stared out towards the matchbox cars. Half-damped, he spun her, pressed his mouth to hers. She showed no sign of disapproval or pleasure, allowed it, did not discourage.

'Give us a kiss,' he said, standing back.

She lifted her cold mouth; he pulled her in. Tongues slid to tentative exchanges.

They kissed, adequately, without passion as the wind battered about them. After a moment or two Elsa moved a yard away from him, patted at her clothes.

'I shall need a visit to the hairdresser's tomorrow.'

'Are you warm enough?'

'Yes.' She waved towards the road. 'It's light out here. Grey or not.' He, immersed in himself, shuffled back into the shelter, shrunken inside his coat. 'We found a dead body in a wood, once.'

'We?' he asked.

'Daddy and I.' She joined him under the trees where though they could hear the riot outside, the calm ten yards deeper seemed secure.

'Come on, then. Let's hear about it.' He had liked her father, Professor Bruce-Grayling, but had never rumbled him.

'He used to make us walk with him in the afternoons, when we were home from school. On this day Octavia was shopping.' She recalled her father's strict habits. At one o'clock he came downstairs expecting his lunch on the table, soup on which he insisted already served. She'd heard that as an undergraduate he slaved from six in the morning until nine at night, and for ten years after he'd gained chair and wife in his early thirties. From then onwards his hours were ten until one five days a week. As a young man he'd produced four books; middle-aged he managed two, both short, both highly regarded. All six were in print still. His lectures to his own students or at foreign universities he'd prepared carefully, but unhurriedly, preferring to repeat himself until he was certain he'd changed his mind. These had not been published, would be on the wish of his executors. A further book grew imperceptibly longer.

Each afternoon, unless it rained hard, he'd set out at two-thirty, taking dog or daughters or both. He said little, mulling over his morning's conclusions, they'd guessed, for he never quite conquered his compulsion to work. When he stopped, he'd point with his stick at a bird, toadstool, rabbit, and grunt. If they pressed him for information, he knew nothing, could not name, merely offered them the chance to share what he saw. He made no principle, no philosophy out of his habit, never sought to impress. Now and then the girls proffered information, flashed nomenclature: he nodded, did not comment.

On that day Bruce-Grayling had a faculty meeting at 3.45, which meant that he walked slightly faster. There was no need for this, since his exercise period never exceeded three-quarters of an hour, but he rammed his stick down more militarily, waved it peremptorily at any slackening of speed by dog or daughter.

'Tansy started to bark. Daddy looked annoyed, because he was in a hurry and didn't like routine disturbed. "See what it is, Pet," he ordered. I went, saw hobnailed boots and trousers. "It's a man lying here," I shouted. Daddy didn't come at once; he'd be pulling faces in annoyance, beating with his stick. The body was face downwards with a raincoat pulled up over his head. Daddy came through the bushes, ordered me to the path. He wasn't there for long and when he did come out he said, "We shall have to go back," pointing to the way we'd come. I said to him, I don't know why, "Is he dead?" "I think so," he answered. He hesitated because he wouldn't want to tell a lie, even to spare me. We returned the way we came, and I remember we passed a phone box we didn't use. We also saw old Philipps who used to dig our garden, but Daddy just wished him good afternoon. When we got home he sent me to find Mummy, and when she came he said, "Violet, we've found a dead body in Thieves' Wood. I'm going to ring the police. Look after Elsa." Then he signalled us out of the hall, and telephoned.'

'Did it frighten you?'

'No. It's funny. I tried to make myself scared, but I'd seen so little. Hobnailed boots, corduroy trousers.'

'Was it murder?'

'No. A farm labourer called Parker. He'd died from a heart-attack. The odd thing was he came from eight or ten miles away. Nobody knew what he was doing there.'

'Was he old?'

'Sixty-two. His wife couldn't account for it. He'd been there two days since Saturday. She thought he was away at a football match. It was never sorted out. They guessed he might have been with a woman, and she'd run off when he was taken ill. There wasn't any proof.' Elsa, walking briskly now, continued. 'For the next month Daddy didn't take me that way again. After that, back to normality. He'd even say a few words about it.'

'Was it a place like this?'

'No. You remember Thieves' Wood. It was very flat. More civilized than this. Beaten paths. Not so much brushwood, tangle.'

They were walking sharply now, on an uphill path, hardly wide enough for one. When Elsa, who led, reached the top, she paused, and panting, hand on chest, laughed at herself. Chamberlain below said, 'I'd have been frightened.'

'I was a scared little monkey. But I wasn't as far as I remember.'

'Did you know about death?'

'Know?'

'Had you seen a dead person?'

'No. I was terrified of the idea of drowning. Or hanged people. But this had no face. I don't remember even hands. Hobnailed boots and trouser legs.'

'And your father?'

'He was either late for or missed his meeting. But he wasn't one to talk. For a literary man.'

They set off again, emerging on the further side of the summit of the hill where again they could see the north road, at much the same distance, with the same bevy of silent, scurrying cars.

'You never told me about that before,' he said. 'I wouldn't mind dying here.'

'Not today,' she ordered.

'What about John?' he asked.

'What about him?'

'Will he be all right? On his own! Down there?'

'Lynette's going to see him the week-end after next. He'll look forward to that.'

'Do you trust her?'

Elsa gestured her annoyance, wheeled, stood dumb.

'Is she carrying on with Boy McKay still?' he asked.

He knew he'd get little sense, began to walk round the edge of the wood until he was arrested by her voice.

'Don't go rushing away just when I'm about to say something.' He turned, found Elsa unflustered, unemphatic. 'I'm as worried as you are. But it's no use making a song and dance about it. She'll chase after men. She can't help it. She's not the right woman for him, but he thinks she is. We'd be wrong to try to argue him out of it.'

He surfaced with platitudes, and she waved him on. Thirty yards further they re-entered the wood, began to descend. A man with a little girl and a dog, in file, met them, exchanged head-movements.

'I wonder what they'll find,' Chamberlain said, out of earshot.

'She'd be seven or eight. I was thirteen. Tansy was a spaniel.'

Put into place, he pressed on harder, slapping his feet. Once they'd emerged into a lane with hawthorn hedges they walked together.

'I don't think I enjoy walking,' Elsa said.

'We've talked. That's something.'

'You hardly say a word.'

'I sometimes want to say something about John. But I don't know what. If I keep appearing with, "I'm worried", you'll think I've gone off my head.'

'I shan't. What about Pamela?'

'She's sane. She's got her head screwed on. I hope so. I tell myself so. It's probably not true, but nothing's happened yet.'

'That's what you want to believe?'

'Why? Is there...?'

'No. Not that I know. You should talk to me, sometimes.'

'What the bloody hell can I say that you don't know?'

'You give the appearance,' Elsa had stopped, in spite of wind and cold, 'of not noticing any of us. They can't confide in you. I can't. You've no interest. You show none.'

'Well?'

'I get it all. They run to me.'

'Isn't that usual? Or right? Didn't you talk to your mother?'

'Maybe so. I could wish it otherwise.'

A lorry churned out of the mud at a farmyard gate, jarring to a halt, reversing with metal-roaring awkwardness, finally blocking the road. The driver violently revved his engine, loosed his accelerator; noise cut out. Three or four bursts on the self-starter wasted themselves in raucous throbbing; the driver jumped out slamming the door.

'Can you get round?' he bawled, cheerfully enough at the Chamberlains, and dashed down into the farmyard, wellingtons flapping.

Elsa jumped across the ditch on the far side of the road, teetered through the grass clumps by the hedge, and, hand on lorry, waited for her husband.

'Why won't it start?' she asked.

'Flooded.'

'Is that why he went back into the house?'

'He's giving it a minute or two to clear. Perhaps he's forgotten something.'

They stood, comically, by the empty mud-daubed lorry before they set off. A hundred yards on they heard the engine fire, first time, and soon the vehicle clattered behind them, hooted. They stepped aside.

The driver, red-faced, deeply furrowed, leaned out from a window already wound down.

'He brought me up also out of an horrible pit, out of the miry clay, and set my feet upon a rock, and established my goings.'

He grinned, under greasy, thinning black hair, a pointing finger raw red. Again he thrashed the accelerator, waved stiff-handed, roared deafeningly off at a clanking waddle.

'Why did he say that?'

'Non-conformist lay-preacher showing off. It's a psalm, I think.'

'Which?'

'I'll look it up for you when we get back.'

Elsa seemed pleased, repeated the phrase 'miry clay', laughed at the 'funny, little man', said it had cheered her up.

'We talked a bit,' she said, in the warmth of the hall. 'In the open air. We don't do it indoors.'

'Lynette said that. The night she demanded to see me. She wouldn't go into the Crown, because we'd be interrupted, or overheard. She drove me up some lane near where her family had lived.' He could speak of the incident, now, without a tremor, shamelessly. 'We're like Midas's wife. There's no bugging in the wind.' He wondered, sure now Lynette had expected him to make a pass at her, had not been disappointed.

'I liked that preacher,' she said. 'He did us good; didn't he?'

'You and I are literary persons.'

He checked the reference for her, the fortieth psalm, came down to show her, his Bible open, stayed to hear her chatter.

11

Four days later at lunch, the postman had only just arrived, they read a first cheerful letter from John. Lengthy, it conveyed his satisfaction with his progress. His thesis, a tutor adjudged, was excellent. He'd given a lecture on it, which had gone down well, caused discussion. The principal had stopped him in the corridor to comment. The weather had been sunny. Chamberlain, willing for renewal, passed the letter over to Elsa, who read it, face straight, laid it by her plate.

'That's good,' he said.

'I hope so.' Snappish. 'Madeleine wants to see you.'

'Why? When?'

'This afternoon or evening. You must phone.' Elsa sat displeased, explained about the morning's call, thought it had nothing to do with Pamela. No, she would not conjecture. The finality was tantamount to an accusation. He obeyed, sheepishly, when his wife was out of the way.

At eight that evening, by appointment, Madeleine Hill sat him down to whisky in her drawing room. She wore a long black skirt, a white blouse with elaborate collar and cuffs; her hair was scraped back from her face.

'I want your advice,' she said, sipping a meagre martini. 'I've not been very well. There's nothing wrong with me physically; not much, that is. But, my doctor, Ron Gilman, says I must talk to somebody. He said to George at first, then some woman friend. I've got none. Not that sort. So it's you; or nobody.'

'I see.' He paused. 'Elsa, though? Elsa. Why not try her?'

'I'd as soon talk to a bean bag.'

That did not please. Madeleine recognized her error, did nothing to correct it or apologize. 'We, George and I, have been going through a rough period. It's six months now. I thought the summer holiday might clear things. It didn't. Things were so bad that I had to go to Ron. He's quite good, really, though he's a bit slapdash compared with George.'

'Is it anything to do with Saul and Pamela?'

'That's a minor part.'

Chamberlain prepared himself for confidences he did not want, found to his surprise that he occupied himself largely with the idea that a doctor's wife had to go out from home for treatment. Madeleine looked harassed, but as it were temporarily, like a film-actress, miming ephemeral distress according to instructions. Her skin stretched sallowly smooth on hands and face; she had disguised the small wrinkles at her eyes.

'George has been acting oddly.' She did not hurry. 'His work's begun to get on top of him. You know what he's like, very thorough, conscientiousness itself, but a bit blunt. He really is quite clever, and he's never lost interest. But last spring he had one or two bad cases. Not mistakes; I don't mean that. These were violent cruelties to children. A woman plunged her baby's hands and arms into scalding water. A father beat a child with a poker. You read the sort of thing every day now in the newspaper. But he was involved with two or three inside a fortnight. Brought into the cottage hospital.'

'I see.'

'He's not easily fooled. He did something about it. Called the police. But there seemed no end. I'm not saying that's right, that's how it seemed. Violence towards children, especially helpless babies, and against women.'

'What sort of people are these?'

'You'd think they'd all be in the mining villages like Cotgrave and Bagthorpe, but they weren't. Nor were they all uneducated people.' She did not raise her voice. 'He began to sleep badly. And he was fetched out once or twice in the night. You don't recover so quickly at his age. I was worried. He talked, now and again. I didn't bother much for a start. He'd always told me interesting things or difficult ones. It helped him put it into words, and he liked to give me an explanation. It made him surer of what he was saying.' She shrugged at the quotation, expecting his scorn.

'Yes.'

'One day he came home from the hospital, sat down and, and, collapsed. Crumpled. Not unconscious or fainting. Just helpless. Couldn't really talk. It frightened me to death. He's strong. He came round in the end. But I didn't get out of him what was wrong. I put him to bed but he wouldn't let me send for Ron. He put himself out with drugs. The police, apparently, had brought a child in. Neighbours had complained, the RSPCA, social workers had all been involved, and still this woman had knifed her daughter. Actually, it wasn't too bad. He dealt with it surgically without much trouble, finished the rest of his work, turned dizzy. He managed to drive himself home, but he couldn't remember how he'd staggered into the house.'

'Well?' Madeleine slopped her drink round her tall glass. He downed his whisky.

'He got up next day. I didn't want him to. Said he was all right. He seemed so. I was worried, rang Ron Gilman up. He said it was strain and I'd got to slow him up. George was back at the usual time, didn't eat much, he often doesn't now, slumped down in a chair. I took his coffee in, started to talk. He didn't say much at first, listened, then said, "That'll do, Maddy, I'm tired." I wasn't having it, though. I told him what I thought. He said, "Shut up." I said now I'd begun, so on, you know. Then he went red, a horrible brick-puce, and started to swear. Shut my stupid fucking bitch's mouth or he'd bang the whore shut for me. Now, you know

George; he can blow his top, but this wasn't the same. It wasn't as if his language was a navvy's. He's always sworn. This was like some other man. Some vulgar, hoarse, oh, lout. It was as if a devil had . . . He looked different. I was terrified and I screamed at him. It didn't go on for long. Bawling and cursing and my crying. Then he suddenly was quiet, and tears poured down his face, not a few, but without any noise, no sobbing, just water gushing, streaming. After a minute he seemed to come into what was happening, and he gulped, and went out. I just sat and trembled, from head to foot.' Madeleine stopped, seemed to withdraw her attention. There was no excitement in voice or gesture, a slight salivation.

'You're not saying anything,' she finished.

'I've no idea what I'm supposed to say.'

She stood, much at ease, wordlessly lifted his glass from his fingers, refilled it, resumed pose, poise in her armchair.

'I thought he'd gone to kill himself.'

'You didn't chase after him?'

'No. I sat there for an hour. More or less. I couldn't hear anything anywhere. In the end I made myself move, go upstairs. I hardly dared open the bedroom doors, but when I looked in he wasn't in any of them. The bathroom door sticks, and I thought . . . In the end I found him in the surgery, smoking a pipe. That's a thing he never does. He doesn't like his patients to know he smokes. Well, he doesn't much now. The odd pipe. I said, "Hello, George." He answered. I asked him if he was all right. Then he apologized, but asked me to go out, leave him. That frightened me. It was this new man, thing, again. If he'd gone on all fours, grunting and scratching, I couldn't have been more terrified. He sounded normal, preoccupied, or sleepy, but he was on his own. My back crawled. Icy. Water. I felt sick, shivering.'

'And?'

'That was it for that day. He took his evening surgery.

He slept quite well. It didn't hit me until a day or two later.'

'When was all this? Before Christmas?'

'Yes. And I'd just finished the breakfast dishes. George was in the surgery, and I could hear the bell, the phone, and Angela answering. I thought, not suddenly, exactly, because I'd been feeling a bit off colour, that's it, the end. George isn't my husband any more. Not a sane man. You see, don't you? You understand?'

'Well. You mean that he . . .'

'You know me, Eric. In some ways I'm volatile. Sexually. I've not been completely faithful. There's no need to tell you.' She giggled, sniggered, out of character with this solemn, sallow face. 'I had one serious affair. George knew. In the end. It was before our little . . . slip. You won't understand this. You're a philanderer. I don't know. You might. However much I played false with George, or disagreed with and quarrelled with him, he was there. I didn't always like that, want it. Sometimes I'd kick, be rude. But now that George, that husband, had gone. Do you see?'

'This is all very interesting,' Chamberlain answered, not rushing. 'But doesn't it all sound like imagination?'

'Maybe. That's probably true. It makes no difference. I was convinced. And not just in a half-hearted way. To the marrow of my bones.' She smirked at her phrase, disdaining it, but straightened her face grimmer. 'It knocked all the energy out of me. I couldn't stand up even. I cried, in an abandoned way. As if it were somebody else. Uncontrolled. There was no centre of control. I knew it was me, but I didn't, if you see what I mean. If I'd have heard someone else howling like that I'd have been frightened, tried to stop her, but now it just went on. I could hear it, and feel the heaving, and big groans, and stabbing nails and patches of tension or shuddering. I'd lost myself. Really. Luckily no one interrupted. Angela sometimes comes through from the surgery for something for George. Not this morning. At the finish, I'd just enough sense to drag myself upstairs, drop on the bed. And I was worse then. Like a lunatic, rolling and squealing and banging.'

'How long did this last?' He sat amazed at her exposition.

'I was an hour in the bedroom, then I staggered off to the bathroom. Angela must have made the coffee. We had a cold lunch.'

'And then you were better?'

'I felt,' Madeleine moved a hand to express the difficulty of achieving precision, 'as if I'd been beaten. Physically. Caned.'

'Did George not notice?'

'He was busy. He asked me twice in the evening if I was well, said I looked pale.'

'But now its over and done with?'

'Sometimes, for no reason I can see, this overwhelming feeling grips me. This desolation. My marriage means nothing. Nor does he.'

'But if you've been unfaithful?'

'You ought to know.' She chipped sharply in. 'When you take up with somebody, the danger, the chance you may lose your first is part of the appeal. You, I, enjoy the deceit. It's shameful, but that's the truth. It is, isn't it?'

'I suppose so.'

'I can't understand it. It's as if George had died. But then I'd have to get over it. Now I haven't the will.'

'What's Gilman say?'

'He talks, sympathetically. Massages my neck. Gives me pills. Now he insists I confess this to somebody.'

'That'll do you good?'

'He doesn't know. He's a pragmatist, he says. But the embarrassment of having to spit it out, word it up for somebody else, not a doctor, will make it clear to me, if it's possible. He suggested a woman, when I said not George, but there's nobody I know well enough. I chose you because you aren't any better, morally, than I am, and you're a cool bastard into the bargain.'

'Thanks.'

'Isn't that right, though? You have women. To boost yourself. And you keep your head, don't shout. I always think Elsa's hands are full.'

He swigged his whisky, savagely, replaced the glass feather-light.

'You've confessed,' he said. 'Has it improved matters?'

'Do you think what I've told you is the truth?'

'Don't see why not. Sounded convincing.'

She rose, this time taking the bottle to his glass.

'You'll have me drunk,' he said.

'You.' The word stabbed, but she eased herself into a chair. 'It sounds so feeble when I tell you. So dull, humdrum, nondescript. But I know exactly how I'd feel if George dropped dead.'

'The point you're trying to make,' he said, 'as I see it, is that there is, or was, a powerful bond between you and your husband.'

'Yes.'

'I'd have thought, at your age, that the bond's more likely to be habit, or convenience. We're used to it. The passion's evaporated.' He smiled at his word. 'I don't mean you can't enjoy the sex. You can, and be skilful, practised, with it. You can admire your partner, think of her as beautiful, but the . . . the wildness, the uncertainty, the dangerous corners have gone.' As he enunciated the sentences, he felt mild pleasure, not because there was much sense in his pronouncements but because she'd listen, might chase off after one or two of the implications and thus ease herself, forget the obsession. If he'd taught her card tricks or a new form of patience he'd have done as well. 'Had you realized that this relationship was so strong?'

'No. I'd have said not. I admire George. Though I see that more clearly.'

'This other man?' he asked.

'Sexual attraction. Guilt. He needed mastering.'

'Is it still going on?'

'No. He married. That altered things.'

'He was younger than you?'

'A bit. Yes.' She opened her eyes wide, as if to enthral perhaps. 'It was as good as over, when you and I . . . I made a pass at you, didn't expect anything. But you were away in no time, knew it all. I was surprised. I didn't think you'd be much use. But you were. An accomplished lecher.' She laughed at the phrase. 'It got my own back on Elsa.'

'Why her?'

'She always seems so sure of herself. And here she was with a husband who went off . . .'

'Don't be too certain of that.'

'I'm pulling your leg, Eric. Both of them.'

After this interlude she relaxed, spoke without strain, though seriously. She admitted it had warmed her to confess, did her best to describe again her feeling for her husband. Chamberlain was impressed; Madeleine Hill was both intelligent and had honestly sorted this into words. For a time he thought of her as apart, above the likes of himself, but set such romanticism aside in the end, deciding that as one so rarely spoke about important matters, one lost the habit of fluency, depending on a code of short phrases, telegraphese, somewhat as Mrs Hill described their adultery. He wondered how she managed to speak so clearly, when and where she had practised, how she broke down the barrier of modesty or embarrassment. He came to no conclusion, but praised her, hoping for enlightenment. She provided none.

'Come and talk again,' she begged. 'You are better than Ron Gilman. He was quite right.'

She slapped his bottom; both were tipsy. As he stumbled

down the path his head jangled with his last words to her. 'Don't be too hard on Elsa.'

His wife had waited up, suspecting news about Pamela. He gave her a guarded account, he could be reticent in his cups, and they drank together, friendly and gently talkative until nearly midnight, when they went to bed to make love. Elsa, compared with Madeleine, seemed young now, innocent, untouched by the world. He dismissed the generalization, blaming, blessing the whisky.

12

Lynette returned from her visit to John. Before her departure she had called on the parents to collect a suit he wanted, a tin of home-made cakes and biscuits, but had refused the loan of Elsa's Mini, though she feared her own banger was not up to the journey. She stayed two hours, made sensible suggestions, talked about John in a way that reassured his father.

'I must say I like her,' he told Elsa.

'You once told me she was commonplace, if I remember. That's just about it exactly.'

'Homely.'

'Isn't that American for "Ugly"? She's pretty, isn't she? So you don't expect her to know about recipes for rock buns? You're a typical man.'

'Unfair,' he said, 'unfair as usual. No, when I listen to her, things sound not too bad, bearable. Isn't that so?'

'She thinks life owes her some sort of entertainment. Do you know anything about her first husband?'

'A student. A research student. He works in an American university now. She seems genuinely fond of John.'

Elsa did not answer that.

While Lynette was down at Leaport, John telephoned to say her car had behaved itself, but then asked if his father would be ready on Sunday to pick the girl up in case of a breakdown. Yes, they were having a marvellous time. The weather was sunny, spring-like. He sounded lively, said they were on their way out to lunch, chaffed his mother.

They did not have to help on the return journey, did not

hear from Lynette until Wednesday when she arranged to call in. Her father was ill with influenza and wouldn't act sensibly.

She looked sick, herself, eyes dark and puffed with sleeplessness. For the last two nights she'd sat up with the old man, but now an elder sister had appeared. Elsa took command, insisting that Lynette stayed to sleep, bundled her into bath and bed, and took keys and car to bring clothes, cosmetics from Retford, provided sleeping-tablets and a promise of more duty as chauffeuse next day. Lynette obeyed, collapsed, sniffed, even agreed when Elsa decided next morning that what the girl needed was a day off work.

In this dominant mood Elsa did not consult her husband, packed him off to his desk, told him not to interfere with Lynette who was worn out. In the afternoon she drove into Retford again, satisfied herself that Mr Smith was in capable hands, a sister-in-law had now also arrived, collected enough clothes to make sure that the guest would last a week with them. She instructed Lynette that she could go to the office if she wished, but she was not to return to her flat.

The girl, smiling prettily, capitulated.

That evening she described her trip to Leaport. She'd arrived at the college in the small hours after a difficult journey in the dark. On Saturday evening the pair had spent the night at a party, drinking punch and dancing. They'd been up early on Sunday to attend Matins in the parish church.

'Whose idea was that?' Elsa.

'Mine, really.'

'What did John say?'

'He was glad. It was so beautiful there with the sun sparkling in the big window. At the east end. Marvellous. John had never been in.'

'Do you go to church, then? Here at home?'

'Not every week. Sometimes.'

'Did you when you were married?' Elsa's question scraped.

'To Joel? No, he wouldn't go. I didn't miss it.'

Chamberlain saw honesty in that, a small sign of distinction. He and Elsa imagined the rest of the week-end, the short walk by the sea, the rapid meals, the hours down on his bed. She had left Leaport dog-tired, dragged herself upstairs for an hour or two's sleep before the alarm clock blasted her headache, had no sooner opened the office mail than a neighbour of her father's was ringing to say the old man was really ill, couldn't get up, wouldn't, shouldn't.

She did her one night's nursing in three, but lodged with the Chamberlains. Her father's illness did not respond to antibiotics; he was taken to hospital where he died five days later. Elsa attended the funeral, impressed Lynette's relations, helped clear the old man's house, enjoying herself. She had also begun a correspondence with Eli which kept her amused and on edge for the postman. Chamberlain did not see the letters, but she passed on information, malicious anecdotes and occasionally tips, afterthoughts about his book. Elsa claimed that she was arranging to visit the Dunnes, but never came round to it.

'I'm too busy.'

'You need three or four hours to get there. They'll make you welcome. She's a wonderful cook.'

Chamberlain wondered what she wrote, certain in his mind that she'd established a relationship that would be spoilt by physical contact. Love involved curious devices. Again he felt slightly superior, as if his wife lived a crippled existence, allowing her nothing beyond a verbal contact. She needed Eli's letters. Beth sent no messages, he noted, or if she did they were not transmitted.

Immediately after her father's death Lynette Rockford moved back into her flat, but spent some time, even nights, with the Chamberlains. At the end of June there was to be a performance of a play and Ernestine Hughes-Edge, who could not be absent from such preparations, pressed the girl to take part. The Theatre Club, the Shakespeare Society, Mrs Hughes-Edge's group, the Thursday Music Circle had combined with the complementary chaos of intention and achievement. No one was certain of the venue of the performance, the hall of the Grammar School, the Park Glade Bingo Hall formerly Theatre Royal, or outdoors amongst the trees and trimmed hedges of Woodborough Grange. An overlarge committee rowed over the choice of play, reduced it to *Mother Courage, The Homecoming, What the Butler Saw, The Rivals* and *Hamlet*. People lobbied, modestly nominating the play they considered they'd be asked to produce. The headmaster of the Grammar School, in the chair, smoked his pipe, encouraged them on their sore ramblings; his only interest was to relieve his boredom with the town.

The week after Smith's death, the committee decided in exhaustion on *Hamlet*, because half Retford could then trail a puissant pike about the stage, and on Mrs Hughes-Edge as co-producer with St John Windsor, a former professional, now working with flexi-time in an oil concern. Ernestine had clinched her place because she made it known that she was to have staying with her from April until July, a cousin, Frank Tobias, who'd played in *Hamlet* at the Memorial Theatre, the prince himself, during a recent bout in South Africa, who was resting, recovering from an illness, working on a television serial, a book of reminiscences, and could be persuaded to lead for this performance. An odd-ball, he was known to have talent. His appointment would reduce internecine warfare at auditions.

Mrs Hughes-Edge bullied Lynette to try for the role of Gertrude; she did. Windsor insisted that she was the Ophelia he needed. Ernestine instructed her cronies that this was what she had intended the whole time. Nobody, least of all the protagonists, knew the truth. Lynette herself hardly cared.

Her father's death had not, apparently, affected her, though she'd shivered thin as a scarecrow in the ghastly cold at the crematorium. She'd been ruthless with the bonfire at the old man's house, had demanded of her sisters and brother what they wanted, and on the least show of pusillanimity had made up their minds for them. This and a cheerful brusqueness hid any sense of loss. The Chamberlains were glad at her steadiness, for she wrote regularly to John, visited him once more and now, encouraged by Eric, mocked Elsa into dragging up her roots to visit the Dunnes.

Just before John's return for the Easter vacation, Lynette telephoned in distress. Elsa ordered her to pack a bag, fetched her at once.

At first they had difficulty in discovering the trouble. The girl's disturbance struck obviously, but she sat quiet, shocked, withdrawn. Her answers made grammatical sense, but none otherwise; they imagined she did not know herself what afflicted her. This seemed impossible. They tried together; Chamberlain left the room to Elsa. On her failure he made the girl sip a small whisky. By ten o'clock she gave the appearance of composure, but it froze, contracted. Her trouble originated, one gathered, from *Hamlet*, though they had no clear idea why. They instructed her next day, when she insisted she'd slept well, was fit for work, to return that evening. Elsa, who drove her in, promised to be outside the office at five, had cut delicious sandwiches, made up three thermos-flasks, was at her best. That afternoon she interrupted her husband's work to check her observations against his.

Lynette, Elsa learnt, had been summoned to the Hughes-Edge's house to receive initial instructions from Madame, with rump-patting from the egregious Emrys. Ernestine had spent her time explaining what a fool Windsor was likely to prove, his choice of Ophelia being its first sign, and filling the rest of the evening with an account of the role, sex-crazed, it appeared, of the Queen she had planned for her protégée.

They must put up with it, of course. She did not want a rift in this lute now. But the fact that he had been convinced by mere age, Lynette was arithmetically closer to Ophelia than Gertrude, instead of by voice, dramatic presence, demonstrated his unthinking mentality, what she called 'by RADA out of provincial rep'. Ophelia was perhaps seventeen, a difference of ten from Lynette's age, while Gertrude was not likely to be more than thirty-seven. Hamlet thirty? He didn't behave like it. Ernestine herself at tragedy-queen's height despised an aesthetic which could not bear a moment's cursory examination, and included innumeracy amongst its minor defects.

This in no way contradicted Lynette's expectations. Amused, rather than otherwise, she waited for St John Windsor.

The producer lived in a large, expensive bungalow, one of a group of new eyesores, on the Newark road outside Retford. Unlike Mrs Hughes-Edge he made no fuss, sat her down, produced a gin-bottle and the cut version he had marked for her, instructed her to read it thoroughly and then let him know what she made of it. 'I've read it five times in the last fortnight,' he said, not boasting. 'That's my job. To know the text back to front before I start putting the actors into it. I've got ideas. But it's quite likely they'll have to go.' He pulled gargoyle, theatrical faces. 'One enigma's Frank Tobias. I didn't want him. There's a lad just left Uppingham, working in our place, Oxford next year, who'd be ideal. Young. Fiery. Introspective. Sexy.' He poked out a left forefinger, the whole body screwed, skewed into hunchback seriousness. 'Nineteen, that's the age for Hamlet. Not bloody near fifty.' Tobias was thirty-six, Ernestine had said. Lynette did not argue. Windsor continued, placidly. He'd met Frank. Oh, yes. He'd talent. No doubt. But he was limited, and in the wrong way. 'We've all got our limits. That's what a producer's for. To get out the box-of-tricks inside them without busting the whole shoot.'

Lynette had left the Windsor household elated. The wife, for instance, had been so amused, so distantly reasonable, so ready to toe-end her husband towards common sense that the designated Ophelia felt the man would cope with the quarrels and lunacies of not one but three amateur societies, drill a performance into or out of them. She'd been further cheered when she'd discussed the part with John by letter. He'd done *Hamlet* for 'A' Level, schoolmasterly suggested some books for her to read. Up to this point she'd been excited, confident, looking forward to the beginning of rehearsals.

She'd expected, she admitted, backbiting and envious scandalizing. People hereabouts did not practise tact. Women quite unknown to her had stopped her in the street, detained her in the Wednesday Club to let it be known that Liz Faulkner, who'd played Juliet last year for the Shakespeare, Tania Grocock so brilliant as Miss Julia for the Club, and Denise Mahoney, antecedents unmentioned, were all better qualified than she for the role. These preliminaries, she claimed, did not disturb her. *Hamlet* is thin in women's parts; somebody had to be disappointed. Many.

Anonymous letters were dropped through the door. These were crudely penned, accusing her of promiscuity with Tobias, whom she had never met, with Windsor, with Hughes-Edge, and in one missive, on creased, lined, dirt-cheap paper, in the hand of an old woman, it was plainly stated that she had a lesbian relationship with Mrs Windsor. The language of this was so obscene that she felt, she claimed, sick, had screwed up, thrown the filthy thing into the fire, then wished she had not, in that she remembered every phrase, hardly believing she had not herself invented the stinking sprue.

When the letters threatened physical attack she showed them to her boss, who'd rung the police. A well-scrubbed young woman in uniform had been sent, read the letters, asked to be kept in touch, said that there was little that could be done, seemed unaffected and unsympathetic. Lynette did not mention the one she had burnt. The policewoman smartly packed up the paper, envelopes, took addresses, adjusted her helmet militarily in a mirror, clumped out, healthy and well buttoned. Now Lynette sagged, degraded, disbelieved, a writer of uncleanness to herself.

By this time she was having trouble, but hung on. The effect on her, she said, was twofold. First she had difficulty in committing the part to memory, which had not happened before. She'd been uncertain whether to start learning so early, but decided in favour because one obstacle in many would be out of the way. The second seemed more frightening though it was intermittent. She'd find herself incapable of walking into a shop to buy a loaf, a packet of tea-bags; it was physically impossible to push open the door, or if the attack were delayed to come out with the words. Then, walking along, she'd find she had to cross the road to avoid greeting a casual acquaintance. 'Had to' exactly described the compulsion; there was no choice, nor appeal to reason. A moment or two later, she would be left trembling, breath tight, amazed at her failure, but still unable to correct it. Behind all, lay the fear that this pattern of behaviour would take over, become her normality.

Her doctor was cheerful, handed out sleeping-pills, anti-depressants, advised against giving the part up for the present. 'You're like me,' was his line, 'a natural conservative. Something different upsets us. Right. We'll redeploy the resources of modern science. We can't sit skulking in the same dug-out all our lives.' She cheered herself by reflecting that he must have taken his metaphor from performances of the war-games society over which he presided locally.

The present cause of distress was her failure to improve. Once a day now she could expect a 'turn'.

Elsa had the story out of Lynette in no time. She dismissed her husband, who'd hovered sympathetically, and acted with aseptic efficiency. In this mood there was no resisting her. Let's get it right, now, and then perhaps we'll be able to do something about it. Lynette wept, was allowed to do so, but slapped straight in a chair and her story extracted. The effect was immediate. The girl acquired something of the clinical manner herself, began to suggest cures. She produced the latest poison-pen effusion, re-read it without collapse.

Elsa summoned Chamberlain, commanded him to phone the police, to prise sense into or out of them.

He did his best, getting hold of a superintendent he knew, who admired Chamberlain's oeuvre. Any new letter must be sent in on the off-chance it tied up with a recognizable hand; they'd give that a whirl, though one couldn't promise anything. After that it was merely chance and time. The nutter would either go raving mad and get treatment, or more likely would clear his own head, hers, and give up. When Chamberlain asked if such persecutions were short, Superintendent Balderstone, hesitated, thought so, though he knew one case that had been going on for four years. 'But there's no reaction from the injured party there. That's the key.' And then there were unusual features. In this particular case, Chamberlain heard the rustle of papers, the loud breaths to indicate close reading, well, one couldn't guess. The young lady, the policewoman had reported, seemed a sensible sort and that usually meant the whole business wouldn't last long. Had they anybody in mind? The super laughed. 'Every street in the place has got its eccentric. Look at the letters in the evening papers, and they're from the sane 'uns.' But Chamberlain pressed: was there nobody, theatrically connected, disappointed? The officer became glum, wooden. 'No, sir.' No, there wasn't. That he knew. 'Just think what you're asking for.'

A new relationship developed between Elsa and John.

They phoned regularly and wrote perhaps three times a week with bulletins or comment. The mother explained to her husband what she tried to achieve: a full picture of affairs this end, and from her son a constant activity that would reassure her about his state of mind. Chamberlain saw in this new Elsa a development he'd wished for with himself. He'd wanted her to talk about his writing, say what she thought, for however inept the word he'd learn something about her. But his habitual closeness, broken only with Dunne, had precluded this, scared her off. The only time she'd offered an opinion was when they had crossed each other, and she, in desperation, had looked about to wound him. So she'd pick out a sentence, rightly claim that its language was thirty years out of date, or seize on some repetition or clumsiness and suggest only the untalented would be capable of such gauche error.

But this Elsa had method and intention. She'd keep John informed and steady. In order to do this she had to mother Lynette, coax her back somewhere nearer sense. The girl spent much of her spare time with them; the two women shopped on Saturday together, and Elsa drove Lynette one Sunday into Retford to hear evensong. This busyness and her consequent need to explain, made the house brighter. Pamela, preparing for an 'A' Level at a night-class was included in the package, rescued from glumness, asked to receive confidences, struck up a friendship with Lynette, in which the older girl guided the younger through the pressures of exams, the pre-final nerves and silences of Saul, the preoccupations of parents.

'Quite the little clinic,' he told his wife, jocularly.

'Don't complain. You might be the next patient.'

'You've rumbled me, at last.'

He even dispatched her to confer with Madeleine Hill and in her present euphoria, he so described it to her, she agreed. The women talked, but that was all. Elsa reported that Madeleine had asked if Eric had sent her, had then said that was typical of him, and thereafter they'd described their ailments to each other. He waited in expectation that he'd learn more from the new, expansive woman, and was disappointed. Finally, he asked outright.

'Is there anything seriously wrong with Madeleine?'

'Nothing that's unusual in a woman at her time of life.' She read his dissatisfaction. 'We don't get on. She won't tell me anything.'

'You didn't get on with Lynette at one time.'

'She's in trouble now. That makes a difference.'

'And Madeleine isn't?'

'I'm not saying that. Just that she thinks it's none of my business. Don't ask me why.'

His work on the draft of his novel profited from the constant activity around him. Now he began to see himself as a writer who performed only in happy circumstances. Certainly the picture of a wife planning to kill was striking; Dunne was enthusiastic beyond belief. He confessed himself shocked by the force of imagination; Cassidy, the agent, a man of percentages, wrote that it was 'the best thing I've read in ten years. I gave it to Margit and she was knocked over absolutely sick with it.' By the time John arrived home the final draft was done, delivered.

Chamberlain walked with hands in pockets amongst the daffodils, watched the fading forsythia, the opening of cherry, and manhandled the motor-mower round the lawns, humming to himself.

13

John Chamberlain was in good health. He had played a lot of squash, walked by the sea, tanning face and hands, had cleared up his work and acquired something of a swagger. Compared with him Lynette was pale, quieter, slightly older, keeping herself in check, expecting trouble. By contrast he shouted boisterously, jumped out, made her run, acted with childish energy.

On the evening of Good Friday, sunny but cold still, they had driven to a Methodist church in Grantham to hear Boy McKay sing. He had discovered his voice in the last year or two, was taking lessons and this was his first engagement, in Maunder's *From Olivet to Calvary*. He himself was amused by his new 'talent', joked that the Law Society did not encourage artists, felt his life as an adulterer branded him as unfit for chapels, but put on his neatest grey three-piece. He talked to Lynette about it, seemed obsessed, sang snatches round the office. In the end, anti-climax, a coolish barn, not a fifth filled, the bunches of narcissi, the over-loud, under-soft wooden bourdon, the enthusiastic ruggedness of choir, exactly suited McKay's pale nervousness, tremor of hand and voice, odd contretemps with the organist.

John puzzled, mocked the enterprise. The building, the choral singing, the work itself belonged to a world he did not know, did not concern him. It was a survival, an atavism, seemingly genteel, among the working classes.

'There were women with flowers in their hats,' he said. 'And men with great red hands bawling away. You couldn't help laughing.'

'If you'd been back last week you could have heard the *St John Passion*,' his mother said.

'That hadn't got McKay in it, had it?'

'It had men with red hands. The women wore black, I'll grant you that. The cathedral bears looking at. The orchestra wasn't too bad. The soloists were, some of them, quite well known.'

'And what, Father, are you telling me this for?' John, lively, rash for argument.

'The place was full. Yet it made up a fraction of the population. You stop the man on the milk-float, cleaning windows, ask him to distinguish between Bach and Maunder, and he can't. And that at the end of a hundred years of universal education. They know neither.'

'You can't name pop-groups,' Elsa interrupted.

'I can. I needed a couple for my novel. I know where to look. Not that I understand a thing about them in any real sense. But I can give the appearance.'

'You're just a hypocrite.' John.

'That's what education's for. That's why I got out.'

'What was Mr McKay like, Lynette?' Elsa asked.

'Very nervous. Not himself, at all. More like a schoolboy or a choirboy. Pale and standing still, but wishing he could wriggle.'

'As if he'd peed himself.' John, confident.

Chamberlain lectured them, claiming that what his son would teach in schools was as irrelevant as that chapel, that oratorio.

'It's not a bad thing to be able to read,' John said.

'That's what you schoolmasters are not managing, if I understand it.'

'It's just come to the surface. There's always been a proportion of non-readers. Nobody bothered before. Now we're trying. Special classes. And we give 'em stuff to read that catches their interest. Based on their lives.'

'I know,' Chamberlain said. 'Low-grade Maunder and Stainer. Bach's too hard for 'em.'

'It might lead to Bach. That's the hope.'

'Don't tell me that. The bloody teachers are half illiterate themselves. Never read anything outside the magazines and the hot-breath paperbacks.'

'As provided by yourself?'

'Exactly. I'm no George Eliot.'

'And not, if I take your argument correctly, educational?' John asked.

'Compared with the ephemera that passes for reading-matter in schools these days, I suppose I do pretty well. But it's not high art.'

'And is that what education's about?'

'Not universal education, as well you know. High culture is élitist. Nowadays we're, you're, so bothered with egalitarian clap-trap that many who would be capable of appreciating the greatest masterpieces are crippled by their schooling at the outset.'

'That's not true.'

'I see the advantages,' Chamberlain hectored. 'Instead of a dozen who can read *War and Peace* you've a thousand who'll manage the print under a nude in a popular newspaper, who can make out the names on a voting-sheet.'

'Look, your purveyors of the best of human culture neglected the other ninety-five per cent of the population.'

'Of course. How else do you train great athletes?'

'Then, if that's the case, I prefer the new system where everybody gets some opportunities.'

'I realize that. But it's the death of high art and, I guess, great scientific advance. Seventy-five per cent of the population will be capable of reading political slogans and advertising jingles on the public hoardings.'

'That's not so. Take America now. Oh, I know what you're going to say about Russia...'

John stopped, aware suddenly in the heat of the argument that Lynette in her chair was quietly crying. Although she tried to hide her distress, dabbing at her face, smiling widely at him, she lacked control. Elsa, who had been watching the girl, as the men set about each other, moved across, sat on the arm of a chair.

'Have you got a clean handkerchief?' she demanded of her husband.

When this was passed across, she allowed a minute for use, then took Lynette from the room.

'What's that all about?' Chamberlain asked.

'She seemed all right earlier.'

They sat, dumb and embarrassed, fumbling after quiet, until Elsa returned.

'How is she?' Chamberlain.

'She'll recover.'

'What's wrong?'

'She couldn't stand the way you two were going on at each other. That's all.'

'We were enjoying ourselves.'

'She didn't think so.' Elsa sat, crossly. 'Neither did I, for that matter. You were red in the face, beginning to shout, shaking your fingers.'

'We weren't too bad,' John said.

'You weren't. But your father was losing his temper. She saw it. Didn't like it. You could have shut up. You know what he's like once he starts to lay the law down.'

'I'm sorry.'

'She's not well, John. Her mother and father going so quickly. I know she says she didn't think much of them. And then this Ophelia. And other things.'

'Such as?'

'You'll have to ask her. Little matters. Not important, but . . . Talk to her sometime, John. Make her. She needs looking after.'

Chamberlain moved away to pour comforting whisky.

'Anybody else?' he called back. The others primly refused.

'There must be something pretty seriously wrong with her, to act like that.' The two ignored him. 'What's the doctor say?'

'She's under a consultant psychiatrist.' Elsa.

'You didn't tell me that.' Justification.

'You didn't listen, you mean.'

'What's he say?' Sharp.

'What we all know. But she attends his clinic. And he prescribes. He hopes in time it'll all be better.'

'Amateurish.'

Elsa turned to John, began to describe an exhibition she'd visited. In time the pair were laughing, thick as thieves. Lynette returned, tremulous, smiling, wishing to shrivel into her armchair.

'I'm sorry,' she said to Chamberlain, at the first lengthy pause.

'Not at all. It was entirely my fault. Can I get you a drink?'

She shook her head. 'Tablets.' The room was weighted with silence. Tears glistened in Lynette's eyes, until Elsa signalled to John, who suggested a trip to the billiard-room.

'I don't like the look of her,' Chamberlain said. 'She's . . .'

'She'll do. They love snooker. It's her therapy. In ten minutes they'll be laughing.'

'Somehow, that seems as bad.'

Elsa squared the room up, removing glasses, returning bottles. He saw her restoring the *status quo*, said as much. She nodded, a mate, told him he could invite Madeleine over for a turn on the table.

On Easter Monday the four motored to Stratford, saw *Henry V*. Lynette, excited, insisted on contacting a friend in the cast, dragged him back for introductions. A tall, silent young man, he was spectacularly unlike the Dauphin he'd played, a sharp, swooping, labile prince, flashily handsome and aquiline then, now nondescript, with a bad complexion. He and Lynne let out they'd acted together, but they, she, talked about a mutual acquaintance, Christine, who'd never settle, couldn't sit still, made one scream with laughter, or rage, lit the sobersided world up.

As Lynette talked she transformed herself, into garrulity, her accent developing histrionic plangency. It was as if she hammered feeble dialogue, battering the silent Dauphin about his head, encouraging them all to irrational audience-gaiety. John looked slightly alarmed. Elsa attempted the impresario, flinging in her quota of questions. They sipped alcohol, and after ten minutes the Dauphin dragged himself up, made excuses and vanished, without trace. It needed a further quarter of an hour to reduce Lynette to normality of voice and gesture. During this time she insisted on exclamations, vignettes, declamatory asides, all without interest, all connected with Thespian activity. Only when they were outside did Lynette inform them that the Dauphin had married Joel's sister, that the volatile Christine was her sister-in-law. Then, deflated as suddenly, she could barely bring herself to answer their questions. Yes, Jeremy was still married to Chris. They didn't live together. She'd left the theatre. Worked for an export firm. In London. But she had quietened down.

A day or two later Elsa interrupted her husband. It was Saturday, and he did not exert himself. She knocked, in the evening.

'Are you busy?' She knew the answer to that. 'Lynette's just told me something about herself.'

He pushed his work, symbolically, three inches away from him, faced her.

'She started to talk about Christine, the actress, again. Apparently she lived with them, for a month or two, when they were in London. She never kept her mouth shut. One day when Joel complained about sandwiches made from stale bread, Chris asked why he didn't get his own bloody food ready. He lost his temper and flung a book at her. It missed, but hit a plant-pot in the window. Down it came and broke pot, saucer, plant. Chris flew at him, and there they were wrestling. Lynne tried to intervene, but by this time he was raving and snatched a cane from a tomato plant. He hit them both across the face; they had weals. Lynne was screaming now, crouching down, holding her face.

'Clean that mess up,' he'd shouted, pointing with his stick at the soil, the shards. 'Do you hear what I say? Get it cleaned up.' He whacked her across the shoulders. The cane shrieked in the air. 'On your feet.'

'Leave her alone.' Chris.

Joel's teeth stood bared, big as fangs, his face cemented in fury. He wheeled on his sister, crouching. She snatched the carving knife from the table-drawer, moved towards him. Nothing could have stopped her, Lynne said. His face changed, sagged and he skittled from the room, right out into the street. Christine was grinding her teeth, swaying.

Lynne pushed herself to her feet. She could neither speak nor cry, only whimper, like an animal. Chris's knife flashed as she jerked the blade over, back, over. Both girls moved to the table. Lynne picked up a toppled chair, and she and her sister-in-law sat down, as if for a meal. After a few moments, Lynette lowered her forhead to the cloth, between her hands which lay flat, palms down. She lost herself, did not hear Chris rise. The other spoke from the window, but Lynne could not catch the words. Christine called again. This time the words hit clear.

'Look at the bastard.'

Lynette raised head, dizzy, sat straight. She noticed the knife, ugly, discarded. Chris stood behind the curtain, the ball of her left thumb in her mouth. She took it out.

'I've cut myself.'

When she moved her hand her chin was daubed black with blood.

'Get a plaster.' She thrust the wound back to her mouth. Lynette staggered for the first-aid box, breath beaten out of her.

'Kitchen. Go in kitchen,' she gasped. 'Tap. Under tap.' The other obeyed. The cut was straight, more than an inch long, deliberate seething, tidal with blood. Lyn dabbed cotton-wool, and as Chris pinched the skin together, she applied the plaster, tremblingly, unstraight. The second time it was placed, pressed perfectly. The water in the bowl was pink, the gobbets of wool still bright with blood.

Christine looked at her hand, laughed, marched to the dining room. Sluggishly Lynne cleared the sink, straightened the box, washed down a great spot of blood, from the draining board. Christine, out of sight, laughed or cried.

'Look at him.'

Lynette joined her sister-in-law behind the curtain. On the far side of the street Joel, in shirt sleeves, stared up at the window, blatantly unable to mask his confusion.

'Like a kid at an ice-cream cart,' Christine said. The two, hysterically, then calmly discussed what they'd do when he crept back upstairs. They'd say nothing, dump him in Coventry to punish himself.

It had ended, Elsa reported, in anti-climax, but was not the last of Joel's outbursts. These were fiercer while his sister, who howled or cursed back into his face, lodged there, but once or twice he'd struck his wife.

Chamberlain patiently asked questions of Elsa. They did not know if this were a cause of Lynette's present unbalance. Talk merely confused them. They moved to the kitchen to make coffee, were interrupted by Pamela who'd spent the afternoon and evening with Saul, not interrupting his revision.

She accepted a cup, sat down with her parents. They waited for explanation.

'We discussed a funny thing at dinner,' she said. 'Saul mentioned the phrase "the edge of the sword", and we talked of the days when duelling and hand-to-hand combat in battle were common.' Pamela spoke hesitantly.

'What about them?' Elsa asked brisk, ready to sort the child out.

'It must have been crueller then. And burning people. Drawing and quartering. All that sort of thing. But Mrs Hill said the Germans had exterminated six million Jews in her time. That led on to . . .' Pamela looked at them. She could not drop the subject, but feared it, or their ridicule. They considered the surface of their coffee. 'Well, we thought what it would be like to be ordinary people in the middle of those nightmares, you know. The Jews were just ordinary, like us, weren't they?'

'They liked Beethoven, or cards, or long walks and strawberries and cream?' Chamberlain supported the girl, who seemed flustered, near tears.

'That's right. But Mrs Hill said when the Nazis carted them off in wagons and lorries in the camps they were covered in shit, and then they were no better than animals. Dr Hill was a bit shocked at her language. But they'd be educated, some of them. Witty. Written books. Some were old and dignified. And they marched them out naked to be gassed.'

'And you wondered,' her father said, blowing across his cup, 'how we'd have fared?'

'When you think of it,' Pamela sat owl-faced with anxiety, 'all sorts of people we know have breakdowns, commit suicide. Well, John. But they can't be as bad as folks knocked up in the middle of the night, and tortured and humiliated, and then . . . ? Can they? Dr Hill thinks people get hardened. In the war, he said, soldiers just ignored all sorts of ghastly sights. Headless bodies. Men blown half to bits and still alive.'

'What's the moral?' Elsa asked. Safety sounded in the word. When one roots about amongst vocabulary, however clumsily, sanity prevails.

'I thought about John.' Pamela advanced very slowly, on forbidden ground. 'And how Lynette is upset, now her father . . . I wondered if they weren't as badly off as people tortured in prisons. In their minds. They look all right to us, but they're as inhuman as people staggering off those trucks stinking, covered with . . . faeces.' She halted again. Chamberlain tested the kettle for water, switched it on again.

'There's no means of measuring,' he said. They sat dumb, hot-eyed.

'I just can't imagine what it would have been like. Hung upside down on hooks to die. In that pain I'd want to kill myself, because I wasn't strong enough to bear it. But John wanted to die.'

'We don't know.' Elsa, pouring into her cup, her husband's.

'You never said anything about it, to me. Really. It was because of Lynette, wasn't it? She wouldn't have him? Is there something wrong? With him? Most people grin and bear. I feel rotten sometimes. I couldn't stand torture. I would kill myself. But they . . . ? Just for love? I mean, does he feel things stronger than we do??'

The distress, the dilated eyes, the trembling hands round the undrunk mug of coffee, pulled Chamberlain to his feet. He stood by his daughter.

'There's no answering these questions,' he said gently.

'I ought to have helped John, when he felt, so, so dreadful.'

'We don't know what he felt.' Elsa. 'Or if he'll ever feel so again.'

'How can I tell?' Pamela barely whispered. 'I ought to find out. There are people round me suffering near death, and I don't know. And if I did, what could I do? What should I have said to John?'

'You could have held his hand,' Chamberlain replied. 'Said his name. It might not have worked. You could have been ready to call the ambulance. But we were like you. We'd no idea. I was hit on the head with a golf ball once, when I was a boy. Suddenly. Out of the blue; it wasn't serious. But it shocks; your nerves shatter. For just a minute. That's how it caught me when we heard about, about . . .' He couldn't speak it. 'Except it kept flooding back, like nausea, like breakers.'

'You never told me this.' Elsa. 'I never asked, I know.'

He took her hand.

'You see,' she said, shaking it like a trophy at her daughter. 'Have you ever felt bad enough . . . ? Suicidal?'

'No,' Elsa answered. 'No,' Chamberlain echoed.

'Will Johnny try it again?' Pamela pressed, unmollified. 'He seems so normal. And Lynne? Sometimes she seems so unhappy.'

'In what way?' Elsa, aseptic.

'Haven't you ever noticed? It's as if she's been battered about the head. She's dazed. She's very lively sometimes, marvellous company, but . . .' Pamela stopped, ashamed to instruct the parents. 'It's awful.'

'You need more coffee,' Elsa said, staid, smooth.

'But it's right, isn't it? What I've said? About her?'

'Yes. It is. Pass your cup. Your daddy and I were just talking about it.'

They heard descending footsteps. Elsa warned with face and finger. Hand in hand, John and Lynette entered, faces alive with quizzical curiosity.

'Undertaker's banquet?' John inquired. 'Coffee among the coffins?'

'We were just discussing you,' Chamberlain answered.

'God save the Queen.'

14

Easter Sunday blew magnificently bright.

Lynette took John and Pamela to church, returning for lunch. Chamberlain, happy to potter, oiled the motor-mower, trimmed the lawns. The Hills called in before noon, unusually, without prior arrangement, planted deckchairs in a sheltered corner, drank whisky and coffee, shouting to the one worker outside. The doctor, pipe alight, went indoors to hinder Elsa, while his wife chased off after Chamberlain.

'That Pamela of yours is a good girl,' she began.

'Only just found out?'

'She's serious. We had a marvellous talk yesterday. About suffering. It's something I'd said to her, before. She's not like a young person. Well, you know. It did me good.'

'You need that?'

'I want to ask you, Eric. To talk to you. I'm thinking of leaving George.'

'Does he know?'

'No. I'd say he'd no idea.'

'How will he take it?'

'He'll manage. He's not helpless.'

'May I ask some questions?' She nodded, utterly chic in a dark costume, red-braided at cuffs and collar. Sallowly, severely beautiful, she stood calmly contained, half contemplative, half amused, in no need of assistance. 'Is it another man?' She smiled that away, dismissive. 'You can't put up with him any longer?'

'Something like that.'

'I see. And where do I come in? Why consult . . . ?'

'You won't let me do anything foolish.'

They argued, almost facetiously, for some minutes before he asked permission to complete his mowing. She watched, from one spot, her shoes fetching her to smart tiptoe. She did not follow him while he ran the machine into its shed, but kept her position, not posing, merely waiting until he returned.

'Well, now,' he said. She seemed to breathe, descend from the high heels. 'You shouldn't do anything drastic till Saul's finished his finals.'

'I'd thought about that.'

'And I'm not sure about George. He's a bit of a baby.'

'That's not so. You underestimate him. You always have.' She smiled, like a neat conjurer.

'How do you know that he'll get along all right?'

'I've lived twenty-three years with him.'

'You haven't left him before.'

'You're wrong again.' She smiled, remembering herself. 'I have. He managed. And he took me back.'

'Yes. What about the economics of it?' They moved, sat down on a wooden seat from where they could see George and Elsa in conversation on the patio. 'How did you live?'

'I've enough money of my own. Until I get a job.'

'What sort of job?'

'Secretary. Receptionist. I've done that often enough. And I've a degree in chemistry.'

'That represents a considerable drop in standards. You'll live in a flat. A bed-sitter. At best a small house, which compares very unfavourably with your present.'

'I'm not mad on comfort,' she said.

'How old are you?'

'You know. Forty-five.'

'You don't look it. But we can't be sure how long that advantage will last. Then you'll begin to get old, be dependent. It's best to do that in comfort with money behind you.'

'You're mercenary.'

'Yes, I am. If you're so unhappy you can't put up with him, go. Or if there is somebody else.'

'There isn't,' she said. Elsa and George had now seated themselves, making no attempt to join the others. 'But I'd better grab somebody while my looks last?'

'With George's income, in this part of the world, you're well-to-do.'

'That's the be-all and end-all of it, is it?'

'It's the beginning. You look that straight in the eye, first, and then see how your nerves or your heart are making out.' She shrugged, amused, detached. 'At your age we consult the bank book.'

They sat now until a gust of wind shadowed the garden, chilling them.

'Thanks,' she said rising. 'You've not much idea how people feel.'

'Not really.'

'I wait every day for something marvellous to happen. For a letter. An invitation. Nothing comes. You think that's mad. At my age?'

'I don't. Time's running out. An old army friend of mine died last week. But look on the credit side. Your house is beautiful. You made it so. Look at those two beautiful Dawson watercolours you bought. Your glass. What you should learn to do is to wring every ounce of pleasure out of them.'

'They're done, dead.'

'They are not. Set your mind to them. Re-learn them. The proportions of your rooms, the chairs, the piano. There's enough occupation there for you.'

'I'm too restless. I want...'

They stood not three yards from the seat, heads down, while the sun danced, exploding brilliance round them.

'Am I different from other women? Elsa? I'd be happier working in a shop.'

'You wouldn't, you know.'

'I'm not idle, Eric. If anything I'm too energetic for what I have to do. You don't understand. I might have guessed. Elsa's taken up painting again. Did you know that?'

'I did. Join her.'

'She's trained. I'd hate her beating me at it. Or showing me how to do it. That'd be worse.'

'Good works?' he said, mocking.

She swore, but did not move away for a moment, when she swung, with a gasp, pelted off towards her husband and Elsa.

'You and the old man look serious there,' Elsa called. 'What's he confessing now?'

'Time's passing.' She looked comically pathetic at her watch. Dr Hill stumbled to his feet; pipe-smoke pothered round him. 'He talks sensibly.'

When the visitors disappeared, Elsa, returning to the kitchen, made no attempt to catechize her husband. At lunch they drank wine and laughed with Lynette, Pam and John. The men washed the dishes while the ladies sipped gin in the drawing room. Outside it was cloudier, with a scuttering of showers, cloud-dapple, ragged stretches of blue. John took over his father's study for an hour or so. As the women were intent on talk, Chamberlain arranged cushions in the breakfast room, fell asleep to the music of Gluck. Half an hour later, awaking in discomfort, he dragged himself to the far end of the garden, where he stood with one foot on the compost-heap bucolically. As he looked out north-west over the wall, a flock of starlings darkened the air. Their number was huge so that seconds later the sky seemed thickly spotted. As he turned, the column wheeled, hundreds by hundreds. The whole garden was disturbed, fluffed by the noise of wings, the air softly battered, brushed, punctuated. Startled, he scratched his face, made for indoors and a book.

He read desultorily.

A party of rich French intellectuals moved about a Mediterranean landscape. Witty and urbane, they screamed like infants when they were deserted, behaved like vandals. The prose shifted, a polished steel with reflection, but dazzling. Letters were exchanged; young people faced the immorality of elders, found themselves wanting, set out to plaster the earth with works of art, architecture intense as tantrums, howls planished into epigrammatic calm. Chamberlain enjoyed himself, ran with the author, astonished but fantasizing. Nothing here sounded false, and yet the book rang foreign, attractively so. It was not the Frenchness nor the literary convention so much as his nagging objection that, real enough though these seemed, he had met no one like them. They could have existed; they did not. Stopping his perusal, stabbing himself into thought, he concluded that art must translate the known into an unknown, the unguessed-at. That did not satisfy. He tried again on his text. A young mother, brilliant, adored, unhappy, talked to her sick child. Tenderness warmed; his heart did not melt. One word was not as good as another here. A sob, a fever, discomfort were measured, defeated by antibiotics. The world runs mad, said the author; the world is safe, said the book. He troubled himself no further; now he would read for entertainment, pass the afternoon in innocence like that of a childish pantomime.

John came down for high tea, thoughtful from his work, then set out with Lynette for the Royal Riders, four miles off in the country. Left behind with the chores, Pamela had disappeared to the Hills', Elsa and Chamberlain took advantage of time together. As they walked round the garden, he asked what Lynette had to say for herself.

'I'll tell you. She frightened me.'

They stood under a tall hedge, cotoneaster salicifolia, blotched with red leaves. He murmured interrogatory noises, and, hands in pockets, watched her. Unlike Madeleine Hill with her foolery, Elsa seemed unguarded and would, he guessed, stamp off in a moment, signalling him to keep up to her shoulder while she muttered confidences.

'She told me about John.' She had not yet moved. 'When he tried...'

'How did she... ? Had she questioned...?'

'He'd insisted. Sat her down one night. Down there. He cried, she said.'

Now she walked on, and he, following, wished he could offer her a cigarette. He dared not take her arm.

'Well?' he said, half irritably.

'It was very ordinary. He'd had days and days of depression and pain. Every bone and muscle in his body. Couldn't eat, sleep. Saw the doctor. A short period of relief with pills, then as black as ever. He described it, she said, flatly. How his throat was raw, the fever, how he'd cry and throw himself on his bed, knock his head on the wall from frustration. Then lethargy but no rest. As if he'd been steam-rollered into soft lead, and if he had the energy to move he'd be slit with pain. So he lay, across the counterpane, his face down to the floor. He wished his brain would burst.'

'How long did...?'

'It was just a day or two. But it seemed interminable. And physical. Like some killing illness. But he was ashamed, disgraced. As if it were a venereal disease. That she'd refused him.'

'Is this what frightened you?' They stood by an oval of longer grass, daffodils, narcissi, dashed about by the wind.

'No, because I could hear John telling it. It was her, her attitude. She wasn't in her right mind.'

'How did you know that?'

'I didn't. How could I? I just thought so.'

'But why?'

'Her body. She twisted like rubber in her chair. And glared. In the end, she said, "I know how he felt." She bit at her fingers, and writhed. I'll tell you something. I thought.

"She's an actress, she can act. But this isn't any good. It's exaggerated." '

'She was putting it on, you mean?'

'It was real. You think we can't tell what people are, are like, inside, inside themselves. I could. I asked her if she'd ever thought of . . . "Sometimes," she said. "Sometimes." And then she was acting, strumming the word. She'd got over it. But that minute or two. Anything could have happened.'

'She seemed right as ninepence at tea.' Elsa didn't answer, tugged at a rambler that had broken from its tie. 'Perhaps it did her good. In there, with you.'

'It's Boy McKay she wants, isn't it?'

'What makes you say that?' Chamberlain sweet in reason.

'She'd drop John straight away, wouldn't she? I don't trust her.'

'Has she said anything?'

'Said. Said. She doesn't need to.' She sucked her finger. He could not tell if the outburst were provoked by his obtuseness or a rose thorn. On her wet forefinger she examined a bright pip of blood.

'Have you pricked yourself?' She turned away, brushed past him, stepped along the path, posed in front of the rhus, dry yet, withered with winter. 'Will they be all right?'

'I don't know.'

Elsa pushed smartly into the house where she prepared drinks.

Out in the fields Lynette and John searched for their path, argued, sheltered, trudged on. For the first mile along a road, then on a clearly defined footpath, they had walked fast, down into the rank growth of a valley where the path petered out at a mud-dark, half-barred entrance to a field. Now they moved without confidence, deducing direction, hoping that when they'd crested the rise they'd see their way. Breathless, disappointed, they dodged to the other side of a hawthorn hedge to seek shelter. Their faces burnt; they shone healthy.

Now hands pocketed, collar steeply up, he asked how she'd spent the afternoon. He gave no indication of pleasure when he found out, muttered a rudeness.

John Chamberlain was afraid.

Though he'd not admit it, he had convinced himself that his attempted suicide had won him Lynette. She responded to a violence of action; now she approached boredom again, demanded further bravura. He felt well, had recovered. As he stood there, the shower almost over, he could barely remember his attempt to kill himself. He could recall actions, label them; indeed from time to time did so, out of caution, to reassure himself they were properly passed. His hand shifted to hers; gloved she allowed the capture, did not encourage.

'It's stopped. Come on,' she snapped. Wind whipped cold drops into their faces as they rounded the hedge. 'God.'

She hated him, he thought then, denied his conclusion, stumbling along the rough grass margin of a field. What he wished most was to impress her, to repay the impact she had made on him. In a powerful sense he seemed not to know her. To a passing stranger they would be young people, much of an age, energetically tramping, vigorous, warmly clothed. To him she was not the woman with whom he'd lain naked, but one who'd married, sailed to America, dismissed a husband, taken to the stage, flitted about the country, seen her mother and father to the grave, craved Boy. He had done nothing but progress sluggishly from school to third-rate college. She owed him nothing beyond bare sexual stimulation, itself fitful. He grabbed again at her hand.

'I love you,' he said.

'Come on. Let's find this path.' She did not rebuff, spoke from determination.

'I mean it.'

'Yes.' Bright nod. 'There's a time and a place.' She handled his golfing cap, friendly. 'For everything.'

That damned. She'd no idea of the surge, the sea-flood in him. Sulking he straightened his hat, quickened his pace to beat her to the top, but failed. On the second ridge, the first revealed nothing, they eyed a random pattern of fields, fences, hedges, oblongs of red-brown, green, straw-buff, with a house here and there blackish, inhospitable. He looked this way, that, uselessly, his eyes watering in the wind.

'That's it,' she spoke incisively. He looked, saw nothing that he had not seen before. 'That'll be the path. And it'll take us by the farmyard, and over to the road.'

'I can't see a road.'

She checked, admitting his objection, a small fierce frown eagling her face.

'No. I'm sure that's it.'

'Why?'

'I've been this way before. We should have gone further down at that gate. I bet the path runs by the stream right at the bottom of the valley.'

Her confidence dashed his. She had been this way. He saw neither stream nor road, only fields, wet warning of trespass, sludging shoes and trouser bottoms. Now they stumbled on, kicking tussocks, climbing through a bedstead in a gap; all seemed endless and damp, until they reached the mud path, legged it out for the farm.

The yard was cluttered, with a rusting car, tyres soggy flat, but windows wound up; rags of washing scarecrowed on the line; puddles sogged in an earth black as coal-dust. Firewood, plastic bags, a snake of rotting hosepipe, a slack heap supporting a shed door, hen-coops with wire ripped loose, hinges, bolts, hammer, crowbars. The asphalt path dripped, ran out, in muddy shreds.

'Who lives there?' he asked, scorn high.

'The Blankleys.' He expected no answer.

'Who are they?'

'My father's cousins.'

'You've been down here before?' She'd said so.

'Must have. I didn't cotton on till I saw the lorry.' At the end of two deep ruts a lorry was parked under a shed; the corrugated-iron roof twisted round ugly gashes. W. Blankley on the tailboard, sludge-daubed. 'I recognized the house, then. We always came the other way.'

'You know where we are, then?'

'Roughly.'

They reached the pitted lane, leading from the farm, and soon were on a B road. The late sun gilded the sky luridly. John, more cheerful, took the lead, kicking about in the verges, once dropping into a ditch from which he emerged grinning. A mile and a half's fast walking brought them to the Royal Riders. Now, inside, sweating at his pint John Chamberlain felt no pleasure as he waited for Lynette to return from the lavatory. Uncertainty suggested that she'd disappear; that, he glanced at the yellow-faced clock, in ten minutes' time he'd be alone still while she was away, on a bus, on a hitch with one of a hundred friends. His beer tasted insipidly sour; the landlord said nothing; the lounge stood empty, but she returned to play with her lager, laconic as the publican.

He hated her quiet. Her face set into a pale hauteur as she considered matters out of his ken.

'Penny for 'em,' he said, jovial with fright. She pitied him, looked away. Her hands were out of his reach. Pretty, she was cold as a waxwork. He was not sorry when she refused a second drink and they set out for home, this time by the road. She walked ahead this time, and in the half-darkness they were unbothered by traffic. He caught up and kissed her; she demonstrated no interest.

'What's up?' he asked.

'Nothing.' They did not start immediately, but hesitated as if to heal the breach. Neither made advance, progress; they took again to single-file. He began an account of his afternoon's work, but she barely acknowledged this even if she listened. Now he scandalized; he'd met a peripatetic violin teacher who'd been full of the story that Eli Dunne had slept at the orchestral school with the woman in charge of wood-wind instruction. Nobody had minded; there had been no fuss. Everybody knew; it added the right Bohemian spice. The girl who had told him had been impressed. 'They wanted each other: they made it clear to everybody. That's how it should be.' Did the children in the orchestra know? His informant doubted it; they were too intent on their own randy jaunts. Would anything come of it? Why should it?

He warmed to the tale, embroidered it, drew alongside Lynette. Now he tried to draw her. Did she think Dunne attractive? Faint assent. 'What about Mrs Dunne?' No offering. 'Wouldn't she be distressed?' Lynette pulled in her lips. He felt she wanted to hear the story, but take no part in its telling. He must work at it, while she idled, but if he fell below standard he risked anger, rebuke. He persevered, making no mark. By the time they reached the A road, could walk side by side on a pavement, he was reduced to silence. They stepped smartly along, too fast for his comfort.

He reached for her hand.

'What's wrong?'

'I've told you. Nothing.'

'You're as quiet as the grave.'

'Yes.'

Now they walked more slowly, as if energy had been thrashed out of them. With troubled concern he stumbled on, looking for opportunity. The world bleakened; cars rushed past like closed boxes; inside, their perfumes or colours were denied to him.

'What's up?' he asked again. 'Come on, now.'

'Nothing.'

'Is it anything I've said? Or done? Not done?' They trailed off.

'No.'

She even seemed unattractive, nose-end reddened, a beak in night air. Her movements pronounced no pleasure; she went forward as one staggers, step after step to restore balance, ungainly. He took her hand; limply she allowed it.

'I don't want to . . .' he began. She did not answer. He stopped, his arms round, turning her, pressing his mouth to hers. Unresponsive she stood in his embrace, face cold, eyes melancholy wide. He covered her face with kisses; she might well have been glazed china. Angered he let her go and as he stepped awkwardly back she shrugged him off, not strongly, but as one shakes a lock of hair out of the eyes. She looked at him, not seeing, then with a jerk, spring released on, shaped her mouth into a smile. Short and mechanical, it twisted her lips and disappeared. He hardly believed in its existence.

'I don't want to talk. I feel so awful.'

'Are you ill?'

'No. Depressed.'

'Why?' Nothing. 'What's getting you down?' Nothing. 'Come on. Out with it.' She stretched her arms, mute. 'Is it me? Have I done anything . . . something?'

'It's nothing to do with you.'

Not quite in step they made their way forward. At any time now he was convinced she'd announce his dismissal. Hollow with fright, pinched, he kept up with her as though her physical presence prevented the expected renunciation. She made no signs of her own distress, neither sniffs nor tears, no wandering gestures of the hands, head jerks, tripping. She walked, humanly steady, inhumanly silent. She did not love him. Under the dark sky trees and hedges stretched leafless. The headlights of cars lit road, verge, the cold air, momentarily and were gone, painful as the lash.

Now they reached the village with its row of electric lamps.

The car park of the Oak was chained with fairy lights incongruously swaying.

'Another drink?'

She shook her head, touched his arm as in apology. The sadness of the woman unmanned him; tears beat him about the chest, the belly. Abandoned, he set his face, threw shoulders achingly back, found his voice.

'I'll look after you,' he said.

They passed St Mary's lych-gate, the lighted windows of houses, once the bang and beat of an over-loud record-player. Neither spoke, but as they turned down the lane from the main road he slipped his arm into hers.

A voice called out to them, startling them into attention.

Chamberlain sat in the darkness on a five-barred gate. He greeted them.

'What in hell are you doing?' John demanded.

'Watching the world go by.'

'Are you going to the pub, or coming back?'

'Neither.' Chamberlain clambered stiffly down, lifted his stick from the gate.

'Is it warm enough to sit about?' Lynette asked.

Chamberlain answered her, cheerfully, and Lynette bothered to answer him, if briefly. John knew satisfaction.

15

Before he returned to college John Chamberlain completed arrangements for his wedding. As soon as he'd taken his final examinations, he and Lynette would marry in the register office in Retford and spend part of the honeymoon setting up a home in whatever town he'd found employment. An announcement was made in the local newspapers, and Lynette withdrew from the summer performance of *Hamlet*. Tongues wagged. Boy McKay sulked.

The parents promised the couple a loan to deposit on a house but Elsa would not allow her husband to name the sum. Though this was sensible, it seemed to him a further attempt at control. She must play her large part or there'd be trouble. In the middle of these negotiations, Elsa suddenly announced that she intended visiting the Dunnes in London. This had been suggested at Christmas, but to the best of Chamberlain's knowledge, had not been taken up. Now it appeared Beth and Elsa had been writing regularly, with the final planning completed by phone.

Chamberlain expressed his surprise, but sorted out a pile of books for Elsa to carry down in the car. That led to conversation.

'She's keen on books. Builds her own shelving.'

'I think I probably know her better than you do.' There was no telling with Elsa; sometimes she'd listen, at others hector without reason. 'We've written regularly, once a week at least, and talked several times on the phone.'

He was intrigued.

Had Elsa any notion that she proposed to stay with her

husband's mistress? He thought not, couldn't be sure. Would Beth let it out? Again he floundered. Mrs Dunne made no demands on him, seemed emotionally uninvolved. In bed she enjoyed him as a thirsty worker swills from the tap, refreshed but unappreciative of quality, willing once the drouth was assuaged to settle for abstinence or careful choice. They expressed love in words, conventionally, as expected, but the relationship lived in naked bodies, in the language of parched flesh. It was a conjuring trick, a beautiful performance one did not forget, but about which one did not rave, translate into literary ecstasy. Beth did not write to him; he enclosed a note whenever he sent books, but that was it. Madeleine Hill bullied him; so had other women, but Beth Dunne kept apart from his soul, a Renoir beauty with no speaking voice. He wondered how this could be so, considered with curiosity whether she had other loves she treated with equal sang-froid. When he thought about her he did not so much picture her amongst the shining cake-tins, the formica tops, the warming odours of her kitchen; she existed as a memory along his limbs, under his fingers, in his genitals.

And Elsa would walk into that house on the Woolwich Road. They'd talk. Elsa would be shown the books, invited to read. They'd shop together, cross the road into the woods, skitter down the hill, watch the broad, shifting silver of the Thames under the pylons, wait for Dunne's return, perhaps attend a rehearsal with him. Beth would explain how she organized his work and they'd laugh at the witlessness of husbands, these two he'd bedded.

While she was away he slaved, sat up later in front of his television screen half-interested in the shapeless plays, the documentaries. Pamela, working hard, beginning examination nerves, talked to him, took to watercolours for therapy. The child had talent, working in thin areas of paint, yellows, greens, mild blues, and the finished pictures swept along the paper, puzzling him. It was as if she'd left the medium, or disregarded it so that paintings seemed both incomplete and overdone. This he imagined to be real skill, to make a worn-out style odd, unusual. But his daughter was a tyro, and these disregarded conventions might be elementary errors corrected in any art school for all he knew. The pleasure was there from ignorance or otherwise.

He spoke to Madeleine Hill.

She telephoned with a gardening question for Elsa which he could not answer. Madeleine clearly wished to talk. Why had Elsa gone? Had he heard? George didn't like it when she suggested such outings. Was he looking after himself? Would he drop in for a meal? Then she admitted she had missed him, not deliberately, quite, but she liked to make a fool of him, not that that was too difficult. He listened, intrigued, he'd done a long day's work, and invited her over. She refused, archly, suggestively. Realizing her error, she sobered herself, said George wasn't well, she had plenty on her hands. She did not mention leaving. He did his best to bring the conversation to an end. When she rang off he felt he'd downed, and paid for, an expensive, potent drink he disliked.

On the second night while he was reading, and relishing, a book for review he heard voices in the garden, saw Pamela walking round with Lynette Rockford. From this distance they looked much of an age, and laughed, walking slowly behind the fruit cages, then out to the furthest point under the hawthorn hedge where they stood by a gate in spite of a wind that flapped their coat-hems. He left them to it, but not long after he heard them on the stairs. Pamela tapped his study door.

Both girls looked healthy, cheeks reddened, finger-nails white.

'Lynette wants to talk to you, Daddy.' He invited them to sit. Pamela said she must return to her work, did so.

Mrs Rockford sat straight, on the edge of a chair, patting

neat hair neater when she'd removed her headscarf. She refused a drink, but complimented him on the warmth of the room. He helped himself to a small whisky while they chatted. She had heard from John, who was well; he had not from Elsa, who would be fit enough. She offered snippets of information about her work, her replacement as Ophelia, and he described the high tea he'd cooked, Pamela's plans for next year in a new job, Elsa's scheme for a rebuilt rockery with steps in local limestone. Invited, she removed her coat revealing a blouse, and dark skirt, smart as a Girl Guide's, feminine, pretty but prim for the styled hair, the knowledgeable, pert face. He enjoyed the exchange; he'd earned it with his work on the review. In his head, he'd written his first three clinching sentences, begged a minute from her to pencil them down, then smiled, chuffed with himself, denying himself a sip of the whisky in his pleasure. She was paler now, outdoor glow wiped off. He inquired what he could do for her.

'There's something I wanted to say to you.'

He sat up. He'd spoken unseriously, in masculine delight at her company. Now he scratched the writing-pad. She did not look at him. Her lower lip trembled as she clutched the chair-arms. He offered her a drink, rising ceremoniously to hover over the bottles. Her refusal was angrily given, dashed out with a shake of her head.

'Shall I put the light on?'

Again she demurred with a shake of the head.

Lynette, fingers meshed, stared down at her feet, shoulders humped, wordless. He waited.

'I don't know,' she said, 'if I'm wise.'

To tell him? He adopted a suitable facial severity, which disappeared in ensuing silence. Now he felt irritated, as at a child whose refusal to reveal its secret did not conceal the insignificance.

'It might make things worse,' she said, in the end, syllable after syllable. She sighed, sharply, thrust out a hand, shifted, crossed, uncrossed her legs.

'You think I shan't be able to help. Is that it?'

'I know you won't.'

'Why do you want to tell me, then?'

'Want? I don't.' Eye to eye.

'Can I give you advice?' She shook her head. 'Is it,' he paused, 'confession?' The question might have been in Hottentot. 'You want to tell me something about yourself?' She did not even move this time, sat, knees together, eyelids down. 'Let me get you a drink. A small one.'

'No. That won't solve anything, thanks.'

He rose, walked to the window, and licking his lips peered down towards the hedge where the girls had stood together. It was not yet dark. There they had laughed. He blew his nose, returned, reseated himself. She jerked to attention.

'It's about me,' she said. 'And Mr McKay, Boy, Robin. We still make love.'

Chamberlain was not surprised, not shocked. Morally inane, he rolled whisky round his mouth, considering its savour. When he did look at her again, she seemed more settled, as if at any moment she'd open her handbag to repair her face. Come to think, one did not see much public cosmetic rehabilitation these days. Or had he lost interest?

'I see.' Deep in his chest.

'It's not fair to John. I know that. I daren't tell him.' She dabbed her mouth. 'Well, it, it could . . .'

'You've no intention of stopping, breaking the relationship? With Mr McKay?'

'I can't. I want to. I keep telling myself. But he puts a hand on me, and . . .'

'He knows you're engaged to John?'

'Yes. I don't think such things matter to him. Marriage is nothing. It's spoilt his life, he says. He's in trouble, but he'll make a pass. At anybody presentable. He can't help it.' She nibbled her lip. 'We're very good with each other. In that way.'

'What will happen when you're married?'

'That's what I don't know. If we go away from here perhaps it'll be all right. But Boy's mischievous. And predatory.' Her eyes widened in apology for the word. 'He's likely to come over for the devilment.'

'If he were free, would you ditch John and marry him?'

'Probably. I'm not sure. But it's not much of a basis, is it, for a marriage?'

'Why did you promise to marry John? What's in it?'

Now she smiled, showing her teeth.

'Oh, I like him. He's a lot livelier than Boy in his ideas. He can be interesting. You underrate him. He's quite a man, is John.'

'Wasn't your first husband?'

'Joel? Not really. He was clever, I expect, at his work. But he'd spent too much time on it. He didn't know about anything else. That and a few jobs about the house. He didn't read much or say anything to make you think.'

'You think your infatuation for McKay will spoil your marriage, I take it. Well, give him up.'

'I can't, I tell you. You don't know how strong it is.'

'You and John have sex? And it's not so good as with McKay? So even if you went far enough away to live, you might hold it against John?'

'I might come running back.'

'It's very important, is it? The sexual thing?'

'Isn't it for everybody?'

'By no means.'

She glowered at him in hate, eyebrows puckered.

'You almost had it with me, Mr Chamberlain. I don't think you've the right to talk.'

'To talk? Yes, because you've asked me. To lay down precise law, no.' He sounded prissy to himself, but guilt needs its stabilizers. 'On that night I judged you were desperate. And promiscuous.'

'It didn't matter that I was to be your son's wife?'

'That wasn't certain, was it? But no, it didn't. It relieved us. We could forget it.'

'And is that right?' she demanded.

'In its context. I don't look down on you, or blame you. Why should I? You did what was best for yourself.'

'When I've married John, you won't be thinking . . . ?'

'Now and then. I don't deny it. You're an attractive woman. But there'll be another ten, dozen, twenty men in a similar position, won't there? It's past. This McKay thing is different. That's here.' He held up a hand to prevent interruption. 'One thing has impressed me and that's your concern for John. That's good. You praise him. And as you get older . . .'

'Older, older. It's now. What am I to do now? If I throw John over, he'll kill himself. And I can't trust myself. I'm as likely as not to go chasing after Boy . . .'

He faced up to her, first setting his whisky symbolically aside.

'If I had any choice, I'd pick a wife for him who was a virgin, who loved him, who continued to do so, whose love and affection and care for him increased. But there are no such choices. There are no such women. Or at least one cannot pick them out. I can't. All I'm trying to say to you, Lynette, is this. All marriages are difficult. You're a fool if you think otherwise. Because divorce is easier, one tries less hard once real difficulties emerge to make the relationship stick. I don't even know if that's good or bad. It's the way it is. I, well, you know it, am not faithful to Elsa. She is bored with me, with life here, but puts up with it. She grouses. She makes me uncomfortable, guilty, but that's my punishment. So we hang on. But it's not even as easy as that. If she decided on a divorce, I'd let her go, but I guess I'd hanker after her. It's as irrational as could be. How she'd feel about me . . . I don't know. This is no help to you, but I don't want you leaving this house thinking there's some simple, black-and-white solution if only we had the wit to see it. There isn't.'

'How do I decide?' She sounded almost cheerful.

'You make up your mind, hope to God it'll work out. That you can compromise sufficiently.'

'If I had some religious principles . . .' She waved.

'You'd be in equal, but different trouble. That's all.' He did not elaborate. 'Listen here. I know a married couple who are, you'd say, well suited. But she has lovers. Tactfully, but I think he knows, well, some of it. He could not bear it, at first. Now he sublimates his jealousy, by bullying her a bit, and in his work where he's very successful. Sexually, he's faithful. Sometimes, now and again, I have a suspicion that he enjoys his wife's infidelities, might even spy on them if he had the chance. His temperament has allowed this. That's his compromise. Now and then he'll hit her, and she puts up with it. Or he'll sell something she's fond of. Nothing violent. He doesn't scar her or flog the house round her. Otherwise you'll see them together at the Conservative garden-party, at concerts, at the tennis-club, even at church once a month, happy as kings. They entertain a good deal. They are middle-aged. They are, you could argue, an extreme case in that they put up with behaviour, on both sides, that would wreck most marriages. But that's the picture. That's what most marriages are like. Papering the cracks. Dulling the senses.' He lifted his glass from his desk, drew figures of eight in the air.

Lynette stretched.

'I feel so down, so ill with it all. I'm guilty. I can't sleep. Or eat.'

'Have you been to the doctor?'

'Yes. He wants to send me to a psychiatric expert. I don't see the use of that. I've got to make my mind up, and then act, one way or the other.'

'You come to me, an amateur.'

She caressed her legs as if to heal a bruise.

'You,' she began, 'always talk sensibly, but I get the impression you're worse off than I am. In your mind. You're suffering, aren't you? Flailing about?' She stopped. 'I'm sorry. I shouldn't be talking like this.'

'Why not? We're both cases. What about that drink now?'

'It won't help.' She shook her head. 'Thank you.' She watched him pour himself another. 'If I was sure John would stand it, it wouldn't be too bad.'

'What would you do?'

'I don't know. The fact that he can't just stops me thinking. There's no choice.'

'Have you talked it out with anyone? McKay, for instance. He's a solicitor. He's no fool.'

'He'd listen for half an hour, and then he'd grab me. I'd either swipe him across the face, or go down on my back. He's good, in this way, but hopeless. Immoral. He gives pleasure out by the minute. He doesn't know how he'll think tomorrow. He'd make love until I was screaming wild for him, then pack me off to John.'

'Have you tried Elsa?'

'She thinks about John as you don't. I'm frightened of her. She doesn't want me to marry him, but, but . . . She's as terrified as I am.'

'Nobody else? Relatives? Some sensible friend?'

'No.

'What's to be done, then?'

She sat upright, hands still on her knees.

'I know what I should do. I can't do it. That's why I lie awake. Going over and over. I'm mad. You don't, you . . .' She broke off, but soberly, face unlined.

'Just put it into words,' Chamberlain said.

'I should ditch Boy, marry John.'

'Do it, then.'

'We might be worse off. There's no telling whether the marriage will work. There's no saying, even, that I'll be able to put up with it.'

'No. But do it.'

'How can you . . . ?' He left her time to complete the sentence; nothing happened.

'Do it. Do as you say.' Now his voice thumped heavily about the room, with depth, with weight. He dared not watch her too carefully, but had the impression that though she sat still, her eyes flickered, with small, unplanned jerks like a child's sparkler. He did not like himself, stood up, made himself a human being again. 'That's my advice,' he said, half humorously, 'for what it's worth.'

Eyes met now, steady, hers accusatory.

'I see. Thank you.'

They worked through the argument again, almost formally, with Chamberlain polishing his phraseology. To him it was an exercise; he made sure she grasped his conclusion. He was uncertain of the strength of his argument and therefore presented it with skill. He persuaded her in the end to take a mouthful of gin, a little triumph, and as she left she promised she'd keep him posted on her thinking. The expression jarred; his mood lightened.

Elsa returned energetic and loquacious.

Things were bad with the Dunnes; Eli was a bastard. He recognized his helplessness without his wife, but wanted to loon about with this clarinet woman.

'What's Beth's line?'

'Shock, as though she's been attacked. Or raped. She just weeps, and wipes her eyes, and packs the music up for his next class.'

'What did you tell her?'

'What could I? She'll have to get a job if she leaves him, and that's not easy. They'd have to sell the house.'

'And her books,' Chamberlain said.

'You're off your head about books. What the hell difference do they make?' He grinned his way out of difficulty. 'She depends on him for money. If she went he'd make a hash of his job.'

'And the other woman?'

'She's up here somewhere. They meet, sometimes, on Sundays. And then there's trouble.'

'It happened while you were there?'

'No.'

'How did Beth find out?'

'He told her. He came back cool as cucumber and told her.'

'That's honest.'

'Honesty is no excuse.'

'And what did he expect?' Chamberlain could not help pressing Elsa while she was in this excited state. 'Did he want her to condone it?'

'He's a funny devil. All smiles. You don't make out what he's doing. Perhaps he hoped she'd just tell him to get on with it. He was wrong. He saw what it did to her.'

'He's infatuated?'

'Put what word you like on it. He doesn't care how much she's knocked about.'

'Did they have a good sexual relation? Before?'

'Apparently.'

'Is this the first time?'

'She doesn't know of any other.' Elsa spoke impatiently. 'You're like all men. You've no idea of the effect of this. She's a strong woman, physically, but now she sits down and cries in the middle of vacuuming the carpet. She's insane. She writes him scrawling letters.'

'Why is she so distressed? Is she . . . ?'

'Pride. She made him what he is. Now he's having a little success, and he drops her. That's unjust. I know what I'd feel. And I've no such control over you. You don't owe what you are to me. I sometimes think I get in your way.'

'That's foolish.'

'I'd like to swipe that bastard. Laughing with his crow's feet. I'd maim him, if I could get away with it.'

'Why are you so worked up? It's not like you.'

'You should see that woman. Her heart's broken.'

'She'll get over it.'

'At what expense? You talk like a man. You side with him. Oh, go on, go on, it's all the same in a hundred years. It isn't. She's like someone who's had a surgical operation that's taken the brain and nerves and womb out of her.'

He stumbled through his ramshackle questions, ashamed of himself. Nothing Elsa said gave her away. Excitedly she flung her banalities, flat enough to mock him. The affair reduced her.

'Has there, has there been any suspicion about Beth's behaviour?' he asked.

'They didn't say anything. Not that she was capable of saying much.'

'Eli didn't talk to you about his affair, did he?'

'Just once he said, "We aren't hitting it off too well." Otherwise eating heartily and smiling.'

'Has she any friends?'

'I don't think so. A relative she visits. No, I'd say not.'

'She's tied up in him?'

'Yes. I suppose so. She keeps busy. She goes to classes. I haven't any friends.'

'Yes?'

'Yes,' Elsa said loudly. 'Well, what do you make of that? What should I do if you deserted me, is that it? What about you?'

' "And in the general censure take corruption." '

'I don't trust you. She did, implicitly.'

He left it, waiting for Elsa's next attack. On edge, she took offence easily, criticized him in crude terms, searched for faults, made no attempt to please. Chamberlain, uncomfortable, avoided his wife, skulked away quickly after meals. She'd now bang into his study, as if to encourage an outburst.

His agent, Bruce Cassidy, had phoned him about his new novel. It was tremendous; it really would go a bomb. He'd already been in touch with Charles Martin at the publisher's to tell him big money was required. The Americans stirred already. This was going to be it. Bruce tried to sound hard-bitten. 'I know you, Eric White-knees, hankering after five words of praise in the *Statesman* or the *Spectator*. You're going to buy a Rolls after this one, boy.'

16

Chamberlain spent time in London.

Agent, publishers, film and television people made much of him. He was bothered by transatlantic calls, and all this before his book had appeared in proof. Cassidy sang small, stood proud, mocked the American scrabble for paperback rights, laughed to see money pile. 'It's undignified,' he said. 'Your father and mine would not have approved.' Bruce's father was a Melbourne joiner who'd once batted with Bradman and drunk with everybody else in the antipodes. His son aped the clerical, the Etonian, fastidious in vowel and tie. But he loved the money he deprecated. Chamberlain found himself constantly excited but warning himself. But each unusual step by vendors and buyers, by financiers convinced him. He woke in the morning on the edge of expectation. Elsa spoke optimistically, refusing to be dazzled, wondered when they'd have to find themselves a tax-haven. Accountants made preliminary colossal calculations.

The weather turned tropical.

Mist hung at dawn, burst Turneresque at eight-thirty, with the sky pale, shadows black. Promised thunder sulked, dropped no spot. Local newspapers featured girls on the steps of lidos; Sunday roads to the coast were jammed; tempers were short as shrubs withered.

Chamberlain sat in his agent's stuffy office deciding whether to call on the Dunnes. He'd heard nothing from them and had brought no gifts for Beth, but as he sipped champagne, considered Cassidy's latest reports from the success-sector, he made up his mind. He pushed into the secretary's corner, phoned, was invited over.

Beth had sounded normal, and acted so when he arrived. She was not in the kitchen but sprawled red of arm and leg in a deckchair on a brown, bent-covered lawn. She mopped her face as she dragged indoors to prepare iced fresh lemonade.

'It's too hot to do anything,' she said. She pulled off broad-rimmed hat and sunglasses, briefly polishing her arms wth oil.

'Eli's at work?'

'Should be.'

The drink was delicious, home-made and large. He ate an oat-cake.

'Do you want to sit in the sun?' she demanded. He decided on the old stone kitchen, cool behind Venetian blind, out of the glare.

He explained his presence in London; she spoke her satisfaction at his success, then inquired after Elsa, Pam's A Level, Saul's finals, John's health. Again he was reminded of her efficiency; she forgot nothing. 'Would you like ice-cream; strawberries?'

Brushing the crumbs from his tie, he crossed the floor, positioned himself by the canvas chair where she was sitting. He bent to kiss her hair, her neck, stroked her shoulders. She gripped his hand, preventing movement.

'No,' she said. Her voice whipped.

'What's wrong?' No answer. 'Beth?' She did not allow his hand to move; hers burned, sweated.

'You've heard,' she said. 'Eli's going to leave me.'

'Why?'

'He says he's fallen in love.' The bitterness. 'With a young woman. From your part of the world.' As if it were his fault. Now she'd make demands on him. 'He's going to leave me.'

'Going to? Do you mean he's hanging on here . . .'

'He's still got his living to earn,' she answered, gently and sensibly. 'Who told you about it?'

'Elsa, I think. I'm not sure. I don't believe half I hear.'

'She's a clarinet player. A young married woman, separated from her husband.'

'Have you met her?'

'No. He hasn't had the nerve... No, I haven't.'

'But he told you?'

'He told me.'

Now she managed calm, stood matronly, challenging him to continue. He had no compunction.

'Has this happened before?' he asked.

'Not so far as I know.'

'Won't this, er, blow over?'

'I don't think so. I hoped it would. But not now, no, not now.' She smiled to herself. 'He's serious. Hugs it all deeply. He wouldn't just fall for a casual number. It's tearing him apart. He needs me, and feels an obligation to me, but he's madly in love. That's all there is.'

'And the woman?'

'She's twenty-four.'

'What does she say?'

Beth shook her head, hopelessly, at loss.

'He's like a madman. He cries. He writes her letters every day, and he'd hardly sign his name to a postcard before. At free week-ends he goes off to her.'

'There's nothing you can do?'

Again, the solemn head-roll.

'What will happen?'

'He'll go.'

'When?'

'I daren't discuss it. It might, might alter things.'

'You'll have to get a job?'

'I've done that already. In my cousin's office. He's a solicitor.'

'Doesn't that make it easier for him to leave you?'
'Maybe.'
'Aren't you going to try to hang on to him?'
'How can I?'

He noticed that she was not wearing a wedding-ring. Fingers naked, whereas he remembered them, flour-daubed, with a gold band.

'You'll have to leave this house?'
'Yes. We shall sell up.'
'You don't mind?'
'It's no use minding.'
'Where will you live?'

'I know where there's a flat going. I start work next week at my cousin's. I've helped them out before. At least it'll give me something to do.'

'Will you divorce . . . ? Consent, you know?'
'I expect so.' Again the small smile. 'In time.'
'Is there anything I can do?' he asked fearfully.
'Go on. You suggest it.'
'You don't want to leave him. Do you?'

She did not answer, this big, sun-dazed woman on the canvas chair. Outside not a leaf moved; heat leapt from the yard; high up the sun scorched, bleached, blinded. Beth pushed herself upright, refilled his glass, thumbed in awkward ice-cubes from the plastic dish. This was not the wild woman Elsa had described.

'I wish there was some way I could help you.'
'There isn't.' She fumbled in the fridge, back to him.
'It's wrong,' he said. 'I like you both. It shouldn't happen.'

Now she sat again, with nothing in her hand, no drink, no comforting biscuit. With a handkerchief she dabbed at her mouth, her temples.

'You think,' she said, 'that you and I made love, don't you?' She sweated, not graciously. 'You can't help it, can you?' She did not speak forcefully. 'That should make a difference. It's different. Between you and me it was a marvellous game. But we weren't serious. We loved bodily, didn't we? It was great. Now I'm paying for it.' Her mouth turned down. 'I shouldn't say that. It isn't true, anyway. I don't believe it, and it'll make you guilty. But Eli's not like that. He can't just do it like an animal.'

'Thanks.' Sarcasm might steady her.

'It's true. He fell in love.'

'That makes him better, morally, than you, or me, then, does it?'

'Not morally. But he was involved. With her. She with him. In love.'

'So that a third person is hurt.'

'If they're honest, it must be so.'

'I don't call that honest,' he said. 'It's self-regard. He leaves you for a younger woman, and tries to make out . . .'

'No, he doesn't. He's sorry. He knows what he's done.'

They talked at, not with, each other, in a sense of irritation such as one might feel during the heat-wave. They did not convince, only contend. She seemed to demand the admission that Eli was different, superior. He wanted to settle her if he could, call her bluff as she confessed her hurts. She would not oblige.

They started tea together as Dunne was late, after she had laid out the evening's music for her husband.

'I'd let him find his own bloody music.'

'No. He's got to pay his way. It's no trouble.'

'Don't you feel a grudge? Aren't you jealous?'

'What do you think?'

Eli was pleasantly quiet, included Beth in conversation. Most of the time he talked of the new book, not surprised at its success. He concerned himself with its quality, not its commercial power. Chamberlain began to feel annoyance.

'There's one thing,' he said.

'What's that?' Eli restrung a violin.

'I wanted to dedicate it to you and Beth.' Eli continued, thrum-thrumming now for A, not looking up, the occupied man.

'That'll be good.' E string last, the fifths perfect.

'Beth's told me that you and she . . .'

'You can put our names together. There's nothing wrong with that.'

'What will she say?'

'You ask her.' Eli cased the violin, looked about for another job. 'It's rotten.'

'I don't want to interfere,' Chamberlain said. 'It seems so . . .'

'There's nothing to be done. I'd do it if I could.'

'It's final, is it? No going back?'

'It is.' Dunne flapped a gesture of annoyance.

'On whose account?' Incomprehension. 'Do you want to leave Beth?'

'I do.' He cut off other suggestions. 'There's nothing else for it.'

'She's pregnant?'

'Good God, no.'

'But you want children?'

'I've no idea whether I shall do better there with Diane than with Beth.' The sentence unrolled awkward as his embarrassment.

'I thought you were happy here.'

'You thought wrong.' He paused, in apology. 'We've got on well enough. It's been comfortable. I've been busy, and Beth can always occupy herself. We were in love at one time, I'd have said. The sex thing worked. But when I met Di, all that counted for nothing. You don't make anything of that, do you?'

'No.'

'You'd call it romanticism or immaturity. This was something . . .' He stopped, again. 'I can list all the objections as well as you. I am in love. It's as simple as that.'

'Only because you allow it to be so. If you knew you'd be shot if you made any move towards Diane, you'd soon recover.'

'I can only say I don't think so.' Eli pushed his hand deep into his beard. 'This has hurt now. Shocked you, I can see. And if you think I don't know what it's done to Beth, you're a bigger bloody fool than I take you for. This is not self-indulgence.'

'What is it, then?'

'Do you believe in compatibility?'

'Oh, God. Do you have to label it?'

'When I first met Diane, I . . .'

'What's her name?' Chamberlain, rudely.

'Diane Pendleton. When I first met her, at that orchestral school, she was just an attractive young woman. We made love, but I expected it to fizzle out, I'll be honest. We'd meet once or twice, send a letter or two, and that'd be that. I can't think now of living without her.'

'And in seven years' time?'

'That's not my concern. It's now. I know what you think.'

'What about Beth? She'll have to leave this house. Does she want to?'

'No. But she wouldn't want to stay here knowing what I feel for Di. And if she did, I wouldn't.'

'I,I,I.'

'You seem very excited.'

'It's so stupid. You're not eighteen. And surely you know what she feels.'

'Look, Eric.' Dunne rarely used the Christian name. 'You're a cold fish. You dip your wick and enjoy it, but there's no more to it than that. You don't understand that I'm lacerated, beyond saving, by what's happening to me. I can no more turn aside from what I'm doing than I could levitate. It's inhuman.'

'To Beth.'

'Not in that sense.' He pleaded for understanding, but even as he spoke, a wall of cold sorrow raised itself round Chamberlain. He could not argue, nor move. The prison was ugly iron, white-daubed and freezing, the air fetid but thin, catching the lungs. His eyes pinned themselves to an etching, but made nothing of its grey and white balance; it was painted in another language. Fatigued pain screwed his legs, ripped sinews loose, demanned him, dried him from mouth and aching throat through parched chest, belly, barren testicles. Condemnation held him not at the extreme of torture so that he'd faint or scream, but in a temperance of distress, a shoulder-hardening grief, a loss of self, of respect, as if he'd been transformed into a thick bolt and nut in the prison door, a pained factory-turned lump, welded, clanged into place. Now he rushed away from himself so that he seemed only a kind of movement, a tunnel dash of destroying grief, hurled off from himself, his centre, his steadiness. All humanity, from deep childhood to the shallows of middle life whirled away from him, spiralling into the empty air, wasted, devalued, dumb.

'You aren't rich enough to behave like this.' Chamberlain.

'You could, but not me?'

'What provision will you make for Beth?'

'Not much. She can have what she likes from here. She'll have to work.'

'That satisfies you?'

'No. But it's what will happen.'

Dunne moved about the room, fetched down a yellow pipe from the cupboard, filled it with mild tobacco he rubbed in his palm.

'I'll have to be off, shortly. Takes damn near an hour to get there.'

'I shan't see you here again.'

'No, it's likely.'

'I can't tell you how sorry I am.'

Dunne nodded, in a cloud of smoke, humming.

The men shook hands. Beth appeared with a register her husband had carried off the week before. They were polite, sadly, sadly.

'Will you be here when I get back?'

'No. I can't stay.'

'I see.' He thrust a hand out. 'I'm delighted about the book. It'll sell a million.'

'And your names?'

'Our names.'

Dunne gathered his impedimenta, went out. Beth rubbed her hands weakly, staring into the distance. She pulled herself together.

'What was that about names?' He told her. 'Just put his.'

'He said both.'

'He's lost all feeling, but the one. For her.'

Chamberlain followed her out to the kitchen. As he put his arm about her, she shoved him off.

'I'm sorry,' he said.

'I can't bear any man.'

'You'll let me know if I can do anything.'

'You can't give him back to me.'

She grimaced a smile.

17

Drought burnt through July.

John and Saul both graduated with good seconds, and John, who had been in difficulty finding work, had three interviews offered inside a week. He accepted a post at a rural comprehensive school in Somerset and pushed a trolley round the General Hospital in Beechnall to make cash. A friend found them a suitable house. Saul and Pamela drove off in a hired car for a week's trip in Scotland, annoying both sets of parents by their secrecy of arrangement, and returned engaged. The Hills, about to leave on holiday, raised no overt objection, joined a party for the open-air *Hamlet* in Retford Manor Park.

They lined up their cars and reached the arena by an avenue of condemned elms. Dr Hill was expansive, explaining why they had decided on Istanbul. As far as Chamberlain could make out, the choice had been taken on linguistic grounds, the attraction of nomenclature, but he found this incredible, took it as a compliment to himself. During the past few weeks, his novel, *The Helmet*, had crazily become a gold mine, so that every post, or ring of the telephone, announced some further expansion of its monetary imperium. He had never known his publishers work so fast; his agent let out that the firm needn't raise a hand elsewhere this year, and refused to go on vacation. With Chamberlain excitement had touched zenith, and now he kept depression at bay by steady reviewing, stolid reading of rivals, diffident judgement. These persons had worked as hard as he; no magic transformed them, though he found, and commended, one book more substantial than his own. But in reviews elsewhere the thing won a dozen lines of lukewarm praise so that he wondered if he had deceived himself.

He had one hope.

Perhaps the large sums of money would impress Elsa. Why he should think this, he did not know, or why he should even want it. Certainly she was now showing excitement, had mentioned a change of house, but had vetoed cruises, a Rolls-Royce, or domicile abroad unless that was forced on them. By the look of it, he would never need to put finger to typewriter again, and perhaps she feared it.

'You and I will be able to see more of each other,' he'd said, whisky-happy, after sex.

'You won't want that.'

She lay naked in his arms, but truth prevailed.

'That's not very kind.'

'You're not sober. I'm not.' A shrilling bedside phone guillotined conversation.

One day in his study he attempted a charitable gambit.

'I'd like to help Beth Dunne,' he said. 'Your friend. How do we set about it?'

'In what way?' Snapped.

'Financially.'

'We've not got the money yet.'

'No. But she'll be living in some poky flat, dependent on her clerk's wages, in trouble every time she's ill.'

'Perhaps that's what she'd prefer.'

'She wants to stay where she is.'

'You can't buy Eli back for her. Keep out.'

But now as they crossed the park, Elsa walked in front with Dr Hill, energetic and laughing, slim as her daughter. The young people danced in a line abreast, with Madeleine and Eric well to the rear. Even so, he dragged some steps behind her.

'Come on, come on, Fido. Heel,' she called. No jollity about that. Brown as a nut, she touched her hair in its black severity. There'd be a thin white strip about her breasts and loins he thought. That diminished her, robbed her of the pagan wooden polish of divinity. It comforted him. Sallow skin, the dark aureolae of nipples, a pallor by the pubic bush. She had no right to talk, merely to loll in her bikini, bronze herself with modern propriety.

'It's going to rain,' she said.

'The gardens need it.'

'That's no talk for a literary man.' She dragged his arm. 'You're here to see *Hamlet*.' Well, yes, Shakespeare made money.

At the entrance to the outdoor theatre, the rest waited until he came up with the tickets. Emrys Hughes-Edge came from nowhere to shake the women by the hand, inform them how well it had gone so far. Lynette edged towards Chamberlain.

'How do you feel?' he asked.

'Nervous.'

'Disappointed? Wish you were ...?'

'I don't know about that.'

As they took their seats, a sniffle of wind troubled the privet hedges which surrounded the auditorium. John inquired if Lynette would be warm enough.

'Suppose I said, "no"?'

'I'd put my arm round you.'

Chamberlain recognized a face or two in the audience, culture-vultures, but no one he could speak to. He settled to observation. As usual with any amateur performance, official figures crossed the grass importantly, papers in hand, sometimes in twos, when there'd be a minute of frowning consultation. A young man in denim moved a spotlight all of six inches, fondled its cable, considered the consequences. Mr Hughes-Edge announced, semi-privately to selected groups, that drinks would be on sale in the intervals in the marquee. Yes, they had a licence. They knew the magistrates. His wife fluttered ponderously in, long skirt voluminous, making certain that all were reassured by her presence. Muzak sounded distantly, was lost. Two gentlemen in tights, cod-pieces and doublets, erected three feet of castellated wall. Grey clouds hovered, but a burst of sunshine gilded brown grass, dusty leaves. Exactly on time a burst of Tapiola wind-screamed the battlements of Elsinore, but the arrival of a charabanc party, loudly led, swamped Francisco and Bernardo, peering at each other over a hedge at the top of a grassy bank.

Uncomfortable on his canvas seat, Chamberlain concentrated. The actors spoke well, fast, but clear, urgent. The poetry touched him:

> We do it wrong, being so majestical
> To offer it the show of violence.

The court of Denmark assembled, huge and glittering round substantial thrones. Hamlet in customary black did not stand apart but stood unsmiling amongst the councillors, the civil servants, one of many, less occupied than Polonius. Claudius was good, everybody's telly-politician, at ease, serious, so that one expected money-flow, foreign assets, wage-restraint to occupy his serious delivery. The producer, St John Windsor, had forbidden parody; divinity hedged this king about, concern, outreach. Polonius disappointed with his saws. He doddered, backing as his Bertrand Russell voice cawed and hawked; he did not believe in himself. Chamberlain glanced at Lynette as Ophelia spoke first to her brother. A small, boyish girl, blue-eyed, blonde hair upthrust, her voice had the innocent strength of a choirboy's, more powerful than that of a man, but unsubtle, speaking part, not heart. That was right, he felt; women were nothing publicly, unremarked until they married incestuously, sang filthily mad, drowned their sorrows.

As the Ghost, plum-voiced, found his son apt, a fine drizzle disturbed the audience. It did not rain much, but people shifted, donned coats, cardigans or headscarves, ruined Shakespeare's horror as they stared rustling upwards, dropped programmes, retrieved, murmured, concerned themselves with their own affairs. By the first interval the precipitation had ceased, though the sky was the colour of scum on a collier's bath-water.

Gin and peanuts cheered them. Mrs Hughes-Edge appeared.

'How is it going?' she asked Lynette. 'I've not had chance to hear a word. St John can't be here tonight.'

Lynette praised; Chamberlain's opinion was canvassed. Ernestine swept on.

'What do you think of Ophelia?' he asked the girl.

'Good. There's a big scene just coming.'

'Would you have played it like this?'

'Not so far.' Lynette looked crestfallen. Perhaps her substitute had found in the part something of significance she'd missed. John fussed her, sensing her unease. Dr Hill lectured his wife and Elsa. Rhus, Snowy Mespilus, guelder roses rumbled past his glass. Gardening.

An official with a handbell jollied them back to their seats.

Hamlet came amongst them, on a draped stool by the front row to deliver 'to be or not to be'. He could not be seen three rows back, but it did not matter; this was thought. Pamela's face set serenely grave; Saul handled his beard.

> The undiscovered country from whose bourn
> No traveller returns...

He was too old, built like a front-row forward. stinking of grease-paint, but the voice caressed them, eloquently puzzling their wills. Ophelia entered, at father's command, a Nurse Cavell, bravely fronting the firing-squad. He went back to insult her, but their commerce failed. To himself he spoke with quiet penetration; now he hectored, so that words sounded, echoed, learnt, meaningless. 'For the power of beauty will sooner transform honesty from what it is to a bawd than the force of honesty can translate beauty into his likeness.' So? It did not matter. 'This was sometime a paradox.' Now it was movement of air. Ophelia's shock was translated into small, dry sobs, catches of breath. Hamlet raved himself off-stage, wild at her painting, but thrusting his barbed 'all but one' at the clearly visible Claudius, to attention behind privet.

By now, the drizzle fell thick and the audience, garbed against it, merely fidgeted or commented. On this account, perhaps, Ophelia delivered her lament on Hamlet's madness briskly, every word bell-clear, but an over-prepared paper. The words did not match the sorrow on her face; her body cringed; her vocal cords rang.

> And I, of ladies most deject and wretched
> That suck'd the honey of his music vows,

and it was raining hard, big drops, straight down. The audience endured a line or two more, and turned disorderly tail. Claudius made a full appearance, with Polonius, sensibly in command, but the rain streamed from him, the people deserted him.

> And I do doubt the hatch and the disclose
> Will be some danger ...

Nobody sat, and Chamberlain looking back, saw Claudius comically throw up his hands, and stump off.

Inside the marquee, crowdedly dark, people talked with excitement, glad for their gardens, pleased even that Shakespeare had been curtailed. Rain drummed the tent roof; the smell of damp swelled; loud voices dulled the trickle of music from one speaker. At the bar service was slow. A bald young man made conversation as he leisurely poured, sought for drinks, miscalculated change, enjoyed himself. The jostle lacked ill-humour. A middle-aged woman joined the barman, seemed puzzled by simple words, lager, vodka, lime, spilt and wiped, simpered and hesitated.

The crush shrugged from time to time, rearranged itself. Chamberlain, whisky in hand, found himself cut off from his family. He stood, hand on tent-pole, listening to the rain.

A young woman placed herself in front of him.

'Good evening.' Not without force. She'd be noticed.

She smiled. Surprised, he answered. He had not seen her before. Small, pretty, with urchin head of black hair, dark almond eyes, she seemed in no hurry. She wore a mackintosh, which was open. Her breasts were small, the hand holding a glass of orange beautiful.

'You don't know me.' He did not. 'You're Eric Chamberlain, the writer, aren't you?' The voice was pleasant, of the Midlands, educated. 'My guess is . . .' A sudden crescendo of talk, as a rigged light flashed on; the downpour muffled the information.

'I beg your pardon.'

She glanced up. In fright? The mouth opened in pretty bewilderment.

'I didn't catch your name.'

'Oh, I see.' Was she not going to tell him now? 'It is a mouthful, I always think. Diane Pendleton.'

The left hand was bare of rings. She'd begin any minute with *God's Spies*, which she'd had out of the library. Let her. She could bear being looked at.

'Eli Dunne,' she said. 'I think you know him, don't you?' So. The clarinet teacher, the adulterous oboist. He nodded, waiting for her. Why had she bothered? 'He often talks about you.'

'I like Eli.' He'd help her out. 'An interesting man.'

'Yes, he is. He comes to see me.' Enthusiasm in the oriental face. She stood on tiptoe, at the honey of music vows. 'We met at the Youth Orchestra course. Last Christmas.'

'They stayed with us.' They. They.

'I didn't realize that.' She laughed. 'We don't know everything, do we?'

'Very little, some of us.'

She complimented him adroitly on *Swarthy Webs*, saying how much he knew there. She asked a technical question about radio which he could not answer. No wonder Eli was taken. Now he advanced a theory of the novelist's illusion of knowledge which convinced the ignorant, and forced the expert to supply, apply his own information. Conversation shouted. In four or five minutes Elsa appeared to announce they'd decided to go home. He introduced the woman, and Diane confessed she'd chosen the music for the production, worked the turntable.

'What's on now, then?' Chamberlain asked, an ear cocked towards the speaker.

'God knows.'

They exchanged views about the production. Diane did not approve of Windsor's cast, who were chosen for acting ability, and as St John was no thinker, there was no coherence about the play. That seemed both clever and just.

'Are we ready?' The jovial Hill, stomaching through.

'We shall get wet.'

'We can run.' Breathy laughter.

'Is there any chance of the performance continuing?' he asked Diane.

'They'd act through the sinking of the *Titanic*.' She saw Lynette, who'd come up. 'Uh. Hello.' Unfriendly greetings, and Diane bobbed away.

'Who's she?' Elsa asked.

'Eli Dunne's lady-love. Do you know her?' he asked Lynette.

'Isn't she a musician of some sort?'

The rain abated until they reached the car park, then lashed down again.

At home, they had not stayed with the Hills who had holiday packing to complete, Chamberlain sat with the unopened morning's paper. Some young woman writer was compared unfavourably with himself. On the next page appeared, much delayed, his account of a stay in Shetland. Deliberately he forced himself not to drink, but had to read the articles slowly, almost out loud, to bring them anywhere near his understanding. Elsa looked in.

'Aren't you coming to bed?'

'Might as well.' She waited as he folded his newspaper, consigned it to the basket, closed and locked his desk, shifted the angle-poise, put out the lights.

'How did you know that girl?'

'I didn't. She introduced herself.'

'As Eli's mistress?' Elsa sometimes mocked herself, but charily, as if truth might be injured.

'No. "Friend" was her word. Then I remembered her name.'

'What did you make of her?' Elsa, very grave.

'Like a little Chinese.'

'She knew Lynette.' He nodded. 'No love lost there.'

'That's what I thought. But it may be nothing. I can't ever tell with these...'

'Did she say what she and Eli were going to do?'

'No.' He loosened his tie. 'I wonder if they know.' He chewed at his lip, scratched his neck. 'When I was there both he and Beth were certain the break was coming. Haven't you talked to her?'

'She doesn't know, now. I phoned yesterday. He won't make his mind up. Or tell her. He's going to run a course in Devon, next week.'

'Will Diane be there?'

'I gathered not. It's impossible to get things out of her, Beth, that is. She's ashamed.'

'She's not taking it well?' he asked.

'She is not. It's a blow to her pride and it's knocked her apart. She couldn't keep her man.'

'That's not her fault.'

'No, but she doesn't see it. She doesn't see anything straight now. What sort of woman would you say she was? Sensible, knows what she's about? Now she's struggling to remember whether or not she's been to the butcher's, or what she bought there. Ask her the simplest question, and she's spluttering and crying and gasping as if she didn't know the language.'

'It's not surprising, is it?'

'It surprised me. He's a nobody. She's made her life round him. It's nothing to do with his qualities.'

'You've taken against him.'

'Not really. It's not as if he's anything to lose. But I feel like screaming when I see the effect on her. And then there's this neat little girl tonight. Neither of them knows what they've done.'

'You think not?'

'Don't be a bloody fool, Eric. They've as good as killed that woman.' He was taken aback by the ferocity. Beth had been, was, his mistress. She'd betrayed her husband with him. That must rankle in her head, partly excuse her husband.

'Strong talk.'

'I'm terrified to ring her up. I used to enjoy it. She'd bumble on, then rush off to look at the scones in the oven . . .'

'And leave flour all over the phone.'

Elsa glared, suspiciously. Fancy glosses looked well in books. She pulled her lips sourly in.

'She's in a bad way.'

'I see.'

Elsa scowled again.

'What do you see?'

'A reed shaken by the wind.' His phrase meant nothing to her. Powerfully she seemed concerned for Beth, while he issued words randomly. He tried to recover his good name. 'Do you think we should go down to visit her?' he asked. 'Together?'

'You haven't the time.'

'I could make it.'

'What good would it do?' She asked the question gravely, slowly as if somewhere an important answer lurked.

'It'd show we thought about her. Support her. Give her something to think about, even. We could ask her up here. If she felt like it. She might even want to turn and talk to somebody about it, get it off her mind.'

'You ring her, then.'

'Don't you think it's a good idea?'

'It won't do any good. But you try. You ring her up.'

'You won't come with me?' He wanted her to do the chores.

'I didn't say that. I will. But you must put it to her. I'll come. It won't do any good, but I'll come.'

'I won't bother then.'

'No. I'll come with you.'

'What's the use if you . . .'

'I've no monopoly of judging right. I don't know what to do. I don't think there's anything to be done. I may be wrong. But don't back out. You're too fond of that.'

'Thanks.'

'It's true. You wouldn't intervene with the children, unless they'd annoyed you. "What can I say to them?" And it was left to me to shout and rave. Or comfort them. So you get on the phone and make the effort this time. It's nasty. You don't know what to say. You don't want to do it, but neither do I.' She spoke with a brusque good humour, not angrily, as to a child-nuisance. She hit somewhere near the truth.

The telephone call was easy. Beth would be delighted

to see them, as long as they understood that Eli was away, wouldn't be back. She'd take two days off from the office. She'd intended doing that, but didn't want to spend them by herself. Their visit was a godsend.

'How did she sound?' Elsa asked.

'Well. Cheerful.'

'What did she say about Eli?'

'That he wouldn't be there.'

'Is that all?'

Elsa spoke scathingly, then insisted that he collect a pile of books for Beth's shelves. He complied, pleased, only to find she changed tack, claiming that the books would be a nuisance, needing to be sold off, whenever she moved house. He guessed that Elsa worried herself about her friend and was determined to take it out on him. She nattered him all the way there, complaining of his high speeds, the excellent lunch, the car seats, the suit he was wearing. By the time they arrived he'd sworn at her, felt murderous.

The Dunnes' garden straggled unkempt, untidy, with the lawns pale-straw. A barrow, laden with sods, stood abandoned; a spade lay on the parched soil. Only the outdoor tomatoes had been cared for, richly green or red. Patchy white cloud moderated the temperature, but dust settled almost yellowly on leaves or paths. Here and there shrubs had died, shrivelled. Traffic thumped past; holidaying children shrilled, but the neglected garden sketched a graveyard silence.

As they parked in the drive, Beth came to the door.

First he noted that she looked no worse. Though she wore an apron, underneath she had a smart navy frock, good tights, fashionable shoes. She and Elsa kissed.

'You wouldn't like to run me down to the shop, would you, when you've had a cup of tea?'

'I'll do that,' Elsa said. 'He can rest from his labours.'

The inside of the house was comfortable, no dirtier,

spacious but cluttered, lived in. He'd expected it otherwise. They drank tea from pint-pot mugs, incongruous against Elsa's elegance of hand and ring.

For the first quarter of an hour he detected no alteration in Beth, as they exchanged pleasantries, news. A jacket of Eli's hung on the back of a chair; clean underwear and handkerchieves, a pair of folded trousers suggested he'd soon be in. A pipe rack, a chin-rest, a music stand added credence. A pair of scarlet braces had dropped to the floor.

Then Beth was silent.

She would answer questions, manage a social smile, but always as if her mind were occupied importantly elsewhere. She fidgeted slightly, with hands and feet, and when she moved to pour out tea she did so sluggishly, let out an involuntary huge sigh. At Elsa's suggestion that they should drive down to the shops while Chamberlain washed the dishes she seemed baffled, uncertain what she wanted, meandering from cupboard to cupboard so that Elsa very gently took to suggestions.

The evening meal was simple and good, but how much was due to Elsa's bustling in the kitchen he did not know. Afterwards he unpacked the box of books; the pile stood substantial, bright with dust-covers, tempting. She made a show of picking up a volume or two, opening, glancing, touching as she spoke her thanks, but her face expressed nothing, sullen, concerned elsewhere.

They pressed her with questions which she answered sensibly enough.

Eli was away until the week-end. That meant he'd arrive home some time on Sunday evening. It depended. He'd no evening work now, but she thought he'd do a bit of quartet playing. That would be casually arranged, by phone. In ten days he'd a further course, but though that was local he might live in, she wasn't sure. He'd take one or two private pupils while he was at home, she was already making out a schedule of work. He'd look after himself because she'd be back at the office, but he was capable.

Elsa chattered, bravely.

First Saul and Pamela were described and analysed. Chamberlain noted his surprise at his wife's acuity. They were a decent pair, but neither was positive enough. They wanted their way only in so far as it did not wreck materialistic benefit. 'They aren't idealists, I can tell you. Not about each other even. They'll get what they can while they can from us, then suit themselves.' This was a fairish judgement, he thought, if hard. He'd never looked on Pam like that. Beth put her fingers together, plucked at her skirt, stared up the wall, or down to the floor.

Elsa's main recital concerned the forthcoming wedding.

Here she was amusingly sharp. The affair was to be thoroughly quiet, ten minutes in the register office, a simple lunch for a few friends in a nearby hotel. That was the beginning. The guests now numbered eighty-odd, as the young couple were angling for wedding presents. 'They're absolutely commercial, the pair of them. They had conference after conference on who it was worth inviting, said so openly.' They'd consulted the whole world. Elsa was malicious about Boy McKay who'd produced lists of wedding presents. These, he said, were part of the services he offered as a solicitor. He made no charge but he'd tell the parents to send the bride along and he'd produce his lists. There were about a dozen, and you trimmed them to suit your needs, but only slightly. What one must remember, or work out, was to send the right list to the right person. 'You don't ask an OAP for a Jensen, do you now?' was McKay's crude advice. 'But you'd be surprised how many people need telling that.' Another of his aphorisms: 'The stinking rich are stinking mean', and he had his method there.

Chamberlain was delighted.

He'd realized that negotiations of a kind were in progress, but it was Elsa's sharp-edged précis that attracted. She had her wits about her.

What he did not know was where truth lay. Lynette and John held hands, touched each other in public, were always off somewhere together, but he took this as expected behaviour. They had the skids under them on the way to marriage. Now that he was subsidizing them in the purchase of a house, he had listened bored and patient to their accounts of hunting and finding and had himself pronounced on agents' literature, even promising to pay a visit to the property they'd settled on. But he was quite unaware of the complications described by his wife, said so. Elsa laughed, brightly.

'You live in a world of your own,' she told him.

'I don't think so.'

'Well, now you know.'

Beth Dunne showed no interest in this exchange, but shrugged herself up to a question.

'Is John all right now?'

'Yes.' Elsa. 'He's very fit. Dashes about. He's had some success. At college. With the wedding. Even at the hospital. They all praise him there.'

'You're pleased?' Slow, bucolic, nasally pinched.

'Of course.'

'It's a success for you.'

'I'm not so sure about that.' Glad she'd prised a word or two out of Beth, Elsa's temper still made demands. 'Lynette's not the one I'd have chosen.'

'So it'll end up in, in a mess?' Beth's hands fluttered as if to suggest her own predicament.

'We don't know. We can't say that.' Chamberlain, glad to intervene.

'Yes.' Elsa's sibilant was strong.

'Yes, what?' he asked.

'It'll end up in a mess. And then we shall have John on our hands again.'

'Why are you so sure of that?' Chamberlain was affronted that his wife voiced this before a comparative stranger, and shivered at the gravity of her expression.

'I'm not sure. How can I be? But that's what I think will happen.'

Now she spoke more lightly, easing them, herself.

Conversation grew patchy. At five minutes to ten, Eli rang. Beth returned from the phone, glummer. He'd be home now on Monday morning, not before eleven. Yes, he was surprised the Chamberlains had come. What did they want?

'And what do we want?' Elsa.

'I said Eric had brought me a great case of books.' She lumbered into a chair.

'How did he seem?' Chamberlain asked.

'Just the same.' The exact force of the question no longer eluded her. 'He, well, he doesn't say anything about this woman.' She blurted the phrase out. 'He talks business. Could I get this, go there? That's all.' She looked up. 'There's no drama.'

The phrase dropped pathetically, so that they were silent. A fat tear emerged, stood, staggered down Beth's cheeks. Her face puckered, crumpled; she covered it to sob. They watched, embarrassed, until Elsa got up, snapped to her husband to put a kettle on, perched on the arm of Beth's chair, put an arm round her.

Chamberlain loitered in the kitchen, in no hurry.

He put out, rearranged cups and saucers, tapped at the drawing-room door. 'Tea, coffee or cocoa?' he called, once he'd seen the women. They sat opposite each other, Elsa had drawn up her chair, both leaning forward. Beth Dunne no longer cried, but fingered her hair, uselessly seeking tidiness.

'Coffee. Black. All three.' Elsa did not look at him.

They went to bed without further ado. Beth, locking the doors, spoke normally. At breakfast talk was desultory; neither newspapers nor letters appeared. After he'd washed up Chamberlain set off on a fake errand to the shops, walked around peering into scorched gardens, sitting for a while in a park watching children slide, swing, shout. When he returned the women loitered in the kitchen, waiting presumably for him, Elsa's face grim, Beth's blank. A quick cup and they were off.

His wife did not speak as they drove; her expression of stone.

After half an hour he questioned her.

'Did she say anything about Eli?'

'Anything?'

'Have they come to any arrangement?'

'No. He's going to stay there. He's fixed his work for next year.' Elsa spoke flatly, with aggression. 'He wants her to move out.'

'Has he said so?' he asked.

'Does he need to? It's obvious. He's waiting for her to pack up. Then he'll instal his, his Pendleton.'

'He's told her this.'

'He hasn't told her bloody anything. That's what so bad. Can't you see? He's dragging his feet, waiting for her to make a move.'

'She should dig her heels in, then.'

'You saw what she was like. You must be blind. She's got no will left, no energy. She can't fight. She just traipses back and forward from her offices, living on coffee and cereal.'

'Hasn't she got anybody to help her?'

'If I left you,' the voice hardened, 'if it bothered you, who would you go running to?'

'The nearest whisky bottle.'

'She goes to the doctor. Her cousin, the solicitor, is decent. But her life consisted of Eli. Eli and nobody.' Elsa's mouth stretched tight, as she laid down these certainties. But this woman, he instructed himself, signalling, smoothly overtaking, had been his mistress. And if his, where else?

'There's not been trouble between them?'

'She says not. I'd judge that true. She's given him her life, wasted it on him, thrown it away. She didn't know that. It's what she wanted.'

'There's not any guilt on her part?'

'For what?'

'Has she wronged him in some way?' A quick glimpse, a second established that Elsa's lips were trembling under the stony face. Her fingers reached, dashed a tattoo on her seatbelt shoulder, were clenched back in the other fist. 'You know what I mean. Has she given him some cause to desert her?'

'Boredom, bloody boredom.' He thought she'd hammer the windscreen. 'She's been at his beck and call too long. Now he wants somebody young and lively to gad round with.'

Chamberlain had to brake, wait for six lorries to sort themselves out.

'How can you be so sure?' Foot down, he skimmed away.

'Shut up, shut up.'

'What's wrong with you?'

Elsa stared ahead, at the traffic lights, at the sun flashing on the screens of southward bound cars. Traffic surged, powerfully active, noise-violent. Dabs of white cloud sailed. She glared.

'What is it, then?' He softened his voice, at the risk of its loss. 'Are you all right?'

'Yes.' A short, neutral, cheerful, lying word.

He did not pursue the matter, pursed his lips to a silent whistle, dismissed other cars with a burst of speed.

A week later they received a short letter from Beth Dunne, written from a mental hospital. It thanked them for their visit, gave no details of her own case except to say that it was restful in the institution, that people were kind, that she had spent her time reading, knitting and watching TV. Its normality seemed unreasonable; she was writing from a lunatic asylum not a seaside boarding house. There was no mention of Eli.

Chamberlain asked Elsa if he should ring the Dunne house.

He was glad of the word, because since their return his wife had kept her mouth shut. There was no deliberate abstention from talk; she'd asked about meals, about some detail of the wedding, about the cars. When he mentioned his book and some development, she understood and answered, but her voice sounded differently. He wondered if he imagined this and listened carefully when she talked to tradesmen or neighbours. Then she seemed herself, but when he was to be answered, the voice seemed lighter, less resonant, delivered unnaturally thin. He could not make up his mind, set little traps of speech to judge her by, failed to reach a conclusion, tried again. He wondered if his own anxiety altered his voice, if in fact he suffered alone. And sometimes when a small exchange between them had finished, she'd walk purposefully away, though she'd nothing special to see to, as if to put space between them was a necessity. She was in trouble.

'What's wrong?' he'd ask.

'Nothing.'

'Are you sure?' He risked a hand on her shoulder, and she made no attempt to shrug it away. She did not respond to it; sex, in its minimal manifestations, was dead between them.

'It's nothing to do with the Dunnes, is it?'

'Not really.'

'Is it the wedding?'

'Among other things.' She'd go away in a moment, not rejecting him, leaving him feeling deserted, half-frightened.

'How do you think John is?' he'd demanded. The boy was doing well.

'He's fine.'

'I met Mrs Smithers in the village, and she says her

daughter tells her how popular he is up at the hospital. He'll do anything for the patients.'

'Yes. He is.'

The withdrawn ghost, shadow of a voice. Elsa, his proper wife, would have informed him that Old Smithers would cackle anything that came into her fanciful head, and her daughter, a ward-sister, had already clashed twice with John.

The son, banging with energy, raced about in the evenings to see Lynette, slept like a log, ate piled plateful, rampaged about the house the short time he was at home. He seemed almost powerful as if success had hardened his muscles. He and his mother laughed together as Chamberlain never remembered before, were pally, had colloquies from which he was cut out, delighted in the other's company, acted boisterous brother and sister. Chamberlain could not but be pleased by the explosive improvement in his son, but suspected that Elsa, consciously or not, exploited the situation to discard her husband. He dared not put it to her.

'Do you think I should ring the Dunnes then?' Chamberlain.

'Please yourself. Will there be anyone there?'

'Wasn't he due for another course?'

'He wouldn't give it up, you think, because of Beth's . . . ?'

'You ring.'

She slipped away.

He tried two days without success. Eli was not at home, or not answering. When he got through to the ward, somebody reassured him. Mrs Dunne was most comfortable, really doing well. He probed. Was he a relative? No. Well, then. She was making good progress.

'Why was she admitted?'

'Her own doctor sent her. And she saw Dr Davies here.'

'Had she collapsed?'

'Yes. In a way. She was rather poorly when she came in. But she's really doing well.'

'Does her husband come in to visit?'

'Oh, yes, I expect so.'

He wasted his time. The nurses or orderly blocked straight questions. Mrs Dunne had been quite ill. Had improved. They were pleased. Yes, she took his name. She'd pass on his good wishes. The middle-aged voice did not seem wary, merely slightly stupid or ignorant, unwilling to admit it. Angry, he dashed down to the village for a get-well card, had Elsa laugh at him for his pains. They each filled a short side; he walked out to the post-box.

That evening he caught Eli in.

At first, Dunne grudged every word, mumbled, paused, stumbled. But after five minutes he began to talk volubly, in a rash of jerks. 'You know what's the matter, don't you? You say you've rung the hospital. They told you, didn't they? She attempted suicide. I found her. She'd been very sick. That had saved her. She knew I'd be home that night. Swallowed damn near a whole bottle. Too many. Lying across the hearthrug up to her eyes in vomit.'

Eli did not stop. In this soft, fast voice he spilt the story. He repeated himself, rushing to reach the next stage. Probably this was his first unbuttoned account. Laconic strong sorrow for hospital, police, the GP. Now this flow, this wash of verbiage, unshaped, detail crowding out or blurring chronology.

What the ambulance men said. Reception in the casualty ward. Back to the beginning. Angle-poise lamp right on her. Empty bottle, only just fetched it, blatantly there. Shouldn't prescribe in those numbers at that dosage. Well, they're busy. Horrible mess. The house stank, reeked. Nearly didn't go home that night. Back earlier than usual. No pub.

The tale sprawled shapeless, but never contradicted itself. In the end, fifteen, twenty minutes later, Dunne blew, sighed. 'Well, that's it, then.'

'Had she left a note?' Chamberlain.

'No.'

'Was it expected? I mean when we came down, she was in a pretty poor way. It worried us.'

'But you did nothing about it. You could have rung her doctor, or me.'

'She'd already seen the doctor.'

'And I was the cause of the trouble?' Eli blustered.

'That's so.' Phone silence. 'Has she said anything?'

Again the flow, the diarrhoea. She was sorry. That's all she could say. He traipsed up to the hospital, and she sat there in a chair, and wouldn't look at him, but said she was sorry. She knew exactly what she was about. She could come home if she wished, but she didn't want. This time Chamberlain interrupted.

'Is she better?'

'She seems all right.'

'That's not the same thing.'

'No. It isn't. I don't know what to do. I'm guilty as hell, but I'm not going back to her. She's got to accept that.'

'But if she can't?'

'She'll have to.'

'Isn't that dangerous?' His bowels cringed at his own question. He could hear Dunne's breathing.

'I've acted like a bastard. But blackmail's blackmail. It's all she can do, I know. But what sort of life would it be if I took her back?'

'The sort she wants.'

'D'you think so? It wouldn't be anything. I'm guilty and whatever she did or said, I'd still feel so. I wish to God I was rid of the pair of them.'

'Weren't you and Beth getting on, then, before this started?'

'Not really.' Dunne huffed, uncertain whether to talk. 'Well,' the monosyllable dragged. 'We kept appearances up. Like everybody else. I'm not telling you I've never shoved my hand up one or two neat skirts, but nothing serious.'

'And she?' Excitement. Voyeur's shame.

'Don't know. Might have. Shouldn't think so. She didn't like muddle. I bloody well thrive on it. Or, at least I thought I did. It's killed me, this. I'm standing here like a kid that's pissed himself. I don't know what to do. I haven't even the energy to do nothing.'

'Go back to her, Eli.'

'Eh?'

'Go back to Beth.' It sounded wrong, removed from all complexity, a matchbox morality. 'It'll be dreadful for Diane. But it's what you should do.'

'She's young.'

'She'll survive.' The triteness singed. 'Young people do.' John, John.

'You know damn all about it.' Anger expelled lassitude. 'You've no idea. You're like a bloody robot. Once, you might have felt things once, but not now. Success has done for you. You're cut off. All you can write about is what's extraordinary. Men murdered by their wives. And it won't be long before you're headlong into fantasy. That's where it's leading. You'll have men frying up their own testicles for breakfast. Then you are lost.'

'What happens in reality is so cruel, and so incredible, that we can only make sense by scrawling crazy muck like that.'

'Perhaps you're right.' Dunne's voice fell drab. Chamberlain was disheartened; a woman had attempted suicide, a woman he'd handled, for whom he had responsibility, however diminished, and all he could manage was literary criticism.

'I'm sorry,' Chamberlain said. 'I shouldn't have said what I did.'

'You talk sense. I know I ought to go creeping back to Beth.' He laughed, embarrassed. 'I'm even considering it.

But what's rotten is that if she'd sat at home breaking her heart and saying nothing I'd have been off without another word. It's not until she tries . . .' He gave speech up.

'If she said nothing, to you, she'd have been coping, wouldn't she?'

There was no answer. Foolery and silence stood twins.

Chamberlain apologized once more. Dunne asked about the financial progress of the book, said why it would be a best-seller, hoped that the current negotiations for film-rights would end in a marvellous picture which was there for the making. 'They'll go on doing it, you know. It'll be remade every fifteen years. You'll never want for bread.'

'I've forgotten the damned thing altogether.'

'Have you started another?'

'No. I spend my time reading and reviewing. I don't want to begin again. I'm afraid. I'm not good enough to come up with something interesting just at any time.'

'Nobody else is.'

'I'm not a writer at all. I'm a journalist. It's not me. It's the subject-matter not me, my treatment, that wins the prizes. The fried testicles, not the pen on paper.'

'Don't,' Dunne's voice became stronger, tauter, 'underestimate yourself. You're very good. Perhaps because you believe what you do. You're somebody. I'm nothing, nobody. And I can't even do my nothing without a balls-up.'

They comforted each other, roundabout.

18

The Hills returned from the Near East.

They seemed rested, even pleased with each other, especially solicitous about Pamela. Madeleine offered her services for the wedding preparations and she and Elsa spent hours in company. They then arranged to go away together for a holiday in September. Both, in their styles, fussed Chamberlain. Elsa had twice spoken to Beth Dunne in hospital, and had both times been rebuffed.

A week before the wedding Eli Dunne rang Chamberlain one evening to announce his wife was home.

'How does she seem?'

'Getting there.' Gruff, taciturn today. 'We've made it up.'

'You mean . . . ?'

'I mean.'

Chamberlain hummed into the telephone, immersed in his own doubts. He dragged himself back.

'How did it happen?'

'She came home from hospital. I'd just finished my course. We talked it over.'

'That's good.'

Again they wasted time.

'Has it, does Beth, has it set her up?'

'She's better.'

'Is she in bed?'

'If you walked in here you'd say she was normal. She cooks. She'd work in the garden if there was anything to do besides tidying and watering at night and we're not allowed to do that.'

'And she's well?'

'That's what I tell you.' Again the pause while one grunted, one sang tunelessly. 'I'm not getting excited, if that's what you're hinting. She tried suicide, and that's serious. When she came back first, she was frail.'

'Elsa rang her up in hospital, got the brush-off.'

'I'm not surprised. Suicide's not done for nothing. She was brittle. I looked after her, and she thanked me, but she wasn't all there. Not mad, I mean; hopeless. I had to lug her out of the bath once. There she was kneeling on the floor as if she was praying, stark naked. She hadn't dried herself. I got her back into bed, but it terrified me. For all I know she was bloody well praying. For me to come back. Then she made me sleep with her. She asked me, begged me. "Beg" isn't the word. She was sing-song, as if she'd disintegrate; like a little girl. High up. We made love. I had to. I know all this sounds mad to you. It's bloody well cracked to me, but I've done it.'

'Why are you telling me?' Chamberlain snapped at him.

'I've got to talk to somebody. And you're a little crabby voice, with a few atmospherics for a change. I don't need to imagine you. It's like talking to God. You'll say something in English that has some semblance to sense. If you were actually here, so I could see you and you me, I wouldn't have the nerve. I'd be too embarrassed. I'm not only a double-stewed bastard, but the world's biggest bloody idiot, as well. Oh, this doesn't make sense. It bloody doesn't. It's too depressing. But I've got to tell you, you you disembodied voice, because if I don't, I shall go off my bloody raving head. I'm sorry.'

'There's nothing to be sorry about.'

'That's what you think. While Beth was in hospital, Di was on the phone every day and then she came here. She knew what was up. She knew why Beth had tried to kill herself. And she acted like a jumping lunatic herself. I'd go up to the hospital where Beth hunched like a broody hen, and then on park benches and caffs with Di, Diane Pendleton, you know, with her crying, and tearing her hair.'

'When I met her she seemed a very composed . . .'

'Composed? She was as composed as a bloody earthquake. She'd had trouble. Some relative, some cousin had lost a leg in a pub explosion in Ireland. Been across on business. She hardly knew him, but it was the beginning of our end. She shrieked in the streets. Made scenes on buses. I tried to get her to my house. Wouldn't go near. We actually came to wrestling and mauling at a bus-stop. Christ, I don't know.'

'What happened?'

'What you'd expect. In the end, between 'em, I lost my head and told Di to bugger off if that's all she could do. Beth was home by this time, and I was at my wits' end. She was calm, then. Di. She shut up. We met again once, a miserable hour dumb as cunts and she wrenched herself up and that was that.'

'You've not heard from her?'

'No.'

'So you don't know what's happened to her?'

'No.'

They lost each other for a minute or two.

'It's the best thing, Eli. Really.'

'Does it occur to you that I feel a lot more for Di than I do for Beth?'

'I took this to be so.' Superior.

'And you still . . . ?'

'I still think so.'

Dunne didn't argue, dictated Diane Pendleton's address, phone number, and asked Chamberlain to make inquiries. Both were sore.

Elsa, oddly, showed no enthusiasm for Dunne's decision. Later she raised the question of Lynette, who'd called in to deliver cuff-links for John. The girl had asked why the Chamberlains looked so glum, and immediately Elsa had outlined the dilemma.

'He couldn't have been keen,' Lynette said at once.

'On Diane?'

'Yes. If he'd have wanted her, he'd have grabbed.'

'Aren't there,' Chamberlain enjoyed attitudinizing with Lynette, 'people whose moral principles prevent them from doing what they'd like to?'

'Not many.'

'I'm thinking of hundreds of people who give up part of their homes to old parents. They don't want it. It's a pain in the neck. But they do it. And I know of women who've never married because they were looking after an invalid relative.'

'It must have been what they wanted. Deep down.'

'There's some truth in that.' Elsa had intervened. 'Perhaps they hadn't the imagination to see what would happen, they hoped it would turn out well, put what society thought before their own convenience. But Lynette's right. It's what they wanted. Not a hundred per cent, perhaps, but then nothing ever is.'

They argued too long, he against the women. Elsa angrily nominated him as selfish, one who chased his own ends mercilessly. She hurt; she knew it, savagely.

'Nothing,' Lynette concluded, uninterested in their bickering, 'could have stopped my leaving Joel. I'd no job, no prospects. My standard of living plummeted. But I wasn't staying with him, not if I had to beg on the streets.'

'I'm not saying,' Elsa took something of his own manner, 'how these desires are arrived at. I wouldn't deny principle plays some part. But in the end we do as near as we can to what we want.'

'That's a poor look-out for humanity.'

'I don't think so. We're due for trouble, anyway.'

Down in the mouth, he left it at that, wondering if it were possible to answer any question sensibly. Elsa's argument seemed not so much aimed at truth, but at maiming him, making him out as the apostle of greed, goading, galling him into self-hate. He barely dragged himself to the whisky bottle, could not read, his head an echo-chamber of her biting sentences, her implications. 'You lead your life according to your wants.' He filled and emptied his glass, condemned, damned in his own sight, as he could hear the two women laughing, below, chattering, the confrontation upstairs forgotten.

When he staggered downstairs both women were friendly. He asked them how he should find out about Diane for Eli. Elsa said he should ring, saying that Dunne had detailed him because he was worried. Lynette offered nothing.

'He'll be devious, you see.' Elsa.

'It's a try-out for his books.'

Elsa was right. He rang the County Education Department where an acquaintance obliged with Miss Pendleton's phone number. The girl answered his first call. Embarrassed he explained who he was and began his lies.

'I've tried to get hold of Eli Dunne, and I can't. You said you were an acquaintance and I thought you might know where he is.'

'He should be at home.'

'He's not on a course, is he? I don't know if you know but his wife's ill. We heard from her in a mental institution, but now she's been discharged. Are they away on holiday? I mean, Beth may not be fit to travel.'

'As far as I know they are both at home.' The girl's voice was as neat as her appearance.

Chamberlain apologized for his intrusion, named his source of information on her whereabouts, suggested to her she'd be enjoying holidays. She answered friendly enough. Was she going away? At the end of four or five answers, she said, as if her mind were suddenly made up, 'You know why Mrs Dunne was in hospital, don't you?'

'Yes. It was very sad.'

'I think she's better now.'

That was it. Diane closed down. She was polite, would agree with him, but say nothing about Eli. It wasn't likely she'd meet him this holiday, no. He'd be busy. She was going off somewhere. They might run across each other next term, next year, you never knew. In their line you bumped into people three or four times, then saw nothing of them for months. Um yes, he was an interesting man. Very good personality, got on well with the children. Perhaps not quite thorough enough, or was it well organized? Yes and no. No, not very likely he'd take the next Christmas course. Miles Teeman would be back, now he was fit again. Yes, *he* was really good.

Chamberlain prolonged his apologies, invited her to call in if she passed. She thanked him, cheerfully it seemed.

He explained to Elsa what he'd done, awaited her condemnation.

'Why didn't you do it straightforwardly? Tell her Eli wanted to know.'

'I was afraid.' He shifted paper-clips about a table-surface when she laughed. 'For all I know it might have started it all up again for her. Just when she'd got it manageable.'

'You might have done that now. Just mention his name. Don't see much difference.'

'Possible. She seemed steady enough.'

Elsa watched his fiddling.

'Why didn't you leave it alone altogether? You could have told Eli you couldn't get through.'

'I don't know. Didn't seem right.'

'You mean you're inquisitive.'

'That's probably it. But I felt so sorry for the man I had to make a move.'

'You trade in imagination,' Elsa said, sententiously. She seemed to mock by parody. 'But you have none. Can't you grasp that the girl whose life you've just been poking into is probably as badly mauled as he is? Don't you see it?'

He did, at her instigation. He feared he could not learn.

Eli heard his report, hardly commented. Beth was miles better, took the car out, was rearranging her books. His thanks were short, dismissive.

Two days before the wedding Lynette drove over to collect a hat. This was being confected by a dressmaker in the next village, who, a fortnight before, had been recommended in irresistible superlatives. Lynette, who did not wear hats, decided she must on this day, while Elsa and Pamela were equally persuaded. Chamberlain enjoyed the episode, feeling superior, fetched back the headgear for his own two, talked diffidently to the milliner, a grey, spectacled woman who knew her mind, and finally admired the products with the women's astonished delight at such good coming out of Nazareth.

Now the bride's bonnet was ready.

He offered to do the errand, but Lynette refused, because she expected some last minute perfecting touch on the spot. She invited him to walk over with her. Elsa said she'd be glad to get rid of her husband, but doubted the sense of Lynette's walking four miles there and back.

'You'll turn your ankle over.' She seemed half-serious. 'Then how will you manage?'

'There's no aisle and only one step at the registrar's office.'

'Were you married in church before?'

'Yes. St Luke's, in Retford. All in white.'

Lynette walked soberly, not sure of herself. She asked about the Dunnes and he reported on the phone call to Diane and Eli's reception of his effort.

'Do you think they'll be all right?'

'I hope so. I've no idea.'

'I don't think he should have given in. It was a kind of blackmail. They won't be able to forget it, will they?'

He was taken aback. This girl was marrying John because he had tried to kill himself. She preferred McKay. She saw no parallel, or betrayed no sign of it. He dismissed these simplicities. They walked under trees at the fenced edge of a wood, their eyes dashed by the jumping light between leaves, while in the distance small hills shone, and further, slightly misted, a pit-tip stretched, large and picturesque as a natural feature. She stopped, staring beyond the wire fence into the fierceness of sunshine, eyes screwed, nearly beautiful, her complexion marred by a cluster of spots at the left side of her mouth.

'I love John,' she said.

That was simple, not sentimental. Some emotional debt needed payment, and there was the best she could do. She needed to sustain him, and thus herself.

'Yes, that's good. When you're sure.'

'How can you be?' She immediately raised a finger for silence. Her hand, her arm were delicate, pale, miracles. 'I mean, I'm not sure. I never was. How can I know? I made such a hash last time. And then there have been, you know, other men, disappointments. I shouldn't be saying this. Not to you. I shouldn't tell anybody these things. Especially not John, because he couldn't bear it.' They walked a few steps in silence. 'You think I'm a funny woman, don't you?'

'That's hardly the word I'd choose.'

'You know what I mean.'

'You're frightened this is going to be another mess, aren't you?'

'Yes.'

'And you're not fifty per cent convinced that you should start on it?'

'No, I'm not. That's rotten. When I married Joel I really wanted him.'

'But not this time?' Chamberlain did not hurry; he did not know the way.

'No.'

'You think you could be just as happy with half a dozen other men you know. Or unhappy. Boy McKay or somebody.' He'd said it now.

'Oh, well. Not Boy, though. He's too selfish. We shouldn't last three months. There is something about John . . .'

'Stick to that.'

She looked up at his interruption in surprise. Perhaps that was not what she wanted to hear. She'd have to make do, with no certainties from him. He wished he'd the strength of mind to pontificate, but he had nothing, shrank inside himself.

'My parents used to quarrel,' she said. 'My mother used to get on to my dad. He didn't say much, unless she goaded him too much, and then he'd go chalk white and swear at her. He didn't curse much otherwise.'

'Then what?'

'She'd shut up. I think he must have laid a fist on her at one time, when they were younger. I never saw him hit her. He was a strong man.' Chamberlain thought of the thin, silent figure, baffled and short of heart, at his fireside last Christmas. 'Do you and Elsa get on well?'

'Not always. We have bad patches.'

'Not bad enough to part you? I couldn't stay with Joel. He'd have killed me.'

'Would he?'

'God knows. He was mad. I was. Nearly.' She ran her fingers through her hair, staring at the darkness of close tree-trunks, the downward light in almost palpable pillars. 'When I ran home my mother said. "You've got to give and take"; I don't think she'd any notion what it was like. She'd lost all her spirit. If she'd had any.'

'I expect your father had lost his. Made it easier.'

Suddenly, Lynette laughed, stageily loud, said 'Aren't we all dull?' and they stepped at that minute into the ferocity of shine, on to a stile, where the sun was heavy on their backs, and the smoothed cross-bar fiery. She fiddled in her handbag, donned dark glasses, slithered down a dusty bank out to the road.

There they walked jauntily while he lamented the dryness of gardens. Pantiles and orange brick glowed in the sun, exactly suited, but the grass's pale brown lacked life and trees already carried yellowing leaves. The village boasted a post-card prettiness, comfortable as a cat. From a side street a youth appeared, a West Indian, hair clipped short on a tapering head, his trousers hitched high from thick-soled shoes. He whistled blowily, swinging arms, ignoring them, mincing athletically on his way, heels and soles thwacking the pavements. They watched him cross the road, pause at the newsagent's, clack on elastically up the main street, turn off, still sounding his progress. Lynette touched Chamberlain's arm pointed to the name plate of the street from which the boy had emerged. 'Dark Lane.' A tractor shattered its way; the driver nodded. A vapour trail divided the sky.

Now they crossed to enter a street, wide as the main road and at right-angles to it. As they turned they were confronted thirty yards away by a hearse and two funeral cars. Lynette sucked in, a sound of dismay. The hearse, with flower-roofed coffin, stood ahead, while round the other cars black-coated mutes moved. Chamberlain touched his companion's arm, stopping her. The front door of a detached cottage opened and a frock-coated man ushered the mourners to the street. No one spoke and the dignity, the slow pace, the best suits were almost comical. The limousines filled, glided away, after the hearse followed by a small blue saloon. Windows were wound down against the heat. The road seemed denuded, nakedly washed by sunlight.

'Do you think that's bad luck?' Lynette asked.

'To see a funeral?'

'Just before the wedding.' Her mouth compressed into a serious, thin line. 'I wonder who it was.' They learnt later from the milliner that the dead man was a grandfather who lived on his own, was a nuisance to nobody but himself, and had died unexpectedly, conveniently, without fuss after the family's summer holiday was over, leaving a bit all round. As one that had been studied in his death, Chamberlain decided. 'I don't think I shall forget this.'

'No.' He grew solemn.

'They looked funny, didn't they? Once they drive off they begin to talk. We did, I know.' He remembered her two recent funerals. 'You're too upset to notice what you're doing. My sister was on about the old school in Selston, and the headmaster. Nobody was very interested. I couldn't remember him. We never went there. Must have been her nerves.'

'I suppose so.'

'If John had, had died, would you have had a religious service?'

'Don't see why not.' Shocked at the question, he answered rudely.

'I shan't forget this. Just before the wedding. I wonder if I shall remember it when John dies. I shall think of this street, and how hot it was. It'll come into my mind. You think that's morbid, don't you?'

She was older than his son.

'We never know what will stick. I can remember the art master ticking us off for making a row when public exams were on. "It won't be long before you're doing them." That four years ahead seemed a lifetime. Or the geography master, he didn't teach us, doing cock-crows. Forty years ago. In the dinner room.'

'When afar and asunder.' She laughed. 'They'd got washing out at the back. In the funeral house. I wouldn't have that.'

'You might not have any say.'

They rang the milliner's bell. No answer.

A few doors up, on the other side, two women who had opened adjacent front doors to watch the funeral, and having disposed of that, scrutinized the strangers, were now deep in an anger of conversation. Their voices twanged loudly as the visitors waited, ringing again. Chamberlain wondered how he'd missed them before. They directed, rammed, their speech straight into his ears.

'Don't yo' put up wi' it.'

'I'm not gooin' to.'

'An' I tell yer another thing. If they don't believe yer, an' there's a lot o' 'umming an' ah-ing, just gi'e 'em my name an' address. I'll tell 'em for yer.'

'I will.

'And don't yo forget, missus. Some o' them there as comes round...'

The milliner opened, breathless. Had they been ringing? The bell didn't always work. She'd been upstairs. Funeral or loo? Chamberlain wondered. Please come in.

There was silence across the way.

Indignant eyes watched the door shut. A sentence or two were wasted, quietly. Plangency resumed.

19

The weather had not broken on the day of the wedding.

At the Chamberlains' there was a house full, but sober, punctuated rarely by bursts of laughter or talk. John had been out with his male friends the night before, but without riot, and these young men had sat about drinking coffee after the pub had closed and were in bed by midnight. This morning breakfast had stretched for two hours, but Elsa had employed three women from the village to look after the visitors.

Pamela called in on her father, reported that she'd rung Lynette and Saul before nine and all was well. She smiled, walked round the study, pulling out a book here and there, spurting banalities about the sunshine before bursting into tears.

'What's wrong now?' he asked.

'Nothing. Everything.'

He put his arm on her shoulder, but she hurled herself away and out of the room. In his swivel-chair he hunched uncertain of himself, watching four young men who stood in a sedate group on the lawn. Ten minutes later, when he was half way further down a short paragraph in the *TLS*, Pamela returned, sorry she'd been such a fool.

'I feel a bit like that,' he said, gruffly.

'I don't know why it was. It just boiled over.'

'This is an important occasion,' he said. 'It ought to be.'

'Not for me, though.'

'You and I,' he said, reaching forwards, 'feel it for the rest of them.'

'I didn't like Lynette for a start, but she's brought John on.

She's got another job, you know, when they move. Mr McKay arranged for her. In a solicitor's office.'

'Yes. Everybody I know gets work in a solicitor's office.' He answered her look. 'Mrs Dunne. Beth Dunne. Here at Christmas. Violin-man's wife.'

'Has she? She just seemed pretty and trivial.' The girl looked embarrassed.

'Wait till you and Saul get spliced.'

'I don't know.' Genuine puzzlement, though her engagement ring shone. 'I'll leave you to it.'

'Have your aunts arrived yet?'

'No. I think John's picking them up somewhere. No, Aunt Alice decided she could drive. Must be somebody else.' She kissed him hastily on his parting. He saluted navy-fashion.

Elsa looked in.

'Don't sit about too long. There are people need entertaining.'

'I don't feel exactly sociable.'

'They're not expecting song and dances. A gracious appearance.' Elsa was at her best, with all the answers right and ample time to dispense them. 'Alice and Elizabeth will be here soon, with old Mrs Court. They'll expect a word with the famous author.'

'Where's John?'

'Sitting about in jeans. Talking about the psychology lecturer. Might be any day. You made it clear that you were paying for the reception, didn't you? John seemed doubtful.' Chamberlain took courage. His son's vagueness was deliberate, a score off his mother. He reassured her. 'He doesn't seem nervous. He's all packed up to go away. Very efficient, our young man.'

'I hope so. Will they be,' she paused, supplicatory, 'all right?'

'Pam thinks so. She's just been praising Lynette to the skies.'

'What does she know about it?'

'As much as we do, I expect.'

'I worry about them.'

'Yes.' He put his arms round her. She shrugged loose. 'I'd better not ruin your coiffure.'

'It isn't done. The hairdresser's coming any minute. If you're going to make all this money, I'm going to spend it.'

'Leave a bit for the tax-man.'

They kissed, loving and cool, proud of themselves, uncertain, ready for loneliness. She instructed him to go downstairs, and he obeyed, wishing he could read her mind. Below, John was not to be found, but Elsa's older sisters had arrived, were making sure that they and Mrs Court were looked after.

'Who's them?' one of the helpers quizzed her daughter: 'Talk about Queen Mary. She's as stiff as if she'd got an icicle up her bum.' She stopped as Chamberlain was noticed. 'Three teas in the best china.'

He talked, was talked at.

The ladies knew nothing of John's attempt to kill himself. They flashed gossip. They had read about the forthcoming book in the Sunday papers. Elsa didn't write to them. They'd only just caught a glimpse of her, but they'd arrived at the same time as the hairdresser, so what could they expect? They demanded, he realized, entertainment, put Pam and a gorgeously-barbered, newly arrived Saul on to them. Who Oh, that's who it was. What was his line? They started on accountants we have bested.

He found John at the end of the garden, kicking his heels.

'Used up all your small-talk, then?' His son grinned. He was very tanned. 'Don't forget to give the aunts ten minutes.'

Chamberlain sat down by his son. The house seventy yards away seemed absolutely still in the sunlight, the ground floor masked by shrubbery, the upper windows blackly blank.

'How are your nerves, then?' His joviality jarred on himself.

'I wish it was over. You won't believe this, but all I'm waiting for is eleven o'clock when I put the white shirt and the grey suit on.' He slapped the thigh of his jeans. The garden, every sunlit leaf, shape of shadow, bole, knot, surface, was frozen in hot morning brightness, without a stir of wind. 'I don't feel excited. Just a bit sick. Like an exam.'

'How's Lynette?'

'Oh, she'll do. She's never short of fizz.'

'She was very down a month or two back.'

'She has her off days.' His son smiled. 'Don't you?' John scratched his face; he'd not yet shaved. 'She's always got some plan that keeps her at it. I'm not saying they're all sensible. They aren't. As soon as we're back from the Lakes we're going to redecorate the dining room. It doesn't need it, but it's what she's decided. One week. Then she starts her new job. I've got a few more days.'

'Pam's been praising her up to me. I was surprised. And pleased.'

'She's not a bad kid, our Pam.' John affected the local accent.

'How do you feel about beginning teaching?'

'Just like this bloody ceremony. I want to get it over.'

They talked, with constraint, solemnly, almost as if at a formal interview, as rarely before. Chamberlain stumbled through a platitude or two on the changes brought by marriage. The father was embarrassed, but determined to waste time until eleven and the white shirt were nearer. In the unmoving garden he spoke without haste but without thought, having nothing to say. His body registered immense care or fright, unexpectedly but powerful, not to be dismissed. Something of importance happened. It was ineffable; he would have been pushed to hint its nature, but his muscles, nerves, bowels were eloquently alert, locking him here. A sparrow dashed dust in the border under a cherry tree, a mad scutter in the wide immobility. He and John watched, then looked away.

Elsa waved to them from an upstairs window. Her sisters were with her, having left old Mrs Court, Elizabeth's husband's aunt, downstairs to keep order with her hen's eyes.

'Their husbands dodged it,' John said.

'Business.' Both laughed.

'Did us well on presents.'

'They're not a bad pair. I quite like your uncle George.' Elsa was making signs. 'What's she want?'

'We should be in the house.'

'Oh, I'll do the rounds again when I've got my breath back. While you plug your shaver in.'

They sat for a few minutes longer.

'Are you going like that?' John asked.

'No. Clerical grey.'

Indoors Chamberlain gave Mrs Court his attention, greeted Saul who appeared all importance with the buttonholes, and hearing a clattering outside found men emptying his dustbins. This delighted Pamela.

'It's an ordinary day for them,' she said, linking her arm through her father's.

Elsa made an entrance, checked a point or two with underlings, acknowledged Mrs Court, became the temporary centre of a group of newly arrived young people, retired elegantly upstairs for what Pam called 'final spit and polish'.

Sherry bottles were open; the time was ripe; laughter and loud voices banged in every room. Pam changed from denim into a long, simple dress, knocked up a new hairstyle within five minutes, and Saul pinned on a rose. The aunts were smiling, flower-decked. As Chamberlain went upstairs to the study to change, he'd abandoned the bedroom and dressing room to Elsa, he passed John on the landing.

'Lost your collar-stud?' he asked. John stared, disbelieving the sentence he heard. He shook his head. Saul chased upstairs with his carnation, ordered John and the best man down for theirs.

The house was alive, noisy, anonymous and loud as a pub.

Chamberlain had changed, pinned his flower into place, was examining the effect in a large mirror, when the phone rang.

'Phone call from London, Daddy.' Pamela, in charge downstairs. 'Don't let 'em keep you too long. We're off in less than fifteen minutes.'

More news of the book; another journalist; he'd be pleasant.

'Chamberlain here.'

'Hello, Mr Chamberlain.' A woman's voice, uncertain, vaguely cockney. 'Is that Mr Eric Chamberlain? I'm ringing for Mr Dunne. He asked me if I would. He's had some bad news.'

'I see.' Chamberlain sat down, waited.

'It's Mrs Dunne. My name's Crawford. I'm his brother's wife. Half-brother. He asked me to ring you specially. Mrs Dunne's had an accident.' She was silent. 'She was run over last night. Right in front of the house.'

'Is it serious?'

'They took her to hospital. She died this morning. In the early hours.'

He mumbled sorrow, hardly capable of coherence.

'She stepped right in front of a line of cars. They go fast here, some of them. Just stepped into the road.'

'Was Eli not at home?'

'Yes. He didn't know she'd gone out of the house.'

Chamberlain, lungs dulled to iron, muttered. The two exchanged words, made sounds together, strangers in helpless intimacy.

'How's Eli taking it?' Chamberlain hauled himself somewhere near sense.

'It's too early. He's calm. He doesn't feel it.'

He managed a phrase or two more, surprised at himself. As long as he could keep in contact with this woman he'd . . . The room swirled round him.

'There's one other thing. Mr Chamberlain. Eli wanted you to know. She seemed to throw herself in front of this car. There were some people there. She stood on the side of the road and just, just . . .' The woman dried up. He made the effort.

'You don't know. She's been ill. She may have been dizzy and fallen. It might have looked deliberate.' He struggled on, believing nothing of it.

'She left a note. In her bedroom.' They must have slept separately. 'She said she couldn't stand any more. She'd had enough. Something like that. It ended: "Be happy".' The voice broke; he could hear the woman crying; tears ran down his own face.

Fighting, he asked where Dunne was staying. The man had refused to leave the house. A cousin from nearby offered to stay. He wouldn't have it. He only found the note this morning. When he came back from the hospital. He saw Dunne traipsing the house, smashed with grief, guilt, remorse, finding the envelope.

'When is the funeral?'

'We don't know. There's an inquest.'

'Will you let me have the details?'

She was ringing from the house on the Woolwich road. No, she wasn't on the phone herself. She was sorry. He'd have to get in touch direct.

'If there's anything I can do, let me know.'

'Yes, I will. Eli wanted you to know. He said you'd probably not be able to come down for the funeral. You'd got a wedding. He'd remembered that.'

'It's today.'

'Oh, I am sorry.'

He replaced the phone. Trembling violently beat his legs. He heaved sick. Tears wet his face still. He levered himself to his feet; supporting himself, on the furniture, opened the whisky bottle, poured without spilling. Carefully, denying himself, he moistened his lips, retabled the glass.

Thank God he was ready. The carnation was beautifully pinned to his lapel. He sipped, returned the glass. His body registered pain in every pore, but he remembered the two. She had been his mistress. It meant nothing now. His mind skidded from him. Minutes later he found himself staring at the stylish figure in the looking glass, the tumbler empty at his fingertips. He pushed himself to his feet, walked back to the whisky, allowed himself a thick finger. He put the bottle away, stood in the middle of the room.

A tap on the door.

Pam came in, marvellous in a broad-brimmed hat. She grinned at the glass in his hand.

'Getting ready?' she asked, nodding at it. 'About five minutes.'

'Where's your mother?' He could speak.

'Sitting room. With the aunts and Mrs Hill. She wants you downstairs. John's going any minute now.'

She saluted, as he'd taught her, excited, in full smile. The child had not noticed anything. Naked Beth Dunne was dead, and it did not show on him. He drank the whisky with distaste, went down.

John at the bottom of the stairs waited for him.

'We're off then, Dad.'

They shook hands, his son rather limply, the best man with vigour. The door banged on them and a shouting group of youngsters. Chamberlain tried the sitting room. Sedate people talked, in knots, ignoring or eyeing him.

The aunts congratulated him on his appearance. Madeleine patted the seat next to her. Elsa approved, regally. He answered them, but knew with one word out of place, he'd break. His best suit held him fragilely together.

Now the room emptied quickly. Saul major-domo'd. Cars sped off.

He and Elsa had a limousine to themselves. He helped her in. She stepped magnificently, artificial, elaborate as a wedding-cake, hardly human, lifted to the gods.

'Are you all right?' she asked, once they were off.

'Yes.'

'Did you have a drink?'

'Yes. A little tot.' He could talk.

'Very sensible.'

She composed herself, ready to be queen.

Misery muzzled, he sat upright.